ELLE HARTFORD

Cinders to Dust

The Alchemical Tales, Book 5

Contents

Preface

Long, long ago, a coven of witches created a world just
beyond ours—
a realm of fairy tales.
In Beyond, humans rub shoulders with mythical creatures,
and magic mixes with science.

There are only three rules:

Happily

accept that we share the same home

Ever

remember that what you take, you must also give

After

struggle will always lead to new beginnings

So, if you are ready . . . you are welcome here.

* * *

Belville & nearby forest

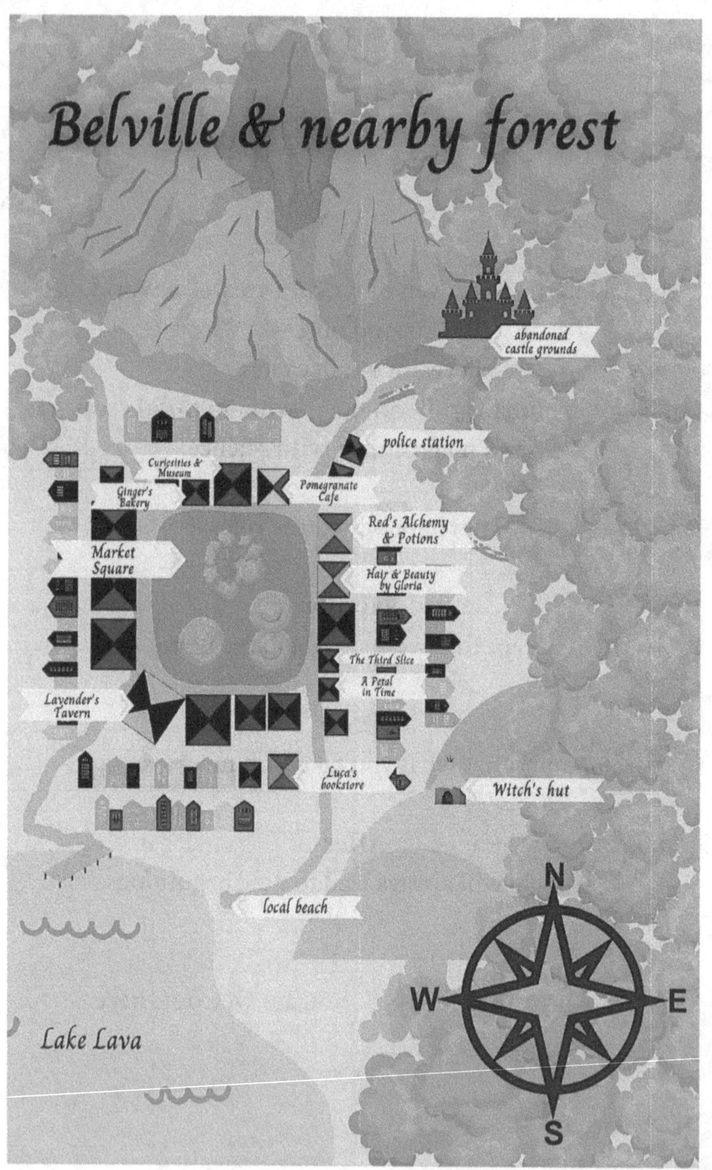

Cast of Characters

Top thirteen, in alphabetical order

Anastasia Willow: once-performer, now helps manage the carnival; mother to Magica, Willow, and Coal

Coal: half naiad; in town with the carnival, looking for new work

Henry Pleasant, Captain: captain of the *Luna II*; experienced sailor

Gus: naiad, works as guard for the carnival; full name August de la Mer

Luca: bookseller and scholar, complicated past; dating Red

Magica Willow: performer in the carnival; step-sister to Coal, sister to Weep

Red: alchemist and child of Seers, full name Cinnabar Sunset; dating Luca

Rowan, Sir: old-fashioned knight; works at Red's Alchemy & Potions

Sakura: nickname Saki; shadow witch; runs the Pomegranate Cafe

Thorn, Officer: half-orc policewoman in charge of keeping law in Belville

Trent: young Witch, lives in a Hut outside of town; eager to help

Weeping Willow: performer in the carnival; step-brother to Coal, sister to Magica

William: canine familiar, capable of protection magic and plenty of sass

1

Just One Bite

If it hadn't been for Sakura's café, I never would have gotten involved.

Well—to be fair to Sakura—if it wasn't for my love of exotic flavored chai teas, I would never have gotten involved. Probably.

"I'm so sorry," I said, to the young person I practically bowled over as I went for a personal record in "popping into the pick up counter at the Pomegranate Café and dashing back to the potions shop." Tea splashed everywhere and the scent of cinnamon and vanilla filled the busy café. I kept talking. "Wow, I really didn't see you there, let me help—"

But the person was already on the ground, and not because I had knocked them over. They were on their hands and knees, sopping up the spilled tea with one of the Pomegranate's handy cloth napkins.

Not only did I feel awful, I realized as I stared down at the unfamiliar gray-streaked head that I didn't know this person at all.

"You should also be sorry because you stole his drink,"

1

Sakura sang out from behind the counter. "*This* one's yours, Red. You ought to know by now that yours is always the gold mug!"

I ought to have, and normally I *would* have. But the truth was, I'd been running around like a headless chicken with an overdue to-do list all morning. I was so behind, I might as well have been operating in last week.

Haste is the enemy of speed, I could hear my mother say. *Look, Cinnabar, you were rushing and you made a mess; now you have to take longer to clean it up.*

I took a deep breath. And when that didn't work, I took another, and reminded myself that the best thing I could do was be present.

"I'm so sorry," I repeated, a little less frantically, to the gray-haired stranger. "Please, let me buy you another one. Saki—?"

"Already on it," the café owner chirped back. Her pale face and pink apron bobbed amid gleaming espresso machines and stacks of ceramic cups as she passed another steaming drink over the counter. "One black cherry coffee with cream for Coal!"

"Coal," I repeated, extending my hand down to the stranger to help him up. "Is that you?"

"Y-yeah. I guess," he said, looking down at his hands as he spoke. He accepted my help as if he thought I might have a tack or a bit of slime concealed in my palm.

I pursed my lips. Four different custom orders were waiting for me back at the shop, plus I had to run out for more sweet moss later *and* I had a date that night; I didn't have time for "I guess." But as I watched Coal, I reminded myself to be kind. He was barely more than a kid, after all, skinny and a little disheveled, only as tall as my chin. His white collared shirt hung loosely on his shoulders, and his leather boots were muddy, tied with mismatched laces.

"Coal came in with the carnival last night," Sakura informed me. Apparently, she was all caught up on her drink orders, because she found a moment to lean over the counter and speak conspiratorially. "He was asking me about work opportunities here at the Pomegranate, but I have a feeling he'd be more interested in *your* line of work, Red. Why don't you two take a seat over by the window and talk?"

If I didn't have time for guesses, I *really* didn't have time for interviews. But just as I was about to refuse, Coal looked up at me, and I clocked two things: first, his eyes looked much older than I'd expected, and second, he seemed to be biting his cheek to hide a smile.

"Please," he said. "I'm a really good worker, but things just aren't good for me at the carnival any more. I have to get out."

I glanced back at Sakura, but the witch-turned-barista was gone. There was nothing left to do but grab Coal's drink and take it to a table to sit with him . . .

. . . Because by this point, everyone in Belville knows I'm a sucker for a traveler in need. Or a newcomer looking for a change. Or even an outsider who ends up accused of murder .

. .

I guess, looking back, I was bound to get involved with the carnival and its silly masked ball—whether tea had been spilled or not.

* * *

A heavy early-summer rain pounded against the Pomegranate's picture windows as Coal and I took our seats. I did my best to set aside my worries and keep my mind open. An open mind is essential in Beyond—after all, living in a fairy tale world may come with magic and fun things like steam-powered traveling carnivals, but it also comes with hidden dangers. Not every tale ends the way you think it will, and not every hero is, well, a hero. Small-town Belville was a perfect example of this. I'd settled in the alpine town three years ago hoping for a quiet place to practice alchemy—and instead I'd run into murder and mystery at every new turn.

And I myself knew what it was like to be the stranger accused of crime. I'd spent years traveling and studying my craft before I'd scraped together enough money to buy my own shop. Not every encounter in a new town had been pleasant. *How much worse would it have been,* I thought, *if the people giving me grief were actually traveling with me, and I could never leave them behind?*

At least, that was my rudimentary assumption about Coal's problems so far. From the way he watched me across the little wooden table, pale green eyes wavering with trepidation, I felt fairly confident about my assumptions.

"Hi," I said, since Coal seemed to be waiting for me to start. "Let's start over. You can call me Red. Yes, that's 'Red' like 'Little Red Riding Hood,' and yes, I know my hair is actually black." I smiled at him, trying to use humor to prove I wasn't going to bite. "I run the potions shop right across the corner from here. However, I feel like I should tell you up front that I don't have the budget—or really the need—for extra staff right now. So that's going to be a hard sell. I can give you advice about settling into town, though, if you need it."

"Are you sure?" Coal leaned forward over his coffee. "The carnival itself is twenty-four new people in town. And that isn't counting anyone who comes to see it. We always draw a big crowd. There might be a rush on things like lightsticks or even mending potions."

Well, he sure knows a thing or two about business, I thought, watching him carefully. We had in fact seen high demand for *both* those things, on top of the usual seasonal demand for specialized fertilizers and water-repelling products. That was part of the reason my shoulders were so tense and my feet were already aching at eleven in the morning.

"I could even mop floors and dust, if you'd just let me work for a few days," he pressed.

I shook my head. "I appreciate your willingness to work, Coal, but I already have two assistants." More like one and a half, technically, since the talking canine-shaped magical creature known as William only worked when he felt like it. But that was more detail than Coal needed to know. "And one of them, Sir Rowan, is very particular about his cleaning procedures." That was true: after a year and a half of working at the shop, Sir Rowan had pretty much taken over all maintenance. "Besides, I have to be pretty careful about the people I hire, even for small things. My workshop is attached to the store, and it's my responsibility to make sure there are no accidents. That makes sense, I hope?"

Coal slumped back into his seat, but he nodded. "Alchemy is the science for people who like adventures and can weather explosions," he said, as if reciting from a textbook. "That's what my dad used to say."

"Well, your dad isn't so wrong about that," I replied, amused. Of course, alchemy was also the science for people who wanted to spend years toiling as an apprentice before they saw so much as a speck of fools' gold, but again, that was detail that Coal didn't need to hear.

"He's gone now, and my mom, too," Coal said. Before I could get out the words *I'm sorry for your loss,* he sat back up and added, "Is it true alchemy is about transformations? Do you think you could teach me?"

I choked back a sip of my tea, a little exasperated. If I didn't have time to hire, I certainly didn't have time to teach. I'd never considered taking on apprentices of my own. And even if I did, Coal was a little older than usual. I would have guessed his age at nineteen—old enough to see independence on the horizon, but young enough to insist on spontaneously-created careers. Rather than refuse Coal outright, I asked, "Is it the transformation part that especially appeals to you?"

Coal nodded, and glanced around the café as though he thought someone might be listening in. Then he leaned toward me again, pushing his coffee mug aside. "I'm half naiad," he informed me. "My father's people could transform into full-on lake guardians. Some of my cousins still work with the carnival. That's how it gets around so easy: they can all manipulate water. But I've never been able to," he concluded.

Naiads, I knew, were water spirits—they are to water what some elves are to forests. It took some piecing together, of course, but I could see what he wanted. "Coal, I understand the desire to explore your heritage, especially when you can see others around you who seem to be more 'in' it than you are." Actually, feelings like that reminded me of my own upbringing with mystic Seers in the desert, who had always seemed far more magical and *perceptive* than me. "But that's not really what alchemy is for. Alchemy is about transformation, yes, but not on living bodies, and not into something you're *not*. It's more about making herbs and minerals into the best versions of themselves."

"But I *am* a naiad," Coal insisted. "I'm descended from Melusine. Even if only half."

"Yes, but—"

"And I don't want to be just like *them* any longer!"

I fell silent, watching him again. Something, I thought, was just a little off. The way Coal was nervous around authority and so eager to prove himself reminded me of my friend—well, to be fully honest, my new boyfriend, Luca. Luca was extremely dear and his efforts to overcome a manipulative former boss meant a lot to me. I wanted to be sympathetic to the desperation in Coal's voice, but there was something in his eyes—a hardness—that I wasn't so sure about. The rain drops outside had eased, and in the wake of that calming sound, I felt uncertain.

"Just say you'll come to the carnival tonight," he pleaded. "Then you'll see. You'll see how it is for me there. What they're like. You'll see why I have to get away."

Well, we'd already planned to go. "Of course," I said, releasing a breath I hadn't realized I'd been holding. "And if there's anyone else in town you want to talk to, I could suggest Lavender, over at the tavern, or maybe Officer Thorn—"

"No," Coal said emphatically. "Only you can help, Red. Please?"

I hid my frown behind my steaming tea. "I'll do what I can, Coal, but I really think—"

"I have to go," he said abruptly, standing. "Now that the rain has stopped, I need to get back. Thank you for saying you'll come. You'll see!"

He left in such a hurry that for a moment I remained

sitting, staring out the gray window, wondering if he'd seen something I hadn't.

2

Love Spells

"Naiads," Sir Rowan informed me, once I'd made it back to the shop, "are naturally volatile, and not to be trusted."

"But on the other hand, they aren't *all* like the so-called 'Lady of the Lake,'" William chimed in. Though he looks just like a big black sheepdog, William often knows far more than I do about old legends. He'd stuck his head through the interior window between the shop and my lab in order to be part of the conversation. "Rumor has it that this carnival was started by Melusine. Maybe she wasn't interested in swords and kings."

Fortunately, the ring of the bells atop the front door interrupted what promised to be a long and tedious discussion of waterfolk-related mythology. But even as William turned to help our newest customer, I could feel Sir Rowan staring at me.

I pulled off my lab gloves, set my chin in my hand, and sighed. My chai was long gone, and lunch time had passed, too. I'd come back from the Pomegranate and managed to get most of the custom orders done or started, and it was time

9

for a break.

No doubt Sir Rowan agreed with me, and that's why he'd come into the lab. Normally he stayed out on the shop floor with William. There was plenty to do out there: floor-to-ceiling shelves lined two walls, full of potions that could always use straightening or dusting; the waist-high shelves and displays of alchemical tools, oddities, and powders in the aisles often needed refilling; and the cozy nook beside the large counter often required straightening. A few armchairs for waiting customers and some free tea waited there—strictly my experimental blends of tea, which sometimes Saki was good enough to purchase for Pomegranate. William remained behind the counter whenever he was working: there, he could perch on an old worn stool and survey everything going on. Right behind him was my window, and a door beside the counter led to my lab. Though it had everything I needed—tile floors, a small kiln in the corner, a back door leading out to the patio, cabinets of ingredients, and a sturdy workbench, my lab did *not* have a lot of space. Normally I insisted people wait for me out in the shop, and I often locked the door.

But Sir Rowan, despite being every inch as polite and demure as one could expect a fairy tale knight to be, sometimes refused to adhere to "normally."

"Rumors about Melusine notwithstanding," he said, clearing his throat to reassert his presence, "I do not believe it wise to become involved, miss."

I shifted to stare down the length of my workbench at him. "I don't know anything about Melusine, and I don't know very much about naiads or carnivals either. But Sir Rowan, you ought to know better than to label an entire group of people as 'volatile.'" *Especially a water-related people,* I couldn't help thinking, *given that 'volatile' usually means fire.* The thought made me chuckle a little, but only internally. I was tired of explaining myself; Sir Rowan and William had already made me go over every detail of my encounter with Coal during quiet moments in the shop.

With pale skin, clear blue eyes, and black hair always impeccably combed back, Sir Rowan could impersonate a statue sometimes. Today, he wasn't bothering. His frown clearly communicated that he didn't feel chastised in the slightest, and instead was about to argue with me. I resorted to the big guns: "What would Daisy say if she heard you talking like that?"

Whatever he had planned to say, he swallowed it. He even managed to look a little chagrined. "My lady is a much better person than I am."

"Well, I don't know about that, but she *is* a sweetheart." I smiled, thinking of the reclusive Daisy—whom Sir Rowan almost always referred to as "my lady." "Anyway, listen. I appreciate that you are concerned. I am too, although maybe not for the same reasons," I admitted, and Sir Rowan nodded— a tacit agreement to disagree. "To me, the whole problem of Coal feeling like he can't stay at the carnival because of someone else seems like a bigger deal than some old stories about naiads. And—" I hesitated, tugging at the edges of my lab coat.

Sir Rowan lifted his eyes to the ceiling, his voice mild. "Consummate observer that you are, miss, I'm sure you're aware that you only perform that particular tic when you're thinking of the local bookseller. When the issue at hand is *not* one of the heart, you generally content yourself with disarranging your hair."

"Flattery will get you nowhere." But the comment broke through my worry, and I grinned at Sir Rowan. "'Disarranging,' huh? I didn't realize that me running my hands through my hair was so annoying to you."

"Ladies," said Sir Rowan, "should always—"

"Oh, stuff it," I interrupted good-humoredly. I had no illusions about being a lady; my hair was held back by a ponytail and my magical safety goggles, for goodness' sake, not a tiara or flower crown. Not to mention that the one special thing about my appearance—the fact that my hair has tiny iridescent streaks woven in amongst the black—was something I usually tried to *hide*, not show off. It was just another way to avoid the subject of my heritage.

"—be aware of the image they present," he finished. "That's all I was going to say, miss."

"Uh huh. Thanks. So I guess you, being the *true* observer here, already have seen the solution to my problem?"

Sir Rowan stood back on his heels—he *never* sat at work, despite William's lazy influence, and my own—and steepled his hands. "By 'problem,' I presume you refer to the uncomfortable resemblance between young Coal's situation and Mr. Luca's former circumstances."

"That, and the fact that I'm going to the carnival with Luca tonight to see the opening show," I added. It was easier to talk about my misgivings when Sir Rowan said them aloud first, but the thought still sat in my stomach like a lump of lead. "And Coal is *definitely* going to find me and want to talk. The kid was nothing if not determined. And so that means he'll talk to Luca too. And Luca will want to help . . ."

"Is that so bad?" Sir Rowan asked gently.

"It isn't bad at all. It's adorable," I said, miserably. "But what if it gets him into trouble?"

"And by 'trouble' . . ."

"I don't mean some sword-swinging contest with a legendary naiad," I supplied, sticking my tongue out at Sir Rowan. "I *mean* that it might—what if it—well, I'm worried that it'll bring up . . . unpleasant memories, I suppose."

For a long moment, Sir Rowan remained silent. He just stood there, tapping his fingers together, one at a time, as if in thought. I knew him well enough to suspect that he wanted *me* to think. But my heart rebelled at the notion.

"It strikes me," he said finally, addressing the ceiling again, "that trying to keep Mr. Luca out of trouble was the reason for your delayed happiness."

"*My*—? You mean *our*—? Oh." I blushed as I put it together. "You mean us dating. I held back for a long time because I was worried about getting him into trouble. Well, yes, that was part of it . . ."

"And how," said Sir Rowan, gravely, "did Mr. Luca react to that at the time?"

"Um, not well," I admitted, my blush now an inferno. "He didn't like it. In fact he might have lectured me about it a few times . . . Yeah, okay, I get your point. No protecting Luca."

"Protection is one thing, miss," Sir Rowan replied. "*Prevention* is quite another."

"Okay, no *preventing*, then. He should be able to make his own choices. I know you're right, I do, but—" Helplessly, I turned, as though I might find the perfect words—and instead I found William panting at me from the shop window. Apparently, our recent customer had concluded their business and left.

"You can't prevent him," William agreed unhelpfully. "Because I want to go look up stories about Melusine, and the bookstore is the only place around here to do that."

* * *

William didn't get his chance for research that afternoon. Shortly after my employees had finished haranguing me about my relationship prowess (or lack thereof), business picked up—with a vengeance. Just like Coal had predicted, many of our customers were strangers, full of talk about the carnival's opening night. They all wanted lightsticks and glow powder, and I was soon sold out of the jokey fake gold coins I kept on hand as trinkets. I quickly abandoned my lab and went out to help Sir Rowan and William on the shop floor. All three of us were run off our feet as, just outside the front bay windows, the sun set over Market Square.

"Fools' gold coins," I murmured to William as we left through the front door. After the chaos of closing and cleaning up, it was our first semi-quiet moment. "Why'd everyone want those? I mean, I put the fake insignia on them quite clearly. No one at the carnival will think they're real."

"It's not just about money, Red," William replied as he lingered on the front step, waiting for me to lock up. "It's about favor. Throwing gifts on stage after a particular performance is like casting a vote for your favorite act in the carnival."

"Alright, smartypants," I said, grinning down at him. "So what was with the lightsticks and glow powder? They aren't planning to throw those, are they?" My lightsticks were made of a specially-reinforced glass that was recyclable, but very rarely breakable, so those wouldn't really be a hazard; but I shuddered picturing a carnival atmosphere full of sparkly dust from all those glow powder vials we'd sold. Sometimes running a business—particularly one with some dangerous wares—felt a little bit like running a daycare. *Do I need to make the vial lids spill-proof, maybe?* I worried.

"You're such a stick in the mud," William told me, fortunately with some affection. He nudged at my leg as we set off down the street, which was still full of shoppers and soon-to-be attendees of the carnival. "No, they're not going to throw those. Probably. That's for waving lights and decorating their clothes while they're watching the show.

"Because it *is* going to be dark by the time the show gets going," he added. "And not everyone is surrounded by the halo of romantic light that you and Luca are."

"You hush," I protested, half laughing, half mortified. I nudged him back. "We are not. I know very well that evening falls around eight these days, thank you very much."

William snorted. "And when's the last time you ate? Or are you surviving on Cupid's nectar?"

"That just sounds weird. Besides, it's because of the shop that I missed lunch. And—shoot. I had hoped to leave earlier, but we're so late as it is. Do you think Luca would mind if we just bring some sandwiches to eat on the way down?"

"You know him better than me," my companion retorted, weaving around a horde of excited children. "I think the real question is if he minds a third wheel tagging along."

"He knew when he asked me that you wouldn't want to miss the carnival's opening night," I replied, grinning. "You'll probably have to entertain yourself afterward, though."

"Gross," William said. "I don't even want to think about what you two will be doing."

"Comparing notes about the performances and debating

the history of traveling theater, of course," I said, innocently. With one last grin at William, I ducked into the local pizza and sandwich shop, The Third Slice, to get some food to go.

For as rural as Belville is, its central park—Market Square—is a true blessing. Not only is there the Pomegranate and my shop at one corner, and Belville's proud tavern sitting on the other, the remaining sides are lined with all kinds of shops. The Third Slice was usually a quick lunch place, especially since I enjoyed cooking dinner at home when I had time. But that evening, it was jammed full. Fortunately, the servers knew my usual order, and were happy to throw in a sandwich for Luca, too. When I rejoined William on the cobblestone sidewalk, we only had a short walk just past the edge of the Square to reach Luca's bookstore.

As Belville's resident scholar, Luca had inherited his shop from his old mentor and boss, Owl. All across Beyond, it was common even for small towns to have at least one scholar, who performed a very specific role: looking after a collection of books, some of which were usually for sale, housing the town's records, and serving as a resource for anyone with questions about local history or lore. With his enthusiastic personality and love of careful research, Luca made a particularly fine scholar—but of course, I may be a biased source. I'd be the first to admit, though, that he wasn't a particularly detail-oriented shopkeeper. Let's just say that Belville's book store could have benefited from Sir Rowan's mania for cleanliness . . . *If* Sir Rowan could ever be convinced to set foot in the dusty, jumbly, full-to-the-brim shop.

"Red, I was just about to come looking for you!" Luca tumbled from the bookstore's front door just as we arrived, and greeted me with a hug that immediately melted away all the tension in my shoulders. I nested my head alongside his and hugged him back one-handedly, clinging to my bag of takeout and smiling like salvation had just dropped from the sky.

William *might* have been onto something about that halo . . .

"It's been so, so busy," Luca continued cheerfully, stepping back to acknowledge William too. "I put up a poster at the tavern advertising these new 'Guide to Carnival' pamphlets I made up, and boy, did they sell! I ran out before lunchtime, and had to get Leo to print me more using the newspaper's equipment. I only just managed to close up, and I was feeling so bad because I haven't had time to change or anything, but it turned out just right I guess! I'm so happy to see you," he concluded, without so much as a pause or hesitation.

"Okay, deep breath," I teased him, as we fell into step. The crowd around us flowed naturally down to the pier on the lake, where the carnival was set up.

"What would you even change into? Another robe exactly the same?" William added, prancing on my other side.

"The same, but less dusty maybe?" Luca confessed with a grin. His scholar's uniform was always long, black robes, usually with the hood up to conceal marks leftover from an old curse.

"I didn't have time to change either," I admitted, also grinning. Fortunately, my outfit of red tunic over brown leggings and tall boots was less work-related than his.

"You look great though," he assured me. "You always do."

"I'm not going to sit with you two if you're going to be like this all night," William complained.

Laughing, I opened up my takeout bag and distributed our

on-the-go dinner. While William loudly chewed on his kabob, holding it aloft with blue magic, Luca took his sandwich with the gratitude of someone who hadn't eaten in days. He immediately promised to buy carnival snacks and dessert.

"I'll hold you to that," I told him between bites of my creamy salad wrap. "Although I have to admit, I really don't know what to expect. Maybe I should have pre-ordered one of your carnival guide pamphlets."

"Oh, Red, you know me better than that." Luca held his sandwich aloft and, with his free hand, drew a crumpled but shiny pamphlet from his sleeve. "I saved you one, of course. But I wasn't sure if you would want it, seeing as you might have already been to lots of carnivals, when you were traveling and all."

"We were always too focused on work," I said, because I knew William would groan if I said what I was *really* thinking, which was *Luca, I don't care if it's a treatise on breathing—if you wrote it, of course I want it.* I took the pamphlet with a smile which I hoped conveyed at least a little of how I felt. Luca's green eyes shone against his dark skin, making me think he got the message.

"That's just her excuse," William declared, jolting me back down to earth. "The real reason is Red hates fun."

"I do not!"

"And steampunk or magitech."

"Well . . ."

"And she never, ever knows when to take a break."

"No breaks tonight," announced a new voice—a brash voice. Officer Thorn. She cut deftly through the crowd, headed straight for us. "Unless it's a break in my new murder case, that is."

3

Behind the Scenes

Luca reeled at Officer Thorn's announcement, but I was more used to her behavior. I narrowed my eyes and waited for more information. By that time, we'd made it down to the dock, the magically-lit carnival ship anchored nearby. The ship's name, Luna II, etched beside a fanciful shark, was visible on the wooden hull; so were multiple signs for the "After Midnight Carnival." In short, we were far too close to the excitement to act rashly.

"So, who got murdered?" William asked loudly. Suddenly, the crowd was giving us a wide berth.

"Keep your voice down, or I won't let you come along to do the magical investigations," Officer Thorn retorted—as though being pressed into police service was a treat. William was such a meddler at heart that in his view, it probably was. I exchanged a wry look with Luca as the officer shooed us onto the beach to one side of the dock, where everyone else was lining up to purchase tickets for the floating carnival beyond.

"The tip came in not ten minutes ago," she continued, her own voice low and rumbly. The four of us huddled together

19

in the falling darkness. "A letter at the police station. Caught me right before I was about to do my rounds and check on the crowd."

She gestured behind her shoulder, where carnival-goers had resumed chattering happily. As Belville's only police officer, Thorn was a common sight at any event. Like Luca, she wore a distinctive uniform—although hers was truly a uniform, a military-esque coat with shiny buttons over perfectly pressed trousers and polished boots. She also stood out because she was literally a head taller than the average person in the crowd. As a half-orc, Officer Thorn had the raw muscular power—and intimidatingly pointy teeth set against mossy green skin—that made her job as a solo police officer go much more smoothly.

Except, of course, when it came to investigations. *All hands on deck,* she liked to say, whenever the possibility of murder reared its ugly head. Given that the carnival itself was *on* a ship—and knowing how much my friend the police officer adored puns—I fully expected to hear that comment at least twice this evening.

"What kind of letter?" Luca asked as I studied Thorn.

She looked at him askance, her long and silky black hair trembling in the evening breeze. "Does it matter?"

"Well, it could," said Luca reasonably. "There's letters that come through the post, of course—those could be traced, and you'd know they must have been sent at least a day ahead of time. Then there's hand-delivered letters, or magically-delivered letters, which some scholars posit are actually much—"

"Luca." I interrupted his lecture with a gentle hand on his shoulder. "Let's focus on the threat for now, and consider the letter more fully later."

"Best idea either of you has had all evening," William grumbled.

Officer Thorn, meanwhile, was checking off details on her fingers. "Hand-delivered letter. Didn't see the deliverer. Says someone aboard the ship's going to be murdered. And that after the show, the body might disappear." Thorn looked up at us over her now-clenched fist. "The way I see it, that adds up to an impromptu raid. I'll need you all to be my support. Red, you'll help with the physical investigation, like always. William, you're on magic duty. Luca . . . you can be crowd control."

Despite the seriousness of the situation, I did raise an eyebrow at that. My boyfriend was very learned and good-natured, but he wasn't exactly the commanding type.

"Stop giving me that look, Red," Thorn told me. "You might be sad to be missing the carnival, but it's even sadder for the pool soul who could be murdered."

"But you don't know who, and you don't know *where* on board the ship?" I asked.

"That's what we're about to find out. Come on."

Without waiting for a vote, Officer Thorn straightened up and started for the ticket booth. *She plays nice with the town council, but maybe she'd be happier in a dictatorship,* I considered muttering to Luca. Seeing as she'd been right about the seriousness of murder, though, I decided to hold my tongue.

Luca, William, and I trailed in the officer's wake. She cut the long line like it didn't even exist. Fortunately, the people we'd interrupted were Belville locals: the baker, Ginger, and his kids. They knew Thorn well enough not to protest.

The same couldn't be said for the two ladies selling tickets, though. At first glance, their identical surprised faces made them look like sisters.

"I'm here in an official capacity to investigate a serious threat," Officer Thorn began.

"A threat?" squeaked one of the ticket sellers.

"I'm afraid we already have most of the audience on board," the other one said quickly. "Beginning announcements have already started. The show must go on, you know."

Safe in Officer Thorn's shadow, I watched the two women carefully. Upon inspection, the quick-talking one looked older—perhaps she was the squeaky one's mother. They both had brown skin and very slender frames, but the daughter wore a brightly-colored leotard that looked like a performer's costume. The mother, with her dyed-red upswept hair and low-cut sparkly crimson dress, looked very much the diva.

"If I uncover anything dangerous, we'll have to get everyone off the boat," Thorn was saying, her chest puffed up in her best you-don't-want-to-question-me stance. "For the time being, I'll conduct my search belowdecks while the show is going on."

"Belowdecks?" the girl in the leotard repeated, shooting a wide-eyed look at her mother.

"Then the threat has to do with the ship, and not with the show," the diva decided. Behind her upturned chin, I thought I could hear a bit of a quiver in her voice. "Very well, I will escort you. Magica, you can finish up here and close the booth before you're due on set."

"I will," the girl replied, as her mother swept out of the makeshift booth.

I was a little surprised when we came face to face with our new guide beside the booth. She couldn't have been much taller than five feet. And in the bright lights of the dock, her dark brown eyes flashed with a peculiar haughtiness—a look that reminded me of someone, though I couldn't quite place *who*.

"My name is Anastasia Willow," she informed us, as though a more cultured group of investigators would have recognized her already. "I've been in the carnival business for over twenty years. I will be able to tell you anything you need to know, I'm sure."

"*I'm sure*," William echoed to me in an undertone as, once more, we fell into step behind Officer Thorn.

"Does she remind you of someone?" I whispered back.

"Yeah. A gossip," he replied.

Well, when it came to gossips, William was the authority. Particularly since he spent so much time in the window seat of my studio apartment, observing their activities to compare notes with his friend Dusty later.

"Did you hear? We're starting by touring the staff quarters," Luca dropped behind Anastasia and Thorn to inform us. "I know it's under unfortunate circumstances, but still—we'd never be able to go back there normally—it's kind of cool, right?"

I gave Luca a teasing eyeroll, and he tucked his hands around my elbow to lean in close. With all the butterflies in my stomach and the bright carnival music beginning on the ship overhead, it didn't feel like a murder investigation—yet.

And I had to admit, Luca did have a point about going 'behind the scenes' on the *Luna II*. I preferred to do my traveling over land, so I didn't have much to compare the ship to; but it was undeniably huge. It looked like an old pirate ship, except that instead of sails, a giant stage ringed with risers rose above the upper deck. A low, constant hum beneath the sound of the crowd confirmed the rumors I'd heard earlier: the ship's floodlights and whatever tricks the carnival needed were run by a steam-powered waterwheel. I couldn't see it, because it was hidden on the other side of the hull, but I did notice the unusually choppy nature of the lake.

A gangplank at the end of the dock took us out over the water and up onto the upper deck. There, we followed Anastasia away from the rest of the audience on board. While they climbed staircases and magical elevators and even ladders to get to their seats, we shifted left and went down a staircase that took us below. The first level, Anastasia explained curtly, housed the ship's galley, meeting rooms, and private chambers for the director and the captain. She insisted that those weren't searchable, but I knew Officer Thorn—if she wanted to see those rooms, she would. In the meantime, though, we took another dark staircase down to the next level, where the crew and performers were housed.

"And the animals, at the rear," Anastasia sniffed as she waited for everyone to squeeze into the hallway. "There's more below this, but it's just the engine room and storage."

"Rooms first," Officer Thorn insisted.

"Many of them will be locked, as everyone is with the carnival. Even the crew."

I caught Luca's eye, wondering, *Why'd she lead us down here just to tell us no?*

"Somebody must have spare keys," Thorn growled, clearly sharing my opinion. "You can retrieve those, or I can start breaking down doors. Need I remind you that this is official business?"

Anastasia hesitated for a moment, looking over Luca,

William, and me as if she might protest. Finally she admitted that the ship's guard would be helpful, and ran off to find him.

"Should've got the guard in the first place," Thorn muttered as we waited in the hall. Though the *Luna II* was as steady as any building in Belville, the lake air and old seagoing lanterns made it feel unmistakably nautical—and a little dismal, in my opinion.

Next to me, William glowed blue, a sign he was checking for nearby magic. "I don't sense anything out of the ordinary yet," he reported.

"Are you sure there wasn't anything more to go on in the letter?" Luca asked.

But before Thorn could answer, Anastasia returned, this time with a muscled naiad in a sailor's shirt and breeches in tow.

That was the first moment I really thought of Coal, and my stomach plummeted. I didn't pay much attention as the guard introduced himself, nor as we began to poke into the performers' rooms. As we went slowly along one side of the hall, each time we found nothing, my nerves went up a notch. By the time we'd reached the rooms in the bow of the ship, my feet were itching to be *anywhere* else. It wasn't intuition so much as a growing dread that I knew what we would eventually find.

"I haven't got the spare for this one," the guard said, as we reached the last room on the left side of the hall. "Everyone's key's different, you know."

"Why haven't you?" Thorn asked, a little more roughly than usual. The tone in her voice snapped me into the moment.

The guard glanced at Anastasia and shrugged. "Never got one. Sometimes they change 'em."

"Then they'll have to change it again," Thorn decided. Shooing Luca and William from her side, she backed up—and with one swift kick, opened the last door.

The room on the other side was so neat and plain that at first, it seemed laughable. For all the trouble we'd gone to get in, there was nothing out of the ordinary to be seen . . .

Until I caught sight of one bare foot sticking out from behind the room's solitary cot.

4

A Chorus of Mice

"Got it," Officer Thorn said grimly, as she followed where my gaze had gone. I'd thought she was being as businesslike and insistent as possible before, but as soon as she saw the body, it was as if she'd turned those qualities up to eleven. "Alright, everyone that's not me or Red, out of this room right now. Don't touch anything. Luca, you stay with our new friends in the hall. I want all three of you to wait there for us—no ifs, ands, or buts. William, you go and watch the gangplank. If anyone associated with the carnival tries to leave, stop them."

"*Everyone* here is associated with the carnival," William grumbled, while the others began filing out the door without resistance. "What do you think I am, some kind of Cerberus?"

"Performers and crew," Thorn amended. "You know what I mean. And I'm sure you're capable of bossing people around."

"I learn by example," William said—but he said it under his breath, so I'm pretty sure I was the only one who heard.

I would have rebuked him, of course, but at the time my gaze was fixed on Luca. As he left, he gave me a little head tilt, as if to say, *you going to be okay in here alone?* I nodded back at him, biting my lip. I wasn't worried about helping the officer with her survey of the room. I was worried about the fallout of this for Luca himself.

It must have shown on my face. Perhaps I was tugging at my tunic, as Sir Rowan had accused me of earlier; or perhaps life in Belville had made me grow soft. It used to be, on the road, that I was able to hide everything.

"Out with it, Red," Officer Thorn said, as soon as the door clicked shut behind Luca and the rest of them. Her voice remained firm, but she'd at least adopted indoor volume levels—what in another person might have been close to a whisper. "Why d'you look like I just kicked your grandma?"

I stifled a sudden and inappropriate laugh. "I do not look like that," I said, pulling myself together. "But the thing is, I know who our victim is. Slightly. I met him at the Pomegranate this morning . . ." Quickly and quietly, I did my best to fill her in.

"'Coal,' huh?" Thorn glanced askance at the body behind the bed. "Some kind of nickname?"

"Could be. If it is, I don't think he told me his birth name. But he did mention his family was descended from naiads."

"That's what made me wonder. Strange name for waterfolk. But, to each their own," Thorn said, catching sight of my pursed lips. "Anyway, set all that aside for now, Red. I need you to go through my checklist with me."

"Checklist for what?" I asked, blinking. A sign of how distracted I was, I suppose.

"For going over the room," Thorn replied matter-of-factly. "Guild policy says one set of eyes is good, but two is always better."

As she pulled a notebook from her pocket and began flipping

through it, I moved to her side on autopilot. I realized that, for all the times I'd helped Officer Thorn with her investigations, I'd never really gone over the scene of a crime with her. Most of Belville's crime so far had happened out of doors, where evidence was quickly lost to the elements.

Thorn's police guild-issue notebook turned out to be full of pre-printed templates, all ready and waiting to be filled in. She flipped to one entitled "STUDYING THE SCENE," holding it down slightly so that I could see it too. The stubby pencil in her hand skimmed over subheadings like "FURNITURE" and "SMELLS" and "POINTS OF EGRESS."

"Stop that," I said, because I could see exactly what she was doing—picking the section that looked most likely to yield something interesting. Apparently, not even a guild form could induce her *not* to go straight for the point. "You have to do them in order. Otherwise, why would there even *be* an order?"

Thorn's pencil drifted up the page to "1: SKETCH THE SCENE," and she sighed. "Red, has anyone told you lately that you're a—"

"Don't you dare say 'stick in the mud,' or anything like it. They're *numbered*," I protested.

"I meant it in a good way," she replied, and to be fair, there did seem to be something affectionate in her tone. As she began sketching out a little rectangle to demarcate the walls of the room, she went on, "So, you're definitely helping with this one, right?"

My mouth opened and closed, but no sound came out. *I don't think she's ever considered that to be an option before,* I mused. *Maybe after that business last fall, she's feeling a little more generous.*

The previous fall, an unknown assailant on the road had appeared to be attacking travelers—particularly travelers with orc heritage, like Officer Thorn. She'd taken that case very personally, and in fact—for perhaps the only time in recorded history—had tried to *stop* everyone else from investigating it. She'd been worried about us.

And now she's giving me a choice. Well, even though Thorn didn't know it yet, it didn't feel like a choice to me. Aside from Saki, I was probably the one person in Belville Coal had managed to talk to. And, given how his situation seemed to parallel Luca's history . . . how could I not be part of the effort to find justice for him?

"Definitely," I managed at last, though it came out with a squeak. "I have a feeling this one's going to be especially tough."

* * *

Officer Thorn's checklist—or perhaps I should say, my insistence on adhering to each section of Officer Thorn's checklist—took the better part of an hour. We weren't able to find anything strange about the room . . . which was perhaps the strangest thing about it. Nothing was out of place, not even the sheets or a pile of loose change on the dresser. Coal's key was on his bedside table. Coal himself was fully clothed and seemed untouched, except that he was missing his shoes and socks. In all, it was like the room was a set for the carnival, not a place where someone really lived.

"As I see it, the biggest thing," said Officer Thorn, scratching her head with her pencil, "is the bars on the window."

"It *is* unusual," I agreed. "I didn't notice them on any other room. That makes the door the only point of entry . . . and Coal's key is right here, but the spare is missing."

"And the door was locked," Thorn continued, stepping toward the offending fixture. As she brought her head down to level with the doorknob, she let out a low whistle. "Fancy custom lock. Looks to me like two or three locks put together."

"Well, the whole ship is kind of that way," I said reasonably. "'Steampunk'—that's what they call it in the city, in Brass. As far as I can tell, it just means they really like extra knobs and gears and overly complicated machines."

"That's as may be, but you weren't at the front of the pack earlier when we were unlocking the other doors," Officer Thorn insisted, straightening. "None of the rest of them looked like that."

"If you think it's worth it, I can take it to my lab and figure out how it works," I offered. When Thorn gave me a look as if to say *what do you mean, how a lock works? It locks things,* I clarified, "There *are* different kinds of locks, you know."

"Of course I know," she retorted. "There's a special class on 'em at the Guild. But I thought you didn't like magitech and steampunk and all this junk."

"I don't," I confirmed, thinking, *and apparently I'm not alone in that!* "But I'm still a tinkerer at heart. Given time, I could probably get it apart and trace all the mechanisms to figure out what they do. Or if I couldn't, Dusty definitely could."

"Put that idea under Plan B, for now," Thorn decided. "We'll see what folks say when we interview them, and decide then if it's worth it to go hacking locks out of doors. For now, it's time to take a look at the body."

Big words from someone who probably damaged the lock to get in here in the first place, I thought, but I followed along. I'd been dreading this part.

And yet, for all my dreading, it turned out . . . simple. Depressingly, frustratingly so. Coal was lying on his side, as though he'd simply rolled out of bed and forgotten to catch himself. He wore the same outfit I'd seen him in earlier, minus the footwear.

I, of course, am not a doctor of any stripe, but in the past I had sometimes been able to help Thorn by finding hidden things in the victims' clothes, or providing some analysis of unknown smudges. This time, there was none of that. Coal might as well have been fast asleep in a glass container, as far as I could tell.

But that's the wrong fairy tale, of course. And Coal certainly wasn't sleeping.

After going through another of her checklists, this time without even a strange lock to comment on, Officer Thorn sat back on her heels. "Nothing," she declared. "The boy's certainly dead, of course. But we've got no injuries, no traces of magic, no signs of a struggle. And the room . . . nothing out of place."

"Which, if you think about it, is exactly what's so out of place," I observed, shivering.

Officer Thorn pointed her pencil at me. "You were right about this one, Red. At this point, I'd be glad of a fairy godmother to help us along."

* * *

After that, the only reasonable thing to do was to begin interviews. With the carnival still going on above us and no reports from William, Officer Thorn decided to start with the two carnival-folk with us: Anastasia and the guard. As she herded them down the corridor, "to somewhere where we can talk," I pulled Luca aside.

"Hey," I said, again as quietly and as quickly as I could. It was becoming a habit. "Listen. There's something I ought to tell you."

I told him everything about my encounter with Coal, and everything Thorn and I had found. It was difficult to get the words out, but I could practically feel the specter of Sir Rowan beaming benevolently over my shoulder.

Luca's brow creased as he thought. "Oh, Red, I'm so sorry, I had no idea," were the first words out of his mouth. "I had no idea you knew him, are you okay?"

And immediately, he threw his arms around me in a hug.

"Luca," I said, surprised and half amused, "I was worried about *you*."

"I can see that," he told me, his voice muffled in my ponytail. "But what about *you*?"

"What about me?" I fell silent for a moment, thinking. Luca held on. "Well . . . to be honest . . . it makes me really angry. Like *really* angry. Not because of Coal exactly. But it's like . . . . everything I never got to say to Owl, about how wrong it was, how he treated you . . . it's all come back. And if that's what it's like for me, then for you . . ."

It must be so much worse. The words hung in the air.

Luca pulled back, and I swore for a moment his green eyes were watery. But he brushed the expression from his face with a sleeve, and smiled at me. "I know. It's okay. We're going to be okay getting through this, as long as we do it together."

5

The Belles of the Ball

Officer Thorn's "someplace we can talk" ended up being one of the meeting rooms on the next floor up. We could hear the boom and applause of the carnival above us—and under that, the low, steady hum of the steam-powered wheel. It seemed far from ideal to me.

To add to that, the room itself was distracting. A hodge-podge of rugs from all areas of the world covered the wooden floor, and the sofas and armchairs didn't match any better. The interior walls were lined with shelves full of strange mechanical trinkets and carnival souvenirs, while the outer wall, lined with portholes, let in a gloomy, shadowy light.

Undaunted, Thorn set herself up on a deep red sofa at one corner of the room. As before, she made Luca the hall guard, and had me stick around. "To take notes," she informed me.

I found myself wishing for the brief days when she'd had an official Guild assistant to do the note-taking. My stomach growled.

But Coal's murder was serious business—and seriously confounding. I had to admit, I was curious to see what the

34

officer's questions would dig up.

We questioned the guard first, while Anastasia waited in the hall.

"Name's Gus," he began, sitting up straight and attentive on an old wooden chair across from the sofa. "That's what they call me here, anyway. Full name's August de la Mer. I've been with the carnival two years now."

He certainly looked like a sailor—tall, and fit, sitting with his chest slightly puffed out even in a relaxed setting. His short dark hair was thinning a little on top but carefully combed, and his button-up shirt and sturdy linen pants were also looked after and tidy. From looking at his pale, slightly blue-tinged skin and watery blue eyes, it was clear Gus was a naiad. I wondered if he'd been any relation to Coal.

"Is it common for everyone aboard to have nicknames?" Thorn asked. Apparently, she wasn't thinking along the same lines as me.

Gus seemed a little taken aback by the question. "I—I guess it is, miss. I can't say I ever really thought about it. It's often the way on ships, you know, and makes everyone feel part of the team. Myself, I was accepted on as a stranger, but I never felt treated that way."

Okay, so, not related to Coal, I thought, disappointed. Officer Thorn gave me a look as though to say, *are you writing this down? "Welcoming atmosphere aboard carnival ship."*

"Welcoming" aside from the murder, I wanted to say. But I bit my tongue and returned to my notes.

"Can't say I knew the boy that well, myself," Gus continued, at Thorn's prompting. "Of everyone aboard, he kept to himself. But that's not to say I didn't care for him. He was a good hand with the animals, and helpful around ship. If there's anything

I can do to help, I'll gladly do it. The strange thing of it all is I just can't think of what to tell you. Right up 'til you got here, it seemed to me this night was going smoother than most. That's not saying we have trouble—usually we don't. Carnival life is more quiet than you'd expect. They call me 'guard,' but really I'm more like a super for the crew quarters, you know, looking after maintenance and that sort. We've never had need for anything more, not in the years I've been here. And between you and me, I'm grateful for it—we don't need the trouble, and the pay would hardly be worth it. Not that I mean to grumble, mind."

"How about keys to his room?" Thorn asked. "Can you say more about that? When did he get that fancy lock?"

Gus tapped his hand against his leg, thinking. "Everyone just has one key to their room, and then I have this ring of spares, just for maintenance or emergencies, you know. You can see it yourself, here. But I never did have Coal's—see, there's only twenty-three there, not twenty-four. Now I think on it, it's always been that way. I think that lock had been replaced right before I came on. The crew mentioned something about it to me, something about it being a family affair. I'd thought Anastasia had the spare."

That's pretty unfortunate, I thought, making careful notes. *Two keys, and one was in the room with Coal, one mysteriously gone. If we could find it, we might be able to wrap this up.*

"And did you notice anything out of the ordinary today?" Officer Thorn asked.

Gus thought about this hard, tugging at one slightly-larger-than-average ear. "He—Coal—wasn't at breakfast this morning with everyone else, as I recall. But that's not too out of the ordinary. In fact, I could be remembering it wrong—it happens often, see. Other than that, it's been business as usual. Everything's especially busy on an opening day, and it's easy to miss things in the rush. I've been busy all day getting orders from the captain and lending a hand in the stables, so I didn't have a chance to notice much. I thought I heard someone say Coal had been into town—I do remember that, because it was a bit of a surprise, see, we usually are all too busy to see a new place until the second or third day. I wish I could tell you who it was who said that, but everyone's been so worked up about the show tonight, that I just can't recall."

Upon ascertaining that he couldn't say anything more useful than that, as he'd last seen Coal the night before, and hadn't kept track of anyone else since, Officer Thorn let Gus go.

"Figured that'd be a quick one," she confided to me. "These unaffiliated 'guard' sorts of positions are like that. Not always attracting the best and brightest, if you get my meaning."

"Don't be rude," I whispered back. "I wonder what else Coal might have got up to in town?"

"We'll sort out the timeline later, once we know more," Thorn said. Then a thought struck her and she called out to Gus as he reached the door: "See to it that any performers or crew who make it off stage are sent here before anywhere else, will you?"

"Sure thing, miss."

I was momentarily tickled by Gus's insistence on referring to Thorn as 'miss.' I had to admit, it *was* pretty clear that Gus held Officer Thorn's position in higher esteem than his own. It was kind of—well, *cute*, honestly, to see her treated with deference instead of the good-natured frustration most of Belville felt for its police officer. But my amusement faded as Anastasia made her entrance.

She exuded waves of condescension, as though somehow the murder was *our* fault. Behind her, trailing in the tide like buoys, two performers in brightly colored leotards bobbed and weaved. I recognized one—Magica—and inferred immediately that the other was her twin.

But why are they here already? I raised an eyebrow at Thorn.

As if he'd somehow intercepted my thought, Luca stuck his head in the door behind the incoming trio. "I didn't know the ship has a wire system! I'm sorry, Officer!"

I didn't grasp the significance of this at first, but Thorn did. She stood, drawing herself up to tower over Anastasia. "Who else did you tell?"

"Everyone will know soon enough," the diva said with a defiant sniff, sweeping to a stop in front of the officer.

"Everyone will know *when it is safe to tell them*," Officer Thorn corrected. "And around here, *I* am the expert on what's safe. This is not one of your carnival acts. This is murder, and I expect my authority in the case to be recognized. Otherwise I'll be wiring to the Guild for special assistance. Did it occur to you that by telling your children inside information, you have put them in danger from a murderer *who is still on board?*"

It obviously hadn't. Anastasia's perfectly made up face scrunched in anger, twisted sourly, and finally fell into a very guilty-looking regret.

Said children, meanwhile, were speechless. Aside from their vibrant costumes and gladiator-style sandals, which were a riot of color-coordinated ribbons and silks, they had identical brown skin, gray eyes, and golden hair. I recognized Magica by the pattern of the leaves interwoven in her long tresses. Earlier, I'd thought the leaves were part of her costume, but I saw that her brother—despite having shorter, shoulder-length hair—sported the leaves too. He remained a pace behind his mother, watching us all from under cover of Anastasia's shadow.

But Magica was staring, not at her family, but at Officer Thorn. Almost as though pulled forward by a magnet, she slipped around her mother's side.

"Simple," she said, almost too quietly to hear. Then she cleared her throat and tried again. "It's a—a very simple system. The wire, I mean. We only ha—have it in the halls and dressing rooms. And the captain's room. It's just for emergencies or—or carnival news. Mostly reminders to be on set. Mother only sent—sent an emergency signal to our dressing room. That's all."

She glanced desperately over her shoulder at her brother. Almost reluctantly, he stepped forward. "She's right. We don't know what's going on."

Anastasia was still floundering, and Officer Thorn did something I hadn't seen her do before. She crossed her arms and backed down.

But she didn't say anything. So this time, I cleared my throat. "Maybe, in that case, it'd be best to interview Magica and her brother first, Officer Thorn?"

"Hm? Oh. Yes. Right now," she replied, gesturing for the twins to sit on the couch.

Anastasia sputtered and protested, and there was a match of wills, but eventually Thorn and I resumed our places sitting opposite Magica and her brother, whom she introduced as Weeping.

"So that's Magica and Weeping . . . Willow?" I asked, struggling to recall Anastasia's family name for my notes.

"Everyone here just calls me Weep," the brother said with a

nod.

Magica nodded, too, and Officer Thorn said nothing.

Frowning, I asked, "And when was the last time you each saw Coal?"

"Is that what this is about?" Weep shrugged one thin shoulder. "Probably at breakfast. Why?"

"No," Magica said uneasily, before trying again. "That is—he wasn't at breakfast. We haven't seen him since . . ."

She glanced at her brother, who looked sharply back at her. "Since last night. That's right."

Officer Thorn was still watching Magica. "What happened last night?"

Magica blushed. "Well—"

"Nothing," Weep broke in. "Just Coal being Coal."

"Could you clarify that?" I asked, when it became clear no one else would.

Weep sighed expressively and waved a hand. "Just, you know. Dramatic, all the time. Always saying how someone did him wrong about something or other."

Given what I'd seen of his mother, I wasn't too certain about Weep calling *Coal* "dramatic." But I kept that to myself. "And what wrong was he talking about last night?"

"Um," said Magica.

"Nothing," said Weep. "It's always the same with him. Why? What's this all about? Did he go missing or something?"

"He's dead," Officer Thorn blurted out.

I tilted my head at her. Sure, I didn't care too much for the Willow family either, but it was hardly fair of her to put things so bluntly!

Magica must have felt the same way, because her cheeks went ashen and her hands flew to her face. She sank back against the overstuffed couch cushions, releasing a cloud of dust.

"What's wrong with her?" Officer Thorn asked Weep, as his sister's eyes fluttered closed.

""What d'you mean, what's wrong?" Weep glared back. "That's our step-brother you're talking about."

* * *

Unsurprisingly, we learned nothing more from the Willow twins.

Still, though—just the family relation was a revelation. And as Anastasia swept into the room her children had just vacated, I could practically hear the pieces clicking into place.

Of course *she's the stepmother,* I thought. And then instantly chastised myself for thinking.

But she made it so easy . . .

"Of *course* Coal is my stepson," she said, the moment Thorn presented her with this fact. "Why do you think I was so worried for my own children? What kind of mother would I be if I *hadn't* immediately called them down? Besides, their act is over anyway. You get a feel for these things when you're with a carnival as long as I have been. But I have never seen a murder here—no, not anywhere—and certainly not of anyone so close to *me!*"

When asked to recall when last she'd seen Coal, she launched into a similar soliloquy. "I don't keep track of the boy's movements. He is much too obstinate. I *tried* with him, really I did, but how much could I do? He hardly ever answered to his father, bless the dear departed man. I'm sure *I* hardly ever had a chance. He was forever getting too full of himself, you see. Always had to have things his own way—neat as a pin, you must admit that—but so particular and *stubborn.* Oh, after a little intermission in his room, he might seem better. He might come to you and seem to reconcile! But then the same problems would always come up again."

Officer Thorn leaned forward, shoulders flexing. "An 'intermission'?"

"Strictly for his own good, of course," Anastasia replied at once. "Not that it ever *did* him any good. But I did try. Oh, how I tried!"

"Are you . . . are you saying you would lock him in his room?" I asked. My pencil, forgotten, slipped to the floor.

Anastasia narrowed her eyes as she turned to me. "I'm sure I never said any such thing!"

"And this afternoon was the last time you did so?" Officer Thorn pressed.

"I never! I haven't seen him since—since yesterday," Anastasia insisted. But her voice faltered.

"Since when, exactly, yesterday?" asked Officer Thorn.

"Oh, you *can't* ask me these little paltry details. Do you know how busy I am, opening the carnival in a brand new town?"

I saw an opening and I couldn't resist it. "Are you saying *you* are in charge of the carnival?"

"Heavens, no. Me? There's the director, of course," said Anastasia. "And the captain. But I'm sure I don't know *where* they would be without me."

"I'm sure," I muttered dryly, reaching down to the green piled carpet to retrieve my pencil.

"Details," Officer Thorn reminded us meanwhile, "about your meeting with Coal yesterday?"

"I'd hardly call it a meeting. I'm sure it was perfectly normal.

There's nothing I can tell you, Officer. You must allow me to see my children—I'm beginning to feel faint."

"One more question," Thorn insisted. "Was the unusual lock on Coal's door your idea?"

"I have no idea about locks and things," Anastasia sniffed. "I really have no time."

"And the spare key?" Officer Thorn leaned forward. "Who has it?"

"I'm sure I couldn't say. *Anyone* on board might. Anyone here could be a murder! Oh, and me and my children with no escape! What if they come after *us* next?"

"We'll continue this interview later," Officer Thorn said, grudgingly releasing our interviewee before she became hysterical. To me, quietly, she added, "Might be worth it to put together a timeline of the family, too."

I nodded and watched Anastasia throw herself dramatically into the hallway, letting the door slam behind her before I replied, "I really think we should take a closer look at that lock. And I'm not sure I believe her about the key, either."

"Funny," said Officer Thorn grimly. "I was just thinking I better get a Guild license to conduct a full search. Talking to our 'carnival matron' gave me exactly the same doubts."

6

The Stroke of Midnight

I f I thought I'd have a moment to investigate the lock right then, it turned out I'd be disappointed. A terrific noise from above deck turned out to be the carnival concluding. In its wake, a parade of performers and crew streamed in for interviews.

To my unprofessional eye, it seemed like many of them were suffering the effects of rampant gossip. They came in wild-eyed and frazzled, still in uniform, each more shocked than the last. It wasn't long before we started hearing hints about "dangerous secrets," but no one was willing—or able—to go into any detail.

We couldn't get much new information, but we did get a good overview of the carnival. We interviewed an animal trainer named Hemming who told us Coal had missed his shift in the stables, then a trio of clowns, a sharpshooter named Siren, an elemental mage, a magitech puppeteer, and Circe, an illusionist who also admitted to being the ship's cook; then on top of that we saw all nine naiad crew members before the night was through. And when the last sailor trudged out the door, it turned out that two of the big fixtures in the carnival had saved themselves for last.

First to come in—or perhaps I should say *penultimate*, the second-to-last to come in—was the captain of the *Luna II*.

"Henry Pleasant," he introduced himself, with an entirely straight face. "My family is from the northern lands, half human, half elf. I've been captain on this ship four years. Most of the carnival doings I leave to the director, but the crew is my responsibility. I'll answer for any of them if they give you any trouble. Anything you need to solve this case, if it is within my power, just let me know and it will be yours."

Captain Pleasant had that weathered, wiry, seafaring look, though his skin was surprisingly pale and unwrinkled: he seemed rather young, actually, to have been captain for four years. He held himself straight and still, only revealing a slight limp when he walked to and from the hall. I could hear nothing but earnestness in his cool, clear voice.

"When did you last see Coal?" Officer Thorn asked him, as she had all the others.

The captain was the only one who could be specific. "Noon, it must have been," he said, holding his short-billed cap over his chest. His clear blue eyes wavered with unshed tears. "Coming back from town, though he didn't take lunch or breakfast with the crew. I—I wanted to speak to him then, when I saw him return, but a question about the engine came up and I . . . I never got the chance."

"And can you tell us anything about Coal's relationships with the others on board?" Thorn asked gently.

"We all have our difficulties, traveling in such close quarters," Captain Pleasant said after he'd taken a moment to get control of himself. "Myself, I always thought of Coal as industrious and—and brave. But I've no doubt there will be others who disagree. I do my best to keep out of the petty squabbles."

"And the Willow family . . . ?" I prompted, curious.

Something flashed in the captain's eyes, but it was difficult to know what it was, especially since he was so obviously grieving. "I do my best to avoid them."

I was still pondering the captain's words when our final interviewee came in: the carnival director. He, too, was charismatic, though in a completely different way.

"I am at your service," he announced, before Thorn had even asked him anything—before he even sat down. "Please, call me Fontus. Just Fontus. Yes, I see you see the joke? Every actor strives for a magical or even deific name, and I am called after a lowly spring. But a spring is ever bubbling, friends. Everything that goes on in this carnival, I know. It has been more than a decade since I took over, and you may trust when I say, we have never had such a tragedy as this, and we never will again!"

I *did* get his little joke: all the clowns and other performers had given us names like Neptune or Circe. But despite his bravado, Fontus actually told us very little of any use. He related the carnival's preparations in detail but readily admitted that none of them had anything to do with Coal, whom he had not seen all day. When asked about Anastasia, he responded like a rhapsodizing knight in a fairy tale. When asked about the ship's security, he tried to flirt with Officer Thorn. He did have dashing good looks—tanned skin, wavy blond hair, green eyes, and just a little stubble around the jaw—but they availed him not.

Not, that is, until the very end of our interviews.

"This has been lovely," he declared, with a sweeping bow.

"How wonderful it is to know that such dedicated, clever officers are on our case. I have no doubt it will be solved before the next day is out. No matter the outcome, I *do* hope you will accept my personal invitation to the masquerade ball at the end of our tour. Naturally we will hold it in young Coal's honor—but it *must* be held, you see, for it wouldn't do to ruin all our livelihoods over one tragedy. Life stops for no soul!"

* * *

"A *ball*?" I whispered to Thorn as the man finally left. "Right after a murder?"

"You heard the man. 'Show must go on,' and all that." Officer Thorn rubbed her chin thoughtfully. "The carnival's scheduled to be in town only the next four days, not counting this one. So that's when this ball will be. It'll be a good chance to see all the suspects together—if we don't have the thing solved by then."

"Since you're saying 'all,' I'm guessing you think it must be someone we just spoke to who killed him," I observed, suppressing a yawn. The night was *very* late.

"Don't see how anyone in town would have had reason—or opportunity, seeing as he was both seen and found *aboard* the ship," Thorn agreed, failing to suppress her own yawn in the process. With a stretch that made her back crack more loudly than gunfire, she added, "Of course, that's before we know anything about the cause of death. Anastasia may balk about our inspecting the body, but we should be able to determine *that* at least. I'll get the Guild in on it, if I have to. Good thing the captain is reasonable."

"What was that sound?" Luca poked his head in the door—and beneath his head, William's furry snout poked in, too. "We thought we heard something."

"You did," I said, waving them in. "It was just Thorn. I guess watching the gangplank got old?"

"Had a nice nap," William panted. He waited just long enough for Officer Thorn to puff with indignation before adding, "Or I *might* have, if it hadn't been so loud. All the audience has gone now, and they're locking up. No one from the crew even mentioned wanting to go ashore for as much as a bit of fresh air . . . except Anastasia. She insisted on going down to check the admissions booth. I went with her," William said, heading off any questions. "There wasn't anything there. Magica, or whatever her name is, locked up."

"I didn't get the impression she trusts them to do much on their own," Luca said very softly.

"Sounds like we have the same impressions all 'round," Thorn declared. "And it also sounds like it's time to leave. Let's get a rest, and come back at it fresh in the morning."

Fresh, with police guild paperwork to throw at Anastasia, I thought. But I didn't want the memory of her to follow me back to my shop. As I handed Thorn's notebook back, I did my best to set thoughts like that aside.

There was a quick pause while Thorn located Gus, and got him to promise to send Coal's lock over to my shop in the morning. That done, we filed back onto the deck and descended to the dock quickly, without much talking. The night was hazy with clouds and firework smoke and the heaviness of the evening. There didn't seem to be much to say.

As we reached the shore, though, it seemed everyone

breathed a little easier. Officer Thorn fell naturally to grilling William about the carnival's 'locking up' procedure. Walking behind them, I nudged Luca's shoulder.

He glanced at me with a little smile. After a pause, his hand found mine. He didn't say anything, and for the moment, I let my worries be.

We walked home like that, together.

7

Down to Work

fter leaving Luca at his bookstore and waving Thorn off from our back stairs, my studio apartment felt like it might as well have been at the bottom of the lake. Usually, the snug second floor above the shop made me feel cozy and at home; but that night, with the fireplace cold and the open curtains letting in shadows from Market Square, it felt anything but homey. I chalked it up to the unsettling mystery of Coal's death—and his troubles at the carnival. Though I did my best to set them aside, I slept very poorly.

A fact William didn't hesitate to point out the next morning.

"No rest for the righteous?" he asked, hopping up on to the chair next to mine.

I put my hand out, steadying the dining table wedged into the front corner of the little apartment. It only held an empty saucer; my mug, full of strong black tea, hadn't left my hand since I poured it. "I was thinking I'd take a moment and watch the Square wake up, since I rose early. But it doesn't seem like there's much going on."

In fact, there wasn't *anything* going on, except for the usual farmer or two headed to the grocer's across the Square. The sun was rising on an empty park.

"The carnival ship's flying black flags," William informed me. Being a magical creature, he didn't have the same need for sleep that I did—at least not at night. He often went for late-night rambles and then insisted he had to nap during the day "to make up for it." I wasn't surprised he'd gone back down to the lake already. "Prob'ly in honor of Coal, though they haven't posted any notices," he added. "The way I see it, most of the town was at the carnival late last night and is sleeping in today, anyway. And those that *weren't* there last night have heard rumors about a murder and aren't feeling too industrious."

"Well, I guess I can't blame them. I'm not feeling industrious either," I remarked, with a self-deprecating chuckle. "I suppose, then, it doesn't matter if we open a little late today."

"You can keep up your gargoyle routine," William agreed, sniffing at my tea. "I want something more substantial than that for breakfast, though."

I shooed his nose away from my cup. "First you call me a gargoyle, then you demand I cook?"

"Admit it, you were going to stay here in the window in your pajamas until you saw the courier from the carnival come up with the lock," he challenged.

"It's cold this morning, and my pajamas are comfy." I shifted self-consciously in my plaid flannel pants. "You didn't see anyone from the carnival on the road, I guess? Gus said they'd send the lock over in the morning, but not exactly *when*."

"No sign of anyone up," William confirmed. "There was barely any action anywhere, even at the tavern."

His words were contradicted by a sharp rap at the door downstairs. In the shock of it, I managed to spill tea down the front of my fuzzy sweater. While I brushed the hot water away, William hopped down and went to answer the knock.

It really shouldn't have been surprising that the person to follow him back up the stairs was Officer Thorn. What *was* surprising, though, was that she held a bulky package under one arm—in addition to a basket of croissants.

"Ginger made 'em for me special and had one of the kids deliver 'em," she said, seeing my look. My stomach rumbled as she set the basket on the table and buttery goodness filled the air. "Guess he figured something must be up, after the way we interrupted him in line last night."

Sometimes, life in a small town was a true blessing. I was halfway through my first croissant—still warm—when I remembered the strange package. "Wait. What else did you bring with you? That isn't the lock from the ship, is it?"

Officer Thorn swallowed half a croissant and said, "It wasn't at my door, Red, it was at yours. Here, have a look."

Setting aside my breakfast, I did so. Naturally, Thorn and William crowded around my side of the table to do the same.

"It's got a note. 'We cut this out first thing this morning like you asked,' no signature." I turned the wrinkled paper over, found nothing, and looked back at the package. It was indeed the lock off Coal's door, wrapped up in a bit of smudged brown paper. "But when did this get here? We didn't see anyone come by."

"More to the point," said Thorn, swallowing another half croissant, "if it's Gus who wrote that, then he's also the one who wrote me that letter about the murder. The handwriting looks the same."

"But it doesn't actually say Gus's name. And anyway, that makes no sense." I frowned. "Gus said he didn't know anything about any murder. He was just as surprised as we were."

"He said the boat'd been quiet, anyway," Officer Thorn said thoughtfully. "I'll put it on the list of things to ask him. Might be he asked one of the crew to handle the lock. I'm headed to the carnival now. I've got a license to conduct a search of the ship, and the paperwork I need to move Coal's body for the investigation into cause of death."

"That was quick," William observed. All across Beyond, it was police guild policy to get permission from surviving relatives before doing anything with a victim's body; that policy had held up Officer Thorn's investigations for days in the past. Fortunately, there was all kinds of magic out there for preserving bodies.

Thorn shrugged, retrieving another croissant from her basket. "I was on the wire with the secretary at the local Guild office last night. Sounds like they've been keeping a bit of an eye on the After Midnight Carnival. Only too happy to give me free rein to search it."

That distracted me from puzzling over the lock delivery. "Is there a history of crime with them?"

"Not as far as we can tell. Not enough to shut 'em down, anyway," Thorn said, sounding a little saddened by the fact. "I better be going—I've got a big ship to search, and I want to get the Witch in on it, too. I only meant to stop a moment."

And to collect a bit of help, I thought, asking aloud, "Do you want one of us to go with you also?"

Thorn flipped her perfect black tresses over one shoulder and eyed my outfit. "Not someone in their pjs, thanks."

I couldn't help it: I chuckled. *Maybe it was a good thing I didn't get dressed right away!*

"I'll go," William volunteered. "I want to see what they're hiding. Besides, someone's got to make sure you don't end up overboard," he added to Thorn.

"I'd like to see any one of those puffed-up actors try," she replied cheerfully. With a wave at me, the two stomped down the stairs—more pushing each other than cooperating, but it seemed to work alright. The door snapped shut behind them, leaving me with silence. And a half-empty basket of croissants.

"If they're going to get to work, I suppose I will too," I mused to the pastries. "And if I'm going to do that, I'd better have some protein. And more tea."

* * *

I brought the basket of croissants downstairs with me, setting it on the windowsill between my lab and the shop. As a rule, I didn't approve of eating in my lab, but the croissants were safer down here than upstairs—Sugar, a tiny pixie who'd taken up residence in my kitchen, had been known to gorge herself on unattended pastries.

I set the lock on my workbench and began collecting tools from the cabinet: a vice, a magnifying glass, a set of various screwdrivers and pliers. Just as I was adjusting the lamp over my seat, another knock sounded at the back door.

This one, though, I recognized immediately. *Luca.* Normally the thought of seeing him put a smile on my face, but this time I felt a little worry, too.

"Hey, Red, sorry about coming over so early," he said as I opened the door. His smile was wan, and his clothes rumpled.

"I know last night I said everything was fine, but I . . . couldn't sleep."

"You can come over any time you want," I said reflexively, pulling him into the lab. "Come on, sit. I actually happen to have croissants on hand. I was worried Sugar'd make herself sick on them otherwise. I can put the kettle on for tea, too, if you want some?"

Luca sat, and I stood. I wasn't just playing with my lab coat; I was actively wringing my hands. And I sounded more like Luca than Luca did.

"That's fine," he mumbled. "That sounds fine, thank you . . ."

I immediately began pulling out the tea things, grateful for something to do. The truth was, for all Sir Rowan's sage observations, I'd been afraid of this from the start. I wasn't *just* worried about Luca reliving his days with Owl: I was also worried because I knew full well skillful I was at consoling someone. That is, how *unskillful*. There'd been a reason I spent all those years as a traveling alchemist, alone except for William. Emotions were not my strong suit.

But it was Luca who made you see the value in trusting your emotions, I reminded myself. *And this is just another part of that. He needs a little care, Cinnabar.*

Addressing myself with my mothers' name for me always snapped me into a broader perspective. As soon as the tea was steeping, I resolved to try an experiment. Luca and I had been dating for about six months—enough for me to know that he was more touchy-feely than I was, on average. That was basic empirical fact, as far as I was concerned. So I decided to build on that.

"Hey," I said gently, reminding him of my presence. I set the tea and croissants nearby, and then sat very close to Luca and put my arm around him.

"Hi," he sighed back. The sound was grateful. He turned into my shoulder at once, wrapping his arms around me. After a quiet moment, he whispered, "I feel like it's really silly for me to make a big deal of all this. But all night every time I closed my eyes I could see Coal lying there and I just kept thinking . . . If things hadn't turned out the way they did for me . . ."

My arm around him tightened, and so did my throat. "You aren't silly at all. That's what I was afraid of. I—I never want you to have to think about that time again."

"Oh, Red." Luca shifted, and suddenly he was the one comforting me. "I do, though," he said, very softly. "I think about him all the time."

"All the time?" I echoed, unable to keep my voice even. I knew without asking that "him" meant *Owl.*

"Less lately," Luca admitted, tucking my head under his chin. "But still sometimes. It's not as bad as you might think. After all, I work in the same bookstore still, and live in the same space. I mean, I *own* it now, and it's mine and I'm happy, but . . . I wonder a lot. I used to wonder about him a lot. What makes it hard," he added softly, "isn't that part. It's knowing that lots of people get hurt the way I did. That's what feels so awful. *Seeing* it. It's like—in my memories—the worst memories are the ones I have as Jade. Because that part of myself knew it was wrong."

All my words were stuck in my chest. I had always wondered how much Luca remembered of Jade, a magical alter-ego created by Owl. I had always been afraid to know.

If Owl hadn't died as a result of his own greedy schemes, I might've murdered him myself right then.

Above my head, Luca shifted again. "But that's why we have to make sure no one else at the carnival is getting hurt, right? That's something we can do right now."

His hold on me loosened, and I looked up. "Are you sure? You don't have to—"

"I do have to," he interrupted, quietly but very firmly. "And I appreciate that you haven't tried to keep me from this one, Red. Now. You were going to take a look at that lock, right? I'll sit with you, and drink my tea."

8

Cleaning Up

As Luca and I sat side by side, slowly deconstructing the lock, my anger began to simmer down. I could tell Luca felt better, too, because he started to joke with me as usual. In fact, when Sir Rowan came to work and found us, we were almost back to normal (and Sir Rowan's deep shock at finding the store not open on time was also fairly normal, I think!). When Trent showed up shortly after Sir Rowan, though, I remembered that the reason for the puzzle before us was murder.

Trent himself, of course, was nothing but amiable. All across Pastoria—in fact, all across Beyond—every little town has an official Witch, and Trent fills that role for Belville. He'd arrived shortly after me, a new recruit fresh out of Witch school, and I'd always felt a little sisterly towards him. Even in his mid-twenties, he hadn't outgrown teenage gangliness and overly pale skin—nor a determination to wear denim and ratty t-shirts. Today's shirt read, "A Witch in time saves lives."

He loped through the store, nodding politely to Sir Rowan and then grinning through the lab window at Luca and me.

Seeing my glance at his shirt, he pointed to the logo and said, "No such luck yet this morning, though. After we turned the whole carnival ship upside down, Thorn was making me do scans and stuff on the body up at the station."

I rolled my eyes at his rather morbid humor and asked, "Did you see William there? He said he was going to take part in the search, but he hasn't been back since."

"He was there. He helped out, actually," Trent said absently, like it wasn't a big deal that my witch-hating magical familiar had warmed up to him enough to assist in spellwork. "He's on his way, but he wanted to stop at the Pomegranate first."

"Why didn't you go too?" Luca asked innocently. Everyone in town knew that Trent had a massive crush on the café's owner, Sakura.

Trent tucked his hands into his pockets and hung his head, almost as though he was trying to hide behind his chin-length black hair. "You remember how Ryuko got hurt when we were trying to fix up the second floor, back when the café was opening?"

"That was months ago," I said incredulously.

"Yeah, and all's good," Trent said hurriedly. "Well, everything's good when we meet up *not* in the café. For some reason whenever I go in there she's still kind of . . . frosty."

Hmmm. As far as I knew, Sakura wasn't one to hold a grudge. I was surprised to hear about their trouble, but also impatient to hear about the results of the search. Besides, when it came to emotions, Saki was much better at navigating issues than I was, so I decided to stay out of it.

And apparently, Trent agreed. "Anyway, I didn't come over here to talk about me," he protested, just as Luca was opening his mouth. "And before you ask, our search didn't turn up anything interesting. No missing shoes, no keys. They're probably at the bottom of the lake by now, and where the boat is parked, Lake Lava's way too deep for any location spell to find them from the surface. That's what I've been telling Thorn all morning. Instead, I wanted to run some stuff by you about the death."

"Coal's death?" I specified, with a covert glance at Luca. I accepted Trent's fatalistic attitude about the boots, because I knew from my own experience that he was right: Lake Lava *did* get extremely deep extremely fast as you moved away from the shore, and sinking evidence would make perfect sense, especially to a murderer who was also a sailor or a performer on a ship. Depending on the time of death, the boots and key had probably been long gone before we were ever on board. Officer Thorn would have to build her case on other facts.

As I adjusted to this, Trent nodded. "I was able to figure some stuff out. But I don't think anyone will like it."

* * *

Officer Thorn might believe in conscripting as much of the town as necessary to solve a murder, but I clung to my belief that investigations were a private matter. (Well, mostly.) So, rather than talk about an active case out in the open in my shop, I dragged Trent and Luca upstairs. Sugar chittered at us from atop the kitchen cabinets, reminding me of my own rumbly stomach. Breakfast had been a long time ago, and croissants aren't exactly heavy-duty fuel—unless you're Officer Thorn, of course. It was definitely time for lunch, though I did wonder about the wisdom of eating while letting Trent talk about murder. Eventually, against my better judgment, I grabbed some cut vegetables, hummus, and whole grain bread to take to the table where Luca and Trent already sat nursing cups of minty iced tea. Just as I was sitting too, William's familiar footsteps sounded up the stairs.

"Nice to see you waited for me to have the meeting," he said wryly, flopping onto the nearby couch. With his paws and snout resting on the back of the cushions, he could watch us and lounge at the same time.

"We kind of did, actually," Trent said. "Red insisted on coming up here and getting something to eat."

"Taking care of yourself comes *before* hearing about police investigations. You can tell Thorn I said that," I challenged the room at large. After taking a large bite of carrot and hummus to prove my point, I gestured to Trent. "Well, okay, then. What was it you wanted to talk about?"

Trent leaned over the table, rubbing his hands on his shirt. At the last minute, though, he paused and looked across at William. "Do you want to go first?"

Apparently, the answer was *yes*. "Saki needs to talk to you," William informed me without preamble. "She wouldn't tell me why, so don't ask. Turns out Ginger told her all about what happened last night. She said to tell *you* not to leap to conclusions," he added to Trent.

The Witch shrugged expressively. "Would she say that if she'd seen what we did? Did you tell her?"

"In the middle of a crowded café? No," William said in his best I'm-not-a-fool-even-if-you-might-be voice. "I just wanted to see if she'd seen anyone else from the carnival, or knew anything more about what Coal did yesterday. The Officer needs help running down loose ends."

"Loose ends? All the ends are on a ship!" Trent scoffed.

I swallowed a bit of buttered bread and tried to get us back on track. "Did Saki say she had? Seen anyone else, that is?"

"Nope. Not a soul," William said, resting his chin on his paws with a dismissive shake of his ears.

Luca leaned back casually to grin at him. "So, how are Glacial's new cupcakes? She was working on a midsummer theme, right?"

"Flowery," William replied—at least, I assumed that's what he meant, as the Pomegranate's resident dessert chef was usually far too proficient to produce *floury* cakes.

"Now we know why you were so interested in helping Thorn chase down leads," I surmised.

"And so uninterested in lunch," Luca added, grinning at me as he took a handful of celery and brightly colored pepper slices.

"Are neither of you interested in hearing what I helped Trent find out?" William demanded in return.

The three of us glanced at the Witch, who hastily brushed crumbs from his chin and chased a piece of bread down with a gulp of tea. "Oh, am I talking again now?"

"Please," said Luca, sounding more amused than worried.

I sighed, reminding myself to let my worries go too. With a clearer head, I could focus on what Trent had to say.

"Cool. It's like this. The murder happened at about two o'clock yesterday, and it was definitely a murder. But that's all I can say for sure. Red, I was wondering if you know anything about magic water," Trent said, leaning forward once more, one bony elbow on the table.

"Magic water?" I wrinkled my nose. This was by no means a professional term, but I knew better than to expect scholarly lingo from Trent. "Why?"

The Witch barely had time to say "Because Thorn and I think Coal was drowned—" before we interrupted him.

"But there wasn't any water in his room!" Luca protested, wide-eyed.

"Not even a glass or empty bucket," I recalled, unsettled.

"Go on and tell them the *worst* part," William prodded.

"—and there's traces of saltwater about it," Trent finished. "You know you all are harder to talk to than Sakura sometimes?"

I ignored this complaint. My mind was racing. Lake Lava is entirely freshwater—or at least, I'd always assumed it was. "I'll test the lake water just to be sure, but I really don't think—"

"Exactly," William said with satisfaction. "We're way ahead of you."

"I mean, still do that, Red," Trent added. "Officer Thorn will want the test results for her reports or whatever. But we don't think it was the lake either. That's why we figure it was very intentional on someone's part."

"I hate to be the one to say it," Luca said hesitantly, "but there *are* magical folk on the ship that can probably manipulate water . . ."

"But they're naiads," William pointed out. "Naiads go with *fresh* water. There's no such thing as a saltwater naiad. That'd be a merperson."

"And even if there was, somehow, I don't think naiads can just *make* water," Trent explained. "They can only shape it or whatever. Like making currents move around the ship. A naiad—or even a merperson—couldn't just conjure water out of thin air to attack someone with."

"So," I mused, "either we missed a source of water in Coal's room somehow . . ."

"Or the murder didn't happen in his room," Luca concluded quietly.

"Or it *did*, and then the murder took it away," William added. "Along with the shoes and the key."

Trent nodded vigorously. "This is all kind of what Thorn was thinking. She's finishing up with the body now, Red, but after that she wanted to go back to the ship. Again."

"And she wants me to come? Well, I guess I can collect water samples while we're there," I said, knowing that resistance would be futile. "And we should probably have a talk about that lock."

"Yeah, she'll be asking you," Trent said with some humor.

"It was locked from the inside," Luca said, still quiet, but steady. "Right, Red? That's what you thought?"

"As far as I can tell," I agreed, nodding in response to Trent's surprised look. "It's a weird, complicated lock—basically two locks in one. There was an external lock too. But when they gave it to us, they literally cut it out of the door frame, and we could see that the *inside* lock was the one that had been engaged."

Trent whistled. "That's going to make things hard to explain."

"Not necessarily," William broke in. "You still didn't tell them the *whole* worst part, Witch. According to what we know right now, the only saltwater creatures aboard the ship are the animals in the carnival act."

"Are you saying you think a sea creature killed him?" I frowned.

"I'm saying that's Officer Thorn's best idea so far," William replied. "And it's going to take a lot of effort to convince her otherwise."

9

Anchors Away

True to William and Trent's predictions, Officer Thorn soon turned up on my doorstep full of suspicions about carnival creatures, itching to go out to the lake again.

William, the little traitor, assigned himself to stay behind and watch the shop with Sir Rowan. I personally didn't think Sir Rowan needed the help—a quiet morning was fast becoming a quiet afternoon—but I had to admit William *had* already done a lot of investigating. It sounded like he and Trent had conducted a full magical sweep of the *Luna II* looking for the missing items—only to come up empty-handed. So, I left him to trade malicious stories about waterfolk with his knightly friend.

Luca, it turned out, hadn't even bothered opening the bookstore that morning. We left him on his darkened stoop getting an earful from his animal-friend-turned-assistant, Frank. Some creatures become wise and learn how to talk simply by living for a very, *very* long time, and Frank was one of those. A three-legged mink with a coat of silvery-white fur and a tendency to sneak up on people, Frank was far quieter than William but just as able an assistant. He couldn't do any magic, but he did have a passion for books—and consistency. I'd really only ever seen Frank speak to Luca, but this morning he seemed to have quite the rant bottled up.

Still, Luca waved us off supportively, promising to gather research materials to pore over later. I doubted there was much scholarly work out there on "magic water," but I knew that if anyone could find some, Luca would be the one to do it.

"What's this, your second time aboard?" Trent nudged my shoulder, knocking me out of my reverie as we walked down the hill out of town.

"Yep. Second. First time was long enough to count as two, though," I added, because I knew that he was looking for a chance to joke around a little before we settled down to serious matters.

"So I hear. William wasn't too impressed," Trent said with a chuckle. "But you didn't get any chance to actually see the carnival?"

"No. We were going to, but Thorn found us on the dock with her news." I glanced at the officer ahead of us; she was leading the way, already acting authoritative and assured. Sometimes she could be a little much, but this time I felt sympathy for her; *the actors are definitely difficult to deal with,* I thought. *It must take a lot of energy to keep up that confident front.*

Or maybe she was just born that way?

"Bummer," Trent was saying. "Last I heard, they were still going to hold the carnival tonight and the rest of the time, unless Thorn tells them not to. I think she won't, though. Unless it turns out that one of the animals really is dangerous."

"I guess their business is their own, as long as none of them leave during the investigation," I mused. "It's not like the carnival ring itself is part of the crime scene. Fortunately. Were you going to see it?"

"Dunno," Trent shrugged. "I don't think Sakura's really into it."

"But you could still go on your own . . ."

Trent gave me an almost pitying look, as though someone like me—someone safely ensconced in a steady relationship—could never hope to understand the intricacies of dating. Or *trying* to date. "I notice you automatically said '*we*' went to see it," he remarked.

I blushed. "Well, yes. Because it's true. But it's not like Luca and I are *always* together—"

"Oh, so this morning was a fluke, then?"

"He just came by because—Trent! Stop being so annoying."

"I'm just saying . . ."

"You're being a nuisance, is what you're doing," I chuckled.

Officer Thorn rounded on us: we'd reached the shores of the lake. "You *both* are being unprofessional. Do you want me to send you home?"

Trent and I exchanged glances. I did kind of want to be working on my summer stock, and I was certain Trent had something else he could be doing—possibly mooning over his not-quite girlfriend. But we knew better than to call the officer's bluff.

Using one of a row of vials strapped to my belt, I grabbed a sample of lake water before we boarded the *Luna II*. Officer Thorn was already halfway up the gangplank, deep in conversation. Not with Gus—he wasn't at his usual post on the deck. It turned out that most of the crew was holding a vigil in Coal's honor, up on the carnival deck. However, Captain Pleasant had spotted us coming, and he'd been the one to meet Thorn as she approached.

"We would have invited you, of course, when you were done with your search," he was saying as Trent and I caught up. "You could come now and see it, if you like. But most are choosing to observe in silence. I'm not sure you'd learn anything new, and I must admit the atmosphere is a little—stifling." He choked a bit on the last word, and I wondered if he meant it was stifling because it was so emotional, or because he was somehow tired of it.

Officer Thorn fixed the captain with a similarly unsympathetic look. "You could have mentioned this earlier, or in the note with the lock."

"I didn't wish to interrupt you," Captain Pleasant said, pale eyebrows disappearing beneath his cap in surprise. "Did Gus take care of the lock already, then? He didn't mention sending anyone ashore. I assumed you'd come to retrieve it this morning, along with everything else. I've been doing my best to keep everyone here, you see. I thought that might make matters—easier for you."

Despite that same choking hesitation in his voice, I thought he sounded genuine. What he said made sense, after all: Officer Thorn *could* have picked up the lock herself this morning—but when we'd arranged with Gus last night, we hadn't known how soon she'd be back with her paperwork. But of course the captain didn't know that. Actually, it seemed like he was doing his level best to accommodate Officer Thorn's investigations. This impression was only strengthened as he led us all over the ship, letting us sample water from the kitchen and the hold before finally ending at the stables on one of the lower decks.

"I'm not often down here, I must admit," Captain Pleasant said. After touring us around for half an hour or more, his voice came more smoothly. "But I do make it a point to know what goes on aboard my vessel. Any questions you have, I will do my best to answer."

"I'm going to need a rundown of what you have, and who can control them," Officer Thorn said, gesturing to the damp stalls around us. Snuffles and snores sounded from behind water-logged wooden doors.

"And what their abilities are," Trent reminded her. A purple glow around the ends of his hair and in his irises told me he was already using magic to scan the stable, looking for traces like those he'd found on Coal.

"If ye're wanting to know," a new voice said from the hall, "then you better be asking *me*."

***

The carnival's animal trainer was nothing like its captain—or the rest of its crew, for that matter.

We had met Hemming the night before, of course. He'd been the one to tell us that Coal had missed a day of work. Apparently, Coal and one or two other crew members worked for Hemming, who was in charge of all the carnival creatures.

Hemming himself looked like he might have come out of an old tome on marine lore. His build was broad, almost boulder-like, and his skin was wrinkles upon wrinkles, like he'd been in the bath too long. His skin was tanned but his long beard was a deep green, and so were his eyes, nearly hidden under bushy eyebrows. A folded bandanna across his forehead did nothing to disguise the fact that he was mostly bald. His clothes were a little large for him, and roughly made—perhaps because we had caught him in his work-and-cleaning outfit, not his show uniform.

Most notably, though, Hemming spoke like words had gone out of style.

"Six ceffyl dwr. One bunyip," he repeated to me at a glacial pace as I scribbled notes for Thorn.

The officer, meanwhile, was pacing the stalls. Trent was moving from corner to corner like a Halloween decoration, still glowing, and Captain Pleasant had respectfully withdrawn.

"Uh huh. And can you describe them for me, please?" I asked, trying hard not to give him the same attitude I might have given William in the same situation.

"Ceffyl dwr. Miniature kind. Some call 'em 'mist goats.'"

"I thought ceffyl dwr were water horses, like kelpies," Trent called, snapping out of his trance.

Hemming shrugged. "Some are."

My pencil paused. "These aren't?"

Officer Thorn decided to put me out of my misery. "They're little ones, Red. Here, look into this stall."

With what I hoped was a polite look at Hemming, I stepped across the dimly-lit hall to peer over the waist-high door Thorn had indicated. She moved aside so I could see, instead of hay or wood, a little muddy pool in which two four-legged, cloven-hoofed, horn-headed little puffs of cloud sat looking back at me with glassy blue eyes.

Mist goats.

I made some notes and let Officer Thorn take over the investigation. We'd gotten halfway through a rather one-sided conversation about the bunyip, a sort of dog-and-seal cross with a booming bark and the creative name *Scylla,* when the penny dropped.

"Comes from lakes," Hemming said. "Same as ceffyl dwr. Me'n the stablehands change their water every day. Take them out for exercise when we can."

"Hold up," said Officer Thorn, raising one large hand. "Lakes? As in, fresh water?"

Hemming nodded. "Freshwater carnival. Freshwater animal crew."

Over Hemming's substantial shoulder, I could see Thorn glaring down the hallway at Trent.

The Witch spread his hands, leaving a trail of faint purple sparks. "Don't look at me! *I* didn't say to investigate the mist goats."

I could practically hear the officer's teeth gnashing. "But you said—"

"There *is* something here that's sea-like," Trent interrupted. "There."

As he faced us, he pointed to his left, across the hall from the stalls. I had assumed there was a tack room or something back there; it was shrouded in shadow. But from the way Trent was pointing so gingerly—not to mention suddenly impersonating Hemming's chattiness—a kernel of anxiety settled in my stomach.

"Ah." Hemming shifted. "Ye're after Sleepy, then."

"We're not *after* anyone," Officer Thorn clarified. "But we do have an interest in creatures that can manipulate salt water, specifically. Can any of your animals do that?"

"No," said Hemming placidly. "Not mine. But Sleepy does."

Seeing as Trent was still acting like a child who'd discovered a bogey, and steam was about to pour out of Thorn's ears any minute, I took over. "Um, Hemming, what is Sleepy?"

"Part of the clown boys' act," Hemming informed me. He shuffled down the corridor and Trent leapt back out of the way. The animal trainer turned to me as he slid open a panel at shoulder height, a sort of window into a large, darkened stall. "See for yourself. He won't bite."

Great, I thought, stowing my notebook. That kernel of anxiety was now a whole corn cob, and it rattled against my spine as I followed Hemming's steps.

I had to pull my goggles down over my eyes in order to see into the gloom behind the window Hemming had opened. As the magic lenses adjusted to the dark, details came into focus. A white fin. A massive, rounded snout. Pale, almost ghostlike, floating in a cloud of water.

Sleepy, it turned out, was a shark. The kind of shark that needed as much space as all the ceffyl dwr and the bunyip combined. The kind of shark which could levitate in its own little ball of saltwater.

And, apparently, the kind of shark that had neither time nor interest for landlubbers. The sleeping creature didn't even blink one tennis ball-sized eye at me as I stared.

10

Smooth Sailing

"I don't get it," Trent whispered to me as Thorn continued to wheedle information out of Hemming. "If you have a massive shark, why use it to drown someone? Why not just have it eat them or something?"

"Maybe it's vegetarian," I muttered back. "You're making assumptions. We don't know for sure that Sleepy was involved in the murder, or even if Sleepy responds to commands."

"You sound like Thorn," Trent complained.

"I'm just saying." I was also trying to remember. We'd interviewed the clown trio last night; they'd come across as a devoted unit, kind of like Magica, Weep, and Anastasia. But they hadn't really had anything to say about Coal at the time. *Maybe that was because they didn't want to incriminate themselves?*

Or maybe someone else gets along with Sleepy?

Or Coal got too close to the shark's stall, and his death was an accident . . . but in that case, why would he end up back in his room?

All this, of course, was setting aside my primary question, which was *how in Beyond is that shark* doing *that?* But I knew that would be a question for William and Luca later. Hemming, it seemed, didn't have much to do with Sleepy.

"I don't keep track of him same as I do the others," he was telling Thorn.

"But you must know what he was up to yesterday. Just in general. Surely a shark bigger than a caravan can't sneak out?" the officer pressed.

Hemming shifted from one foot to the other, and finally admitted, "Coal was on stall duty yesterday."

"But he didn't show up for work," Officer Thorn remembered. Hemming nodded. Thorn went on, "Was Coal what you would call a dependable worker?"

Hemming shifted again. "He was a busy kid."

"But not busy with the work you gave him? With looking after the creatures, seeing to their safety?"

"He had a lot on his mind," Hemming insisted, his voice strained. "I wish I had done more."

"More in what way?" Officer Thorn asked, her eyes sharp.

Hemming shrugged.

"The things on his mind," I suggested from behind Hemming. "Do you mean family matters? Something to do with Anastasia, maybe?"

"Anastasia?" Hemming's eyes widened as he turned to include me in the conversation. "I—no. Not that I would know."

There was something there, some edge in his voice, but I couldn't figure it out.

"Is there anything you do know that you would like to share?" Officer Thorn asked, resuming control of the conversation.

Hemming shook his head. "Only—"

"What?" Thorn asked.

"The ceffyl dwr and Scylla," Hemming said. "They could do with some air. You don't mind I take them out tomorrow?"

"Keep to the lake and you're fine," Officer Thorn said, not showing any disappointment she may have felt. "Nearby you'll find Cactus Island. That'll suit you well, I imagine."

Hemming nodded his thanks, and Trent began crowding me, eager to leave the stalls.

"One more thing," Officer Thorn decided. "Were there any signs of disturbance here yesterday?"

"Never," Hemming said firmly. He straightened his normally bent shoulders, and for a moment I could see how he might be a stern taskmaster. He certainly seemed to take care of his creatures seriously.

Seriously enough to warrant murder?

I did my best to dismiss the thought, but the fact remained that Hemming hadn't quite managed to clear his name . . . or Sleepy's.

* * *

"Alright, here's the deal," Officer Thorn said when we'd emerged onto the main deck of the ship to get a little air ourselves. "I'll go hunt down the shark trio. Trent, I want you to come with me."

"If I go too, we could all interview them separately," I suggested.

Under the stormy afternoon skies, Officer Thorn gave me a particularly cool look. "Nice try, Red. I need you to speak with Anastasia and the twins again."

"What? Why can't you do it?"

"Because I don't want to hear any more complaints about

our search, and I don't want her to take hold of the saltwater lead and run with it," Thorn returned matter-of-factly. "I need you to see what you can get out of her while seeming casual. *Sea*-ming casual, if you like."

"No, I don't like," I muttered. But I knew it was a lost cause. And furthermore, Officer Thorn made a kind of sense. If a police officer questioned the carnival dame about saltwater, no doubt she'd think up twenty different dramatic scenarios, and have the whole place in an unintelligible uproar. But if I just came across as a nerdy alchemist asking random questions, she might not remember what I'd wanted to know.

She probably doesn't even remember my name, I thought as Trent waved merrily and our two parties went separate ways. I sighed, and turned to practical matters. Officer Thorn and Trent were headed below deck again to find the clowns in their quarters—*not* a scenario I'd ever imagined myself thinking through, much less standing in!—and I had to decide where Anastasia was likely to be. The twins, I figured, would be in her shadow.

She's probably at the vigil still, I thought, glancing up at the carnival ring rising behind my head. *Even if everyone else is breaking up, she'd probably be there 'til the bitter end.*

As I climbed the wide stairs that led up to the raised deck, and from there to the grand ring, I wondered what exactly had given me such a negative impression of Anastasia so quickly. Her attitude, surely, but maybe something else, too . . . the fact that I expected Coal's story to be a twist on old Cinderella tales, perhaps? Or even just the way Coal had talked, back at the Pomegranate, about *them* . . .

I didn't have much time to mull the matter over. Standing at the head of the grand staircase put me on eye level with the carnival's central ring. The ropes and magical barriers were down, so I was looking straight out over a polished wooden platform at not only Anastasia and the twins, but Fontus as well.

"Oh, Red! Come, do come!" Anastasia called, her stage voice echoing around the empty seats that circled the stage.

Well, that's one thing she remembers, I thought, willing my feet to take me out into the ring.

It was a little smaller than most carnivals I'd seen before— no doubt being portable and on a ship meant it had some limitations. The ring itself was perhaps twenty yards across at most; big enough for a clown act—or even a massive magical shark—but small enough that, with the stories of seats towering up to the sun, it felt intimate. In the very center of the stage, marked out by concentric circles of blue and gold painted on the floorboards, a temporary altar of sorts had been set up. I recognized a picture of Coal and a few candles and bunches of flowers as I strode up.

Anastasia was in her show attire. I doubt she had any other kind. Today's dress was ornate with buttons and even a useless gear or two, in true steampunk style. The outer layer of deep purple velvet was cut away in strategic places to reveal black blouse and petticoats. She continued talking as I walked up. "How good it is of you to pay your respects to our grieving family during this very, very difficult and tumultuous time! What a sense of propriety you citizens of Belville have!"

I couldn't resist. I eyed the twins—dressed in nearly-identical black breeches and somber shirts—and Fontus, who stood confidently in a dark blue pinstripe suit. "Wasn't this vigil for everyone? I'd hate to intrude on a family matter."

"Oh, but we are *all* part of the family in the carnival," declared

Anastasia, clinging to Fontus's arm. When the black ostrich feather on her tiny hat brushed his cheek, he blew it away good-naturedly.

"Aye, that much is true," he assured me with a smile that seemed a little out-of-place at a vigil. Even the remains of one. "Traveling life teaches you to live fast and move ever upward."

"Huh." I hadn't necessarily learned that lesson, myself. I actually *liked* the slower pace of life in Belville. But, I knew that Fontus's view was a popular one amongst travelers, nevertheless. "Well, I *do* wish to pay my respects to Coal. I see maybe I should have brought something. You even have fresh flowers there . . . ?"

"We all contributed tokens we received from the show last night," Anastasia told me hastily, and a bit theatrically, given that she herself had not performed. "It seemed only right that the favors go to honor Coal's dear, departed memory."

I wasn't sure it was his *memory* that had departed, but I bit my tongue. *So the flowers are from last night, not from someone on board going ashore today. Hmm.* "Well, that's very nice, I'm sure. I've just been down to see Coal's old workplace—you know, the stables," I added, when my little audience collectively gave me a funny look. I did my best to play this off as a totally normal thing to do. "Just helping Officer Thorn with some loose ends, and all. I had no idea this ship housed such a huge shark!"

"Oh, you mean Sleepy," Anastasia purred. "That old thing. Barely moves a muscle, did you notice?"

"Unless—" Magica started, and immediately stopped, at a glance from her mother. "I just meant, he does a good job, in his act I mean."

"The trio's act is a showstopper for sure," Fontus agreed

gallantly. "And the stables are well worth a visit. I myself like to check in on the animals each morning before breakfast."

"Ah, the trio reminds one of our old acts of grand years gone by, does it not?" Anastasia glanced up at the director, eyes alight again. "Why, I remember once, I had the honor of traveling with—"

"It *is* very impressive," I interrupted, a bit loudly. "So, what does Sleepy actually do, then?"

I directed the question at Magica; she seemed like the weakest link in their collective story chain. Weep was impassive, standing next to his sister.

But, of course, it was Anastasia who answered. "Oh, that's right, you poor thing! You never got to see the show last night, and that handsome man with you neither. A pity you had to miss it—all our acts are *marvelous*."

"I've invited them all to the ball," Fontus assured her, not me. "And of course, they can have free admission to come back any time they like."

"Thanks," I said, relatively certain they wouldn't notice how half-hearted I sounded.

"We never deal with Sleepy," Magica said quietly, her large eyes fixed on me.

Well, that saved me the trouble of bringing up the shark again, I thought. But there was something faintly ominous about how focused she was on my face.

"Us? No, of course not," Anastasia said, tossing her loose red hair. "The Willows perform strictly acrobatic acts, of course. And then, I *was* known to sing in my day . . ."

"And a wonderful singer you were, too," Fontus added, smiling down at her.

Bleh, I thought. And then, *is there no way to keep this group on topic?* "Well, Luca—my boyfriend—he loves animal acts," I improvised, feeling rather proud of myself. "I'll have to tell him about Sleepy."

"He floats," Magica told me, a little unnecessarily, and still with almost creepy focus. "He can spit water jets. The acrobats ride on top."

Hmm. That didn't sound like very much action on the shark's part. I was starting to understand his name.

"Of course, just bringing him out makes the crowd go wild," Fontus said good-naturedly. "In between every one of the main acts, he's sure to get his own round of applause! He's a crowd favorite."

"Just the way I used to be," Anastasia sighed, with eyes only for Fontus.

I was saved from rolling mine as Captain Pleasant hailed us and hurried across the stage. "Fontus, Caty wanted me to tell you she's got an early dinner started. A true feast, to follow the vigil," he announced as he came up. "Everyone's invited, of course. Including you." The captain turned to me with a bow.

"Oh, that's alright, really, I ate at home, and I have dinner plans," I managed to say, in the time it took Anastasia to make her goodbyes, gather up the twins and director like so many swirling skirts, and sweep down the staircase toward the next event.

In her wake, I raised an eyebrow at Captain Pleasant. He fiddled a little and almost looked like he might bow again. Finally, he blurted, "I'm not—I must say—I'm really not a big fan of theirs either."

My skeptical look broke into a grin. "Thank goodness. I was having a hard time keeping it in."

"Yes, I—I know what you mean." The need to be diplomatic still seemed to wear on the captain a little, but he did give me a charming smile in return. "I was never with a carnival before this one, but I am told that such shows generally attract . . . these sorts."

"I can imagine," I said sympathetically. "I had actually come up here to ask them about Sleepy. You don't know of anyone who's taken a special interest in him lately, do you? Aside from me and Officer Thorn, of course."

Captain Pleasant tilted his head in thought, throwing soft shade across one side of his young face. He couldn't possibly have been any older than me, I decided.

"I can't say I have," he said finally. "Coal always says—that is—Coal always told me that the shark was the nicest one aboard the *Luna II* to work for."

"Oh?" I prompted, doing my best to sound gentle.

"Yes—and I would say to him, 'well, aside from me, I hope.'" Captain Pleasant's face shifted like the clouds above us, moving through nostalgia, grimace, and loss. He looked down at his polished boots for a moment before meeting my gaze again. "I suppose I—well, it might not come as any surprise to you. I really did *wish* to be professional, when I took this job, but it wasn't long before I realized—Coal—he was . . . very dear to me."

Oh! Captain Pleasant instantly clicked into place in the story for me. *Prince Charming.*

But even as I made the connection, I could see I was doing him a disservice. Captain Pleasant was truly grieving; that was probably the reason he'd come across so strained earlier.

On an impulse, I reached out and touched his elbow. "You don't have to justify it for me. I understand."

He looked up gratefully, a brief smile coming and going. "Thank you. But I'm afraid I must ask you—not to tell any of what I have said to the performers, or the crew. They're all on edge about the search earlier, and even at the best of times, they wouldn't understand. They—many of them—they never seemed to like Coal. It was almost as though they treated him as a criminal, for having dreams of getting away."

"I won't repeat anything," I promised. "Except to Officer Thorn. Since I'm helping her investigation, I have a duty to tell her."

"Yes. That I understand," said the captain with one last solemn nod.

11

A Love in Disguise

"Sounds like you learned about as much as we did," Officer Thorn grumped much later. She'd insisted on waiting until we were ashore to compare notes. Then, the moment we'd set foot on dry land, the town council had found her and begun demanding answers. It wasn't until our collective research "date" with Luca that Thorn, William, and I got to sit down in one place. The officer went on, "Fruitless search, saltwater leads drying up, and barely more than seeds of doubt from the examination of the body. I could do with dinner."

"That comment about Sleepy being the best one aboard to work for sounds ominous, though," Luca said as he passed out polished wooden plates laden with pizza.

"Yeah, but then again, sounds like 'Sleepy' is a well-deserved name," I remarked, accepting a slice of veggie pizza and plopping down on the carpet. "So Coal might have been talking more about him being undemanding, not necessarily about him being, you know, a shark. No one else seemed to know much about it. Any luck with the trio? Or how about the lock?"

"Negative on the clown trio," Officer Thorn replied. She presided over our little meeting in an old armchair. Whenever we met in the bookstore, we took over the back room, where a fireplace and overflowing shelves made for a cozy atmosphere—even when the subject was murder. "They did warm up to Trent, but they still didn't say anything of use. Clammed up whenever Coal's name was said."

"Must have been pretty discouraging," William muttered beside me. "Otherwise she would've gone for a shark pun instead of the clam thing."

Officer Thorn glared at him across the hearth, but then distracted herself with basil and tomato pizza. In a more light-hearted voice, she said, "I did find Gus again, though, and questioned him more thoroughly about the lock. Said he *meant* to run it over to us himself, but never got a chance. He'd assumed the Captain had dealt with it."

"So no one knows who delivered the lock, which means we still don't know who wrote both notes," I concluded. "I have to say, you look surprisingly positive for having hit so many dead ends, Thorn."

"Dead ends are par for the course in a murder case. Means we're doing it right," she told me through a cheesy grin.

I groaned and turned to Luca. "Tell me you had better luck?"

"I had lots of luck, but I don't know if it's any better than what you all found," Luca told me, eyes twinkling. He sat cross-legged in the center of our little circle, piles of books behind him.

"Where's that mink?" Officer Thorn interrupted, looking around the dim room as though Frank might be hiding in a dusty corner.

"He likes to go to bed early. He's usually up before dawn," Luca explained. "Says it's an old habit. Why? Were you hoping he'd know something about Sleepy?"

"Not like you have a magical familiar to ask questions of," William groused.

I chuckled, putting an arm around his fluffy neck. "I was hoping *both* of you, Luca and William, could explain the shark. I didn't even think of Frank."

"It's a good thought, because they probably *are* somewhat similar," Luca began seriously. "William, you can tell me if you agree, but it sounds to me like Sleepy is an actual animal, rather than a familiar. The specificity of Red's description, and Sleepy's characteristics, suggests that he's a very ancient shark who's learned to manipulate water within his own gravity field, or aura, if you like. I could probably find out what species he is if I looked through the natural history section. Ancient animals who develop uncommon abilities, like Frank, are still at heart wild creatures. On the other hand, familiars, like William, aren't necessarily defined by being a particular species. They tend to have much more individual personalities."

"Basically, I'm still the most interesting creature around, and don't you forget it," William sniffed. I elbowed him good-naturedly and he added, "I think the scholar's right. Sleepy's just an old and somewhat magical shark. A lot of mythical beasts are just unusual animals who've managed to survive for so long that they become powerful. But the point is, there's no reason a shark would care enough about Coal enough to kill him."

"Not a well-fed one," Officer Thorn mused, wiping pizza grease from her chin with a flowery cloth napkin.

"Will you stop with that? You and Trent," I complained, more teasing her than anything else. "It's not like Coal was bitten."

"Which, again, either means someone manipulated Sleepy, or Sleepy isn't your murder weapon," William pointed out.

"Where *is* Trent?" Luca piped up suddenly. "I got an extra pizza in case he showed up."

"Standing friend-date with Ryu at the tavern," I explained. "I did ask him to join us, but he said he didn't have anything to contribute. In fact, he said an empty vacuum of space would have been more useful than the jumbled-up traces on board the ship."

"He's just too distracted by a certain shadow witch," Officer Thorn observed. "And that means I'm expecting *you* all to pick up the slack!"

I rolled my eyes at William, who panted, a doggy grin.

And of course, there was Luca, ready to lead us forward. "So, actually, I did research freshwater and saltwater spirits," he said brightly. "This stack here"—he gestured to a leaning pile of well-worn tomes by his right knee—"is all about naiads and the legend of Melusine, who was quite well-known in her day. The stack behind that is all similar types, too. And—"

"Hold on," Officer Thorn interrupted. "What do you mean, 'similar types'?"

Luca paused, thrown off by the question, and while he drew breath, William beat him to the punch. "The whole story with Melusine was basically a star-crossed lovers drama," he said, tail wagging at the chance to show off some knowledge. "She's a naiad, right, and she agrees to marry a human, but because naiads are very reclusive, she makes him promise never to reveal what she actually is to anyone. He promises and everything's hunky dory for a while, but then of course he ends up spilling the beans accidentally, and she leaves him right then and there. Apparently to go set up a carnival."

I glanced at Luca, eyebrow raised. "Essentially, that's correct," he agreed. "I mean, it's the kind of story where there are many different sides, of course. Some people say that the human tricked her into the relationship from the beginning; some say that even *he* didn't know what she was; some say that she was heartless and ensnared him from the start."

"Okay, so, mistakes were made," I said. "And this is so common it's a *type* of story? Or spirit?"

Luca nodded. "Particularly in waterfolk lore. There are lots of water spirits who prefer to keep their true identity secret and consider betrayal the ultimate insult. Not just naiads, but also aloja, and—"

"So what I'm hearing," Officer Thorn weighed in as she polished off her third slice, "is a strong cultural reason for murder."

"Assuming Coal knew someone's secret. A secret we haven't caught wind of yet," I reminded her.

"The sharpshooter did catch us in the hall this morning and suggest Anastasia might have some such family history," Officer Thorn informed me. "You weren't there for that, Red. You didn't miss much; she wouldn't elaborate at all. It's basically another rumor."

"There's also a lot of water spirits out there who are straight-up dangerous," William reminded both of us. "You ought to remember the kelpie, Red. Ceffyl dwr might be cute, but they're very similar. Lots of water animals will lure you into touching them so that they can drown you. Some human-type water spirits are that way, too, like the aicha kandida."

"Right. That's this pile," Luca nodded, gesturing to a lump of books and scrolls behind his right shoulder. "But I also looked up 'magic water,' and—"

"Anything? Maybe a magical object? That'd be a lot easier to find than searching through everyone's personal history and identity," Officer Thorn said.

I frowned at her. "Will you at least let him finish a sentence?"

"I know you're protective of your boyfriend, Red, but this is *mur*—"

"Excuse me!" I blushed furiously. That one was a little too true for comfort.

"Both of you are missing the point," William said, munching on a pizza crust.

"What I was *going* to say," Luca said, raising his voice over all of us, "was that the idea was a little too vague to be much use. I did find *lots* about it, though." Officer Thorn's eyes widened and my jaw dropped as we registered the three towering piles at Luca's back. "There's a lot to go through, and most of it probably won't be useful . . . but many hands make light work, right?"

* * *

Eons later, the evening was finally coming to a close, and I was stuffed to the gills with new knowledge on magical water jugs and watery potions and even a couple legendary water squirt guns. Like Luca had predicted, I doubted much of it had been of use. But the quiet hours had given me a chance to think something else over and come to a decision.

As we wrapped up our research, putting things into piles Luca dictated, I pulled William aside.

"Hey," I said, watching Officer Thorn scoop up a dozen ancient scrolls with the swipe of one arm. "Do you mind going ahead without me? You can keep telling Thorn all about ancient animals or Melusine or whatever."

"I'd prefer to get a head start on my stargazing," William sniffed.

I grinned. "Up to you. I'll be on my way back home in just a little bit."

Luca refused to let Officer Thorn actually put the records away—not that I blamed him—so in a mere matter of moments, he and I were left alone in the bookshop.

And suddenly, I felt tongue-tied. It's not like it was my first evening alone with Luca—far from it. But recent events had definitely thrown me for a loop.

"Here," I finally managed, blushing. "Let me help you *actually* clean up."

"Sure, thanks," Luca smiled back. Something in his green eyes made me think he knew what I was thinking, but he didn't let on. Instead, we each took a few books and I began to follow him through the shelves. "Was it a good thing I did this, do you think?" he asked as he worked. "I didn't mean to derail your investigation."

"No, it was perfect. Even being able to rule things out is helpful," I said, thinking, *who knows where the investigation will lead next, anyway.* "But we don't have to dwell on the case if you don't want to. Maybe . . . tell me about your day?" I tried, hesitantly.

I hadn't been entirely sure how to make him feel at ease, but I must have hit upon a good idea, because Luca beamed at me as we went to collect more books. "It actually wasn't so bad. Finding all these old records kept me pretty busy, and did you know Saki had some tea and a cupcake delivered?"

I didn't, and come to think of it, I wasn't sure how Sakura knew of Luca's involvement in the case at all. But then, her store *was* very close to Ginger's, and they did trade gossip sometimes. When Ginger wasn't feeling ornery about Sakura competing with him for Belville's sweet-baked-goods market. If Luca's sweet tooth was any indication, though, that market could stand the competition.

"It was really good. She used one of your blends again," Luca went on, loyally. "That was around lunchtime, I guess, and after that it was quiet for a bit until school got out and some kids stopped by."

We paused at the front of the store, having put away all the books. Luca lingered a moment, his gaze on my face. Finally he said, "You know, Red, you don't have to. Worry about me, I mean."

"But I care about you," I protested, confused.

"I know, but—I just meant—you don't *have* to worry. Like, it's not required. I know you *will*, but maybe—you just don't have to make it your primary focus, I guess. We can still just talk, or just . . ."

"Clean?" I supplied, smiling crookedly. "Okay, I think I see your point. Not everything has to be a huge deal, just because this case is going on." But mentioning the case again made my shoulders tense, and I ran my hand through my hair, sighing. "It's a little hard to keep everything straight," I realized. "I'm not sure when to be worried and when not to, or when to focus on being Thorn's helper versus focusing on being your—your overprotective girlfriend."

"Or even when to focus on being one of the last people Coal spoke to?" Luca asked kindly. He hopped up to sit on the desk that served as his sales counter, and patted the spot next to him to invite me to do the same. I took the seat gratefully.

"I hadn't really even thought about that part," I confessed. It was Coal's murder, yet somehow I hadn't spared the poor boy more than a few passing thoughts!

"I could tell." Luca's voice was gentle, and his arm remained behind my back. "To be honest that's why I'm a little worried about *you*, Red. Normally you think of everything."

"Maybe not everything," I corrected automatically. But seeing the lift in his eyebrows made me laugh, albeit weakly.

When I didn't go on speaking, Luca did. "It seems like maybe you're a little stuck on worry this time around."

"I always worry. Just ask William." But again, I sighed. How could I explain this to Luca, when I myself usually chose not to investigate these feelings?

Deep down, I knew the truth stemmed from old, tired habits. Even as a child, I'd worried a lot about the people I cared for. Back then, I worried because I was such a misfit in a clan of Seers, and I wanted to fit in, if only for my mothers' sake. I wanted them to be proud. Just like I wanted Luca to be safe and confident and happy . . .

. . . But again, I couldn't possibly voice such thoughts. Not in any coherent manner, anyway.

"Red," Luca said softly, in that voice that always said to me, *I already know.*

I wanted to tell him that it was hard not to worry because he was my priority. More than the carnival, more than the case, Luca was what was important. I could feel that innately, deep in my heart. But the words couldn't make it past the lump in my throat.

"It's just hard to keep my role straight," I managed finally, in a whisper.

I'm not sure it made sense, really, but Luca seemed to get it. He hugged my side into his. "I'm right there with you. I know exactly what you mean."

"Yeah." I let out a deep breath, for the first time feeling a little relief. "You know, you are—you are—"

When I went quiet again, Luca nudged my head with his. "I am what?"

"I don't know," I lied weakly. "I guess I just meant—well—I'm glad."

"You're glad?" He chuckled a little.

"Not about the murder," I protested, poking him. "I'm glad that you're—okay. As okay as you can be, anyway. If you want—do you want to come over to my place tonight? We can make popcorn and just sit on the couch and read, if you want."

"That sounds amazing," Luca said, kissing my hair. "And I totally would take you up on it, but after last night, I'm beat. I think between the exhaustion of being up so much and all this research, I'll be asleep in under a minute."

"Alright, if you're sure," I said.

"Unfortunately, I am. And I know you should get some sleep too," he added, giving my shoulder another squeeze. "Don't worry, Red. We'll make it through this before you know it."

12

Intervention

Needless to say, I wasn't feeling "peachy keen" the next morning. No matter how Luca tried to reassure me.

And that was part of the problem, if I'm honest. Because wasn't *I* supposed to be the one supporting *him*?

No doubt Sir Rowan would have had something sage to say about this, or at least about how my lab coat and hair were suffering for my distress. But it was his day off, which meant I was alone in the lab that morning. I'd opened the shop, but business was hardly booming. I kept one ear tuned for the ringing of the shop bell. Mostly, I fiddled around with the lock on my workbench and started the tests on all the water samples I'd collected the day before. Testing for salt is actually quite easy; when the water is evaporated away, say by boiling, you often end up with a white salty residue. Though Thorn hadn't asked me for anything more than that, I decided to test the water samples for other contaminants, too, just in case.

"That doesn't look like putting the finishing touches on my weekly soap order," someone grumped at me. Instead of from the shop, as expected, the voice came from the back door.

I turned to see that Gloria had let herself in. That alone made me smile. Gloria had been my neighbor in Belville since the very beginning, but way back then, she'd been so prickly and standoffish that I was lucky if she deigned to yell at me from her salon's front door. Now she was not only coming on to my property, she was letting herself in!

"Are you grinning at me like that because you're about to make a long-winded excuse?" Gloria crossed her arms over her black leather jacket, leaning one ample hip against the end of my workbench. An elf with phoenix magic in her blood, Gloria had flawless burnt-orange skin and a plume of red feathers rising above her brow instead of hair. As the salon's owner, she was always perfectly made up. And usually her eyes were as dark and unforgiving as her choice in clothes . . . but today, her gaze softened a little as she added, "Or are you too wrapped up in your latest mystery?"

"You've heard all about it, I suppose?" I asked, tugging at my ponytail.

Gloria nodded. "Johann spends most of his nights at the tavern these days, and he always reports the gossip when we're slow at the salon. Last night he got Trent talking all about the case, apparently, so I've already heard it all this morning. He just likes the excuse to talk. He knows I don't care." She yawned, and then glanced at me again. "Although, in this case, I could make an exception."

Of course, Johann. Gloria's secretary was relatively new in town, but he'd settled easily into daily life. Actually, Johann was part vampire, and known to be practically nocturnal . . . my mind wandered as I wondered if he might have seen anything down at the docks, particularly this mysterious courier that had delivered notes.

But the carnival isn't at all in the line of sight from the tavern, I reminded myself with a sigh. "Well, I appreciate the offer. But don't worry about your order. You know Sir Rowan would never let us fall behind on our commitments," I told her with a weary smile. Reaching under the workbench, I produced a basket of the specially-prepared soaps Gloria used in her salon. Sir Rowan had, naturally, finished the labels and arranged them all perfectly yesterday afternoon.

"Huh," was all Gloria said at first. She accepted the full basket for me, and motioned to where she'd left last week's empty basket by the door. Then she glanced down at the soaps again. "I remember when he was a stranger illegally interfering with soaps."

"Much better to just let him be in charge of them in the first place," I agreed, my smile becoming more genuine.

Gloria watched me, lingering. "You're getting too involved."

"With Sir Rowan?" I blanched. Visions of an angry dragon—not to mention an angry bookseller—crossed my mind.

"No, you fool," Gloria said, with just a hint of affection. "In the case."

"Oh. That. Yeah." I was unable to disagree. "How'd you know?"

"Experience." Gloria set down her basket of soaps and finally dropped into a seat on the bench, facing me head-on. "I saw how you were with Snow. And Luca, the first time around. And me," she added softly. "So I figured this one'd be hitting you hard. And I was right."

"Congratulations," I said, leaning my head on my hand. "Want a fools' gold medal?"

"No. I want you to spill your guts," she said, leveling a

pointed look at me. "Keep in mind this is a one-time offer."

I blinked. And then, gratefully, I did exactly as she suggested. I told her all about my meeting with Coal, finding him on the boat, and what we'd learned so far of his situation in the carnival. And then, more hesitantly, my worries about Luca. Gloria was aromantic and notoriously unsentimental, so I wasn't sure she'd want to be bothered by all that—but I should have known better. Prickly as she might be, Gloria and I were friends. And she was an intensely loyal friend.

"Obviously *something* is going on there," she agreed as soon as I finished. "Sounds like a classic case."

"Yeah. Something Luca said the other night . . ." I bit my lip. "Do you ever wonder why so many fairy tales start with unhappy families? Like—why is that so common?"

Gloria shrugged. "I'm happier than ever with the family I've got now." She kept her gaze on me until I'd pulled myself up out of my wallowing and realized what she meant: myself, William, Johann, Luca, even Sakura—we'd all forced our way into Gloria's life and embraced her fully, whether she invited us or not. "Maybe that's the point you should be focused on."

"I get the value of looking on the bright side. But how does that help in a murder case?" I asked, confused.

"Look at it this way," she said, shifting on the bench. "People who are stuck in Cinderella story lines, or any kind of depressing situation like that, usually have a benefactor. Right? A 'fairy godmother' character. Someone or something is in the background trying to help pull them out of the mess they're in. You ought to know," she added reproachfully.

"You're not saying *I*—"

"Yes, I am. Who was it who confronted the fairies when I was laid up in bed? And who was the first person to confront

Owl? Have you ever stopped to wonder where Luca or I would be without you?"

"I'm sure you'd have sorted it out," I said, but my voice wavered. "It—it's not like I have magic or anything."

"Right now you're not acting like you have much brains, either," Gloria retorted—but again, there was affection in her voice. "You're not getting it. Obviously the fairy godmother doesn't *need* to have magic. It doesn't even need to be a person, or just *one* person. The fact is, someone was looking out for Luca and me, and that changed our stories. So now before you go getting sentimental, think logically about this situation with Coal. Someone was probably looking out for him—or maybe they *wanted* to, but something else got in their way. Either way, if you can find out who it was . . ."

". . . then I'll get a completely new perspective," I said, straightening up.

"And you'll also see where the danger was," Gloria concluded. "Someone looking out for Coal probably would have known who his enemies were. And if an enemy got to him—which obviously they did—then it must have been through some way the benefactor couldn't control."

Oh, my gods and goddesses, I thought, as Gloria's insight settled in. *She's right—I haven't been looking at the full story. How could I hope to see the end of the experiment if I can't even look at all the component parts?*

"That did make sense, right?" Gloria asked after a moment. "I'm not as good with all this metaphorical problem-solving as you are."

"Gloria," I said, smiling in earnest now, "did you just acknowledge I have a skill?"

"If only you'd use it," she muttered. With a sly grin back, she went on, "I guess my work here is done, then. Come by the salon when you're done sleuthing. You look like you could use a break."

"I'm ignoring that slight against my appearance!" I called after her as she picked up her basket and made her way to the door. "Thank you," I added, though I knew she wouldn't hear.

I'd been letting this case get to me. But now, I saw that Gloria was right. I was missing pieces, and it was time for action. My water tests were already telling me that none of the samples I'd collected were salty, so I wouldn't be able to rely on that evidence. But fortunately, thanks to my neighbor, I knew exactly where to look next.

13

The Magic Words

After changing out of my lab clothes and badgering William into looking after the shop, my first stop was the Pomegranate. Sleuthing needs fuel and, after all, the café was right across the corner, so how could I pass it up?

"Let me guess." Sakura grinned as the line at her counter finally dwindled down to me. It was early in the day yet, and the Pomegranate Café was busy in a cheerful, competent kind of way. Its owner looked my outfit up and down and then decided, "Chai latte with a dash of cinnamon cream, in one of our secure travel mugs? Large, I'm thinking."

"Extra large," I agreed, handing over the mug I'd remembered to swipe from my kitchen counter. "But don't bother getting out a new travel mug—I brought this one back. Cinnamon chai sounds perfect. You have a gift."

"I have experience," Sakura giggled as she rang me up. "You *are* one of our best customers, after all."

"Just 'one of'?" I teased as I glanced idly around the café. Amid the crowd I noticed that another regular, Belville's local postmaster, sat in the couch nook by the front windows.

"I'm glad to see you're doing well," Saki added, keeping up the conversation over the noise of her magitech coffee machines. I followed her along my side of the counter. "Ginger told me all about what happened at the carnival. I'm so sorry your date was interrupted like that!"

"Do you know, I hadn't really looked at it that way," I mused. *Maybe Saki has a point—maybe that's part of why I've been feeling so miserable about the whole thing, and Luca being involved too. We were supposed to just have fun, for once!* "Mostly, when I have a moment to think, I've been feeling bad about Coal."

"Yes, Coal," Saki agreed. But the tone of her voice caught my attention. I glanced over to see a clouded expression in her bright blue eyes.

I tilted my head. "What is it? Do you know something?"

"I felt something," she corrected, expertly finishing off my drink. "Just a feeling. But I've been wanting to talk to you about it. I can't spare the time now, but could you stop by after work? Or I'll stop by your place."

"I'll come to you," I decided, thinking it over. "I'm going to be on the move today, I think, so I'm not sure when I'll be home. But I'll try to make it here in time for closing."

Sakura and I exchanged thank yous and, laden with a drink that smelled absolutely heavenly, I turned to go. Normally I wasn't an expert on feelings—the past few days had proved that—but Saki's, I trusted. As a shadow witch by training, Sakura often had insight into the darker side of human nature. Her deductions had been useful, if dangerous, in solving previous mysteries.

See how much progress you make by letting your friends in? I could practically hear my mother's voice say in my ear. It *did* feel good to have some extra perspective, and it made me feel a bit more bold, too. Making a quick decision, I headed for the postmaster on the couch rather than the door.

Mel had only been in town since the new year, but she'd settled in rapidly. Though her expensive clothes and the jeweled headband holding back her short brown hair spoke of city life, she'd embraced Belville whole-heartedly—joining clubs, sponsoring the café, even dating Saki's melancholic brother, Ryuko. It was her membership in the Belville Boaters club I especially wanted to talk to her about.

"Red, please, sit with me," Mel smiled as I came close. She politely closed the book she'd been reading—a dusty classic, no doubt from Luca's bookstore—and moved aside a china plate so I had room at the little tea table. A forest elf with light brown skin and deep eyes, Mel seemed right at home in the café. She smiled as she added, "I guess you can tell I've just been enjoying a late breakfast."

"Day off from the post office?" I asked, taking a seat.

"Yes, I traded with Abi. He wanted yesterday morning off so that he could go to the carnival and then sleep in, believe it or not." Mel's friendly face took on a troubled expression. "Of course, we all know how well that went. You more than anyone, I suppose. I'm sorry if bringing it up brings up unpleasant memories."

"Oh, don't worry," I assured her. "It's actually about that that I wanted to talk to you. There's someone from the carnival that I'd like to interview, and I think I know where to find them. Trouble is, they said they'd be out on Cactus Island today."

Mel's smile returned. "'Interview,' is it? Ryu told me you often help Officer Thorn. So, I guess you need a boat?"

"That or a way to walk on water," I answered, grinning. I

chose not to second-guess my use of the word 'interview,' which Mel had pointed out.

"Well, I can't help with that," she laughed, "but I *can* help you if you're looking for a canoe. We rent them out down at the Boater's dock. Have you ever paddled before?"

"I'm not at my best on the water," I admitted, trying not to grip my travel mug with white-knuckled anxiety.

"You and Saki both," Mel said, affably. She waved to the café owner as she stood. "Come on, I'll go with you. I'll do all the paddling, and you can be our navigator."

"Are you sure?" I asked, rising hopefully.

"Absolutely," Mel grinned. "I need the exercise, and I was going to end up at the lake sooner or later anyway. Ryu calls it my second home. Besides," she added, with a charming confidential air, "I just am happy to be involved."

* * *

I'm going to gloss over our stint on the lake. Mel was the perfect escort, really, and it was clear she knew her way around a canoe. But even the smoothest of journeys over Belville's Lake Lava makes me a little nervy, perhaps because of a misadventure under its waters shortly after I'd settled in town.

In any case, we made it to Cactus Island in record time with Mel on the oars. Once we'd hauled the boat ashore, Mel stretched out on a sunny rock and produced that dusty classic again—this time out of a waterproof pouch. I managed to catch my breath and compose myself enough to grin down at her.

"Good thing you showed me that," I said, gesturing to the

pouch. "Because you know I'm obligated to report book abuses to Luca."

"I had a feeling," she replied, laughing along with my teasing remark. "I figured I'd sit here and read until you get back. I wouldn't want to compromise the investigation, and besides, I was just getting to a good bit earlier."

"Suit yourself," I said, shaking my head and barely remembering to add, "Thank you. I'll try to be quick."

Cactus Island was only the size of Market Square, once you were on it. However, unlike the park, the island boasted a steep hill and a collection of water-worn boulders that could put a mountainous mine to shame. We hadn't seen any sign of Hemming or his troupe as we approached, but I had a feeling they'd be easy to find by ear. Leaving Mel to her quiet morning, I took a fortifying sip of chai and began clambering over the rocks along the shoreline.

Five minutes' walk later, I'd rounded the northern tip of the island and could confirm my theory about Scylla the bunyip's locatable voice. Forlorn booming, not unlike the sound of a foghorn, drifted along the waves lapping beneath my boots. I followed it to find Hemming and his herd of creatures resting along the rocks in a small, natural bay.

"Red," the animal trainer said, his head lifting at my approach. For a moment, he looked so much like the alert mist goats around him that I had to stifle a laugh. Hemming, on the other hand, was grave. "Thought on the other side of the island, the town wouldn't notice Scylla singing. Sorry for any disturbance."

Singing seemed like a particularly optimistic label. Or was it wry sarcasm? I still couldn't quite read Hemming. Still, I smiled and did my best to be reassuring. "Oh, I'm not here about that, don't worry. Actually, I didn't hear her at all until I'd rounded the point."

"Go, then, friends. Play time," Hemming said to the mist goats. They scattered gleefully into the calm waters of the bay, but Hemming himself sounded—if anything—morose. He sighed. "I'd hoped it was Scylla. If not her, you must be here about Coal."

I studied the man a moment before responding. Away from the gloom and sparkle of the carnival, Hemming looked even older than I'd imagined. His green beard seemed to be the only color about him. "I am," I admitted finally. "I know this is a tough time, and I don't want to make it worse. But it's occurred to me that Officer Thorn and I, as outsiders, need to understand more about the carnival if we're going to get to the bottom of this."

Hemming shrugged. The movement only underscored how much like the boulders his rounded, rough-clad shoulders looked. "I keep clear of politics."

"The politics of running the carnival and captaining the boat, you mean," I guessed. *Politics* was exactly the right word for the impression Anastasia and Fontus and even Captain Pleasant had given me. When Hemming nodded, his eyes on the cavorting mist goats, I pressed, "But how about the politics surrounding Coal, specifically?"

"You think the boy was in danger, even before?" Hemming's gaze moved slowly to mine.

"You don't seem surprised by the thought," I returned gently, dropping to sit on the rocks beside him.

Again, Hemming sighed, and he returned to watching his goats. "I told you, I wish I could have done more. I wish I *did* do more. There's not a quiet moment I don't think of it."

"But why exactly did you feel that way? Because of Coal's stepfamily?"

"No." The sudden curtness of Hemming's voice startled Scylla, who dove into the bay. I had to admit, I was surprised too. But I waited until he explained, "There's people who say too much, and people who say too little. Booming bunyips and ceffyl dwr, hiding in the mist. It's how all the world is. Carnival folk, they tend to say too much. They tell me I say too little. Coal was more like me than like them."

"Do you think someone was *keeping* him from speaking?" I asked quietly.

Once more, Hemming shrugged. "Never thought it through that far. Only thought as how I ought to help him—show him things I'd learned. When it counts to speak up and make a show of yourself. Some people know that from the moment they're born. Some don't."

I bit my lip. So far, Hemming fit more and more into what Gloria might have called "the godmother type." But his musings on the nature of advocating for oneself weren't exactly getting us anywhere. *What would Gloria do if she were here? What would* Luca *do?* Thinking of my friends gave me an idea. "I think I know what you mean," I said suddenly. "I have friends like that. I wouldn't say I have anything to teach them, exactly, but I've always hoped that they could at least speak up with me, if not to a whole . . . audience," I ended a bit lamely, circling back around to the carnival metaphor.

Hemming sighed, and this time it seemed like it actually did him good—like pressure escaping a valve. "I'll admit I hoped that," he said gruffly. "That's why I took the boy under my wing. The true reason. I'd ask him sometimes, if he had one thing to say . . ."

"Did he ever answer?" I asked, hardly breathing.

"He did not." Hemming shook his head sadly. "I never did learn why. Should have pressed him on it. Should have known why there was that cloud looming over him. *Was* it jealousy of Magica and Weep? Was it the loss of his father? Or was it something else—someone on board, maybe, someone higher up . . ."

I tilted my head, thinking. Hemming didn't seem to want to discuss Anastasia, so I set her aside. "Probably not Captain Pleasant, right? I mean, he told me the other day—well—"

"It wasn't such a secret," Hemming agreed thoughtfully. "But often these affairs of the heart turn dangerous."

His sadness took on a new tone as he reflected on love, and I realized perhaps *that* was why he didn't want to talk about Anastasia. Of course, she seemed much younger than he did, but that might be exactly why he considered love 'dangerous.' It could also be why he took a special interest in Coal and the twins in the first place . . .

But that's speculation, I reminded myself. And even though Hemming had opened up a little, I doubted he'd open up enough to confirm the details of a doomed romance.

"If you want to know about the running of the carnival," he said eventually, stirring, "then you could study how it actually runs. Don't listen to any of us, over-talkers, under-talkers. Use the evidence."

He was speaking my language, I must admit, but I still didn't get it. "Evidence like—"

"Here," Hemming interrupted. He settled back onto his rock, and as he did so, he dropped an overflowing pack into my lap. "That's my office. It isn't much. But I'm the only one who keeps records, aside from the Captain. I do it for the animals.

Feed receipts, daily logs, notices. I don't know if it'll help. But you take it."

"Take all your paperwork?" I asked incredulously, sorting through the pack gingerly. Despite the weathered appearance and its haphazard delivery, the papers inside actually seemed to follow an order of sorts. "Don't you need it?"

"Not as much as you do," Hemming said. A note of determination had crept into his voice. "Maybe something in it will help you."

"Well—alright then," I decided, looping the strap over my neck. "Thank you. You don't mind if I share it with Officer Thorn, right?" As the actual investigating officer on the case, she could probably have demanded to see it. In fact, I was surprised she hadn't already . . .

. . . But the blithe look on Hemming's impassive face answered my question. She could have asked a million times, and he'd have just pretended he had no idea what she meant.

"Do what you must," he said finally. "I trust you with it more than me. You'll do the greatest good."

"I—I will," I promised, a little shaken by his words. His faith in me. I was glad I'd decided to open up to him—but also saddened by his own frustration with himself. Unsteadily I rose, but before I turned to go, I blurted, "It wasn't your fault, you know. Maybe he just wasn't ready."

Hemming's head snapped down, and I almost thought he wouldn't answer. But then, just above a whisper, he said, "Knowing the timing's half the work." An old axiom common in sea-faring coastal societies. Even as I wondered about Hemming's past, my heart ached for him.

"You may be right, lass," he added, still looking down. "But maybe the timing's just not right for me, either."

It could be, I wanted to say. But I didn't want to overstep this fragile moment. Instead I promised, "Timing or no, we'll get to the bottom of this. We'll figure out what happened to Coal, and why. You can count on me and all my friends, too. The last thing we want is for something like this to happen again."

And yet, I thought as I took my leave and walked away, *why does it always seem like these things* do *repeat, over and over, time and again?*

14

And Magic Letters

Mel dropped me off at the shores of the lake and pulled away again, saying she wanted to do yet more rowing before lunch. I wished her luck, and hurried off to the police station—mostly because of the news I had to share, of course.

I hadn't wanted to invite Thorn along on my hunch, but I knew better than to plow ahead alone. The right thing to do was share the papers, so I was going to do it. Looking through Hemming's paperwork *without* Thorn looking over my shoulder just felt like prying. I'd tried it already on the boat ride back.

Because it was almost lunchtime, as Mel had pointed out, I decided to swing by my shop. It was on the way, and it gave me the chance to grab some snacks: early cherries, cheese, and leftover falafel. It wasn't the croissants Officer Thorn was known to love, but it *was* some protein to tide me over. William and our mutual friend Dusty were busy gossiping— or rather, testing tea blends in the armchair corner—so I left them to their business. After I slipped out the lab door, it was a brisk two minutes' walk to the police station.

Belville's police station was very in keeping with the rest of the town. The front of the building served as a public space, while the local officer was expected to live in a separate building behind. I'd never known the squat wooden buildings to house anyone but Officer Thorn. Indeed, with their prim yard and perfectly upkept exteriors, they seemed tailor-made for her.

I pushed my way through the front door and found Officer Thorn exactly where I might have expected her: sitting behind the reception desk in the front room. She had an office and storeroom in the back, but clearly, she'd decided that the front room was the perfect place to polish her boots.

I stopped in front of the desk and put my hands on my hips. "Shoe maintenance?"

"It has to happen some time," said the officer defensively.

"During a murder investigation?" My eyebrow rose.

"You have to make a good impression to get anywhere with these carnival people," Thorn muttered to her boot.

I shook my head. "Well, would you mind moving your polish? I brought food, if you're interested. And also a break in the case—maybe."

Thorn, whose dark head had perked up at the mention of a "break," stowed her boots beneath the desk and seemed to return to her normal bossiness. "What do you mean, 'maybe'? I want a full report."

"You can see it for yourself," I told her. As I put the pack on the table in front of her, I explained my meeting with Hemming, and everything he'd said—as best as I could remember. I skimmed over the godmother parts and instead focused on the idea of 'politics' within the carnival.

"Good work," Thorn said as I finished. She was already rifling through the papers. "You take this stack, and I'll take this one. If we finish up in time, we can swing by Lavender's for the lunch special."

"But I brought food," I protested.

Thorn gave me a long-suffering look. "Investigating is hungry work. You'll learn if you stick around long enough, Red."

I shook my head, unsure whether to laugh or feel offended. In the end, with a grin, I pulled a chair up to my side of the desk and settled in to work. Hemming's careful records of daily activities seemed promising, but I quickly found that Sleepy's log was unvarying: *8am, fed, 12noon, check, 8pm, lights out.* There was never any other note except on carnival days, when the trio took him out of his stall promptly half an hour before the show and returned him as soon as the encore was over.

I almost made a disparaging comment about it to the officer, but I looked up to see that she was more hopeful.

"Hold up," Thorn said, popping a falafel in her mouth. After a moment of busy chewing, she explained herself. "This handwriting *is* familiar. I know it."

"Because we've been looking at it for the past half hour?" I suggested wryly.

But she shook her head, unaffected by my humor. "There's something about it that's been bugging me all along."

"Hmm. Let me see." I leaned over the table to take a look at the note Thorn held. While she reached for another falafel, I quickly scanned the contents. "A note about the feeding schedule," I mused. "I was just looking through Sleepy's log. Seemed like all the notes were half this handwriting, half in another handwriting."

"Should we bring Luca in?" Thorn suggested, swallowing the last of the snacks.

I hesitated, setting aside the warmth in my chest at the mention of his name. "There's a little work left that we can do. One of the handwritings, the one that I have that *doesn't* look like your note, is Hemming's. I know that because he wrote a label on the inside of his bag. See?" I twisted the pack around on the table to show it to Thorn. "The handwriting's really obvious, even to me. It looks a little like—like something old, I think. Kind of like—"

"Runes," Thorn agreed, nodding. Catching my surprised look, she added, "What? I knew a guy in the guild who wrote runes on the back of his hand. New one each week. Hard to forget that kind of thing."

"Okay, well, runes aside, we can agree that Hemming isn't the one who wrote the note you've got," I said, ready to continue with my reasoning.

But again, Officer Thorn interrupted—this time with a snap of her fingers. "The note I've got," she repeated. "That's it!"

"What's it?" I echoed. I should have known it was a lost cause. Thorn was already up and out of her chair, striding back to her office. There was a shuffle and the sound of a heavy file cabinet drawer being slammed shut, and then she returned with a triumphant gleam in her eye.

"*This* is it," she said, waving another note at me. This one was carefully pressed between two clear panes of magicked glass, the common police guild method of preserving paper evidence. "This is why the handwriting looked familiar. This is the note I got, warning me about the murder."

"Days ago, then," I said slowly.

"And yesterday, the note about the lock. Same handwriting—I'm positive. Now we just need to figure out—"

But now it was *my* turn to interrupt. "If you had let me finish earlier," I said, standing and smirking at my friend, "I was going to say that given that the notes are about feeding schedules, and we know Hemming is so particular about the animals' care, the note writer had to be someone he trusted. And since Coal was still working his way up, the only person Hemming trusted to feed his animals regularly was—"

"Zale," Thorn concluded. She'd already set down the note and reached for her jacket. "His other assistant. I remember interviewing the boy our first night, but then he said nothing. Come on, Red. Time to visit the carnival again."

15

Shadows Dance

I had to admit, I didn't remember much about Zale, Hemming's apparent second-in-command. That just goes to show you why, of the two of us, I'm the potion-maker and Thorn is the actual police officer. Nonetheless, I was glad she'd asked me to come along to the carnival. While normally I wasn't a fan of being pulled into investigations, this one was different. Not only was there Luca to think of, there was the strange effect the carnival seemed to have on Thorn. Even the previous fall, when orcs and their families were being targeted by a murderer, I hadn't seen her so . . . variable.

Fortunately, there was no one about in town to distract us—everyone was inside, probably enjoying a late lunch with a side of fearful gossip about the steampunk ship on the lake. The ticket booth on the pier was closed and unattended, but the gangplank was still down. Officer Thorn charged straight up it and rounded on Gus, who stood at his usual guard position on deck.

"We need to see Zale," she announced abruptly.

"Hemming's still out on the lake," Gus replied, confused. "So are all the animals."

"It's the assistant we need, not the trainer," Thorn reminded him. "Where can we find him?"

"It's hard to keep track of the crew," Gus admitted, shifting a little as though embarrassed to acknowledge this shortcoming. *Poor Gus,* I thought. Officer Thorn had clearly given him every impression of being omnipotent, and he was struggling to keep up.

That could spell trouble for anyone left aboard, I realized, my thoughts taking a darker turn. *I wonder if any of them have thought of that? Aside from Anastasia, of course . . .*

Once again, I wasn't sure if it was suspicious or shrewd that she'd thought immediately of her own safety.

"But I'd bet he's down on the stable deck," Gus added, his head tilted up like a hopeful child. "Want me to go look for you?"

"Not necessary," Thorn decided. "We'll go. We know our way around, and we're perfectly safe. We'll be in and out."

I nodded when she looked back at me. Though I wondered if we would be safe *for* the carnival folks or *from* them, I kept my sudden misgivings to myself. When Officer Thorn plunged down the staircase to the lower decks, I followed.

The *Luna II* smelled and looked exactly as it had the night and days before—only eerily silent, with its audience and Trent's carefree attitude gone. I crowded behind Officer Thorn, my unease growing as we descended. The gentle shift of the deck below was unnerving now, and the gloom seemed to press on me the same way I pressed the police officer.

"What's your problem?" Thorn asked as we hit the bottom of the stairs and I ricocheted off her back.

"I don't know," I said, shaking my head to clear out thoughts of paperwork and shadows and "politics." "Somehow it feels different now."

The downside of talking to Gloria and Luca about it so much, I decided. *It all feels so much closer now.*

But that means it's more important than ever to face it, I reminded myself, squaring my shoulders. "It's fine," I told Thorn, who hesitated watching me. "Nothing to worry about now."

She shrugged and, with a characteristic toss of her long hair, led the way down the hall.

The stable quarters were strangely spacious without the animals themselves. We found Zale immediately; he was the only thing in the dim hallway making noise. Without pause, Thorn and I rounded the corner to see him in a stall, scrubbing Scylla's holding tank.

"Officer!" Zale looked up before Thorn could speak. Seeing him now, I wasn't sure I'd met him before; his loose, dark shirt and breeches marked him as one of the crew. In the dark it was hard to tell, but no doubt he was at least partially a naiad. My first impression of him was one of surprise. The small pot of coarse white scrubbing solution he'd been using plummeted to the bottom of the shallow tank with an unsubtle *thunk*.

"Zale," Thorn said grimly, when the assistant didn't add anything to explain his shock. "Is this your handwriting?"

She produced one of the notes from Hemming's pack, drawing it out of her uniform pocket like it was a secret key. Zale certainly reacted as if it was. He gulped, his lightly tanned skin going gray in the darkness. Immediately, the determination was gone from his pose, and he glanced around aimlessly.

"That seems like a yes," Thorn said to me dryly.

"Zale, you aren't in trouble right now," I said, feeling it was high time to intervene. *Why would he be feeling so guilty anyway? If he was the one who wrote the note warning us about the murder, he wouldn't also be the murderer himself, would he?*

That's when I realized—he wasn't *guilty*, he was *scared*.

"We just have a few questions," Thorn said, as Zale refocused on us.

"Maybe it would be best to talk at the station," I added. Officer Thorn glanced at me and I did my best to convey *if he's scared to be overheard or revealed, the station is the safest place*, without words. It probably didn't work, but the officer did shrug in the face of my determination.

"The station," Zale repeated, rising shakily to his feet. "Okay—I'll come."

"You will?" Officer Thorn appraised him.

"Well—it's not like I have a choice, do I?"

"Nope," the officer decided cheerfully. "Alright, then. Let's go for a walk."

* * *

When the three of us poured into the station, I had to admit I felt relieved. The warm sun of the afternoon had finally wiped away the shadowiness of the carnival; even Zale seemed to be standing a little taller, the longer we walked. He did falter as we made it into the station, but Officer Thorn took over at once. This was her territory, and she had a plan—as always.

That little feeling of relief as Thorn arranged us in her office and opened the interview was probably the highlight of my afternoon, though. Zale confirmed that the writing was his, of course, and after that he had to admit that he'd written the warning note. But every question afterward seemed to lead us in circles.

"Why'd you send the note?" Thorn asked.

"I—I couldn't say," Zale replied.

"But if you wanted us to know about the murder, then surely you'd also like us to find the murder," I said.

"I do, I do! There's something wrong going on," Zale replied.

"What exactly is wrong? What made you reach out?" Thorn asked.

"I can't tell you. I don't know," Zale replied.

And so on. This little scene must have repeated itself three or four times over before Thorn had had enough. She offered Zale a glass bottle of water from a cabinet behind her desk, and then she tugged me into the front room for an unceremonious chat.

"This is why you're here," she hissed as the office door swung shut, separating us from our tense witness. "Why is it so hard to get anything from these carnival people?"

"Well, it's not actually the fact that they work at a carnival," I said, reasonably. "William and I met several troupes when we were traveling, and some of them were quite talkative, actually. So it's not like they all take a vow of silence or something."

"A vow of silence would be more useful," Thorn grunted. "Then at least I'd know not to waste our time trying to get something out of him."

"It's got to be something specific about the *Luna II*. Or someone on it," I continued reasoning.

"That much is clear from the fact that he wrote the note in the first place. But why write to us if he won't talk?"

"Maybe he wrote because he feels like he *can't* talk about it,"

I countered, thinking hard. *What would Luca do?* "Zale wants the murder solved. His actions show that. But there must be something going on beyond the murder. Someone who makes him feel unsafe."

"The *murderer*," Thorn supplied impatiently.

"Yes, that, but think about it. No one has actually tried to leave the ship. No one's showed up in town asking for sanctuary, except Coal that first day. No one except Anastasia has mentioned feeling unsafe because of the murder. They all seemed to believe it was a private matter. And then, that first night, they talked about dangerous secrets . . ."

"Blackmail." Officer Thorn had lost her air of impatience, instead tugging thoughtfully at her ear as she considered this added layer in the case. "You're guessing that someone has something on Zale and they're making him keep quiet."

"Now that I think about it, I bet someone has something on a *lot* of people on board," I said, recalling the frazzled interviews. "And if it's been going on for a while, then that could explain how scared Zale is. And probably others, too. They don't want to speak up, because someone's listening."

"But they did speak up. In the interviews. In *writing*," Thorn insisted. "Why?"

"Murder is serious," I reminded her. "More serious than blackmail, maybe?"

"But so far, as far as we can tell, this particular murder is also motiveless," she reminded me right back.

"It's like a vacuum," I said, struck by the thought. Trent's words for his fruitless investigation came back to me. "A *vacuum.* That could be why everyone's so uneasy—but also not trying to leave the ship. That's how they might act if they *were* being blackmailed, and then suddenly—"

"Suddenly, now, they aren't," Thorn agreed, letting go of her ear as she stood up straighter. "That's why Zale felt the duty to write a note, but now not *enough* duty to speak up. He wouldn't want to admit to being blackmailed, naturally. But also he wouldn't point the finger at someone, suggesting they're a murderer, if they'd saved his hide by committing murder. And all that suggests an obvious conclusion—"

"—Coal was the one blackmailing him," I concluded.

16

Brand New

The pause was quite the showstopper.

"But that's a lot of conjecture," I hastened to add.

Officer Thorn's eyes were still gleaming, though. She rubbed her hands together. "Come on, Red. Break time's over. I've got a good feeling about this one."

"You and I have very different definitions of 'good,'" I muttered. Still, I obediently trailed Thorn as she let herself back into the office.

Officer Thorn plopped herself back into her office chair and rubbed her hands together. She spoke fast and to the point, as though to make up for lost time. "So, Zale. Was Coal blackmailing you?"

Zale reared back like a frightened kelpie, and I couldn't blame him. I made a face of disbelief at Thorn as I, too, slid back into my seat. But she, as usual, was hyper-focused.

The silence was airless. For a moment Zale gaped at me, as though he was hoping I'd throw him a line. But when I held my tongue, watching him, he finally gave in. With one last gulp, he made the plunge.

"Yes," he said, a watery heaviness in his voice. "For—for months now."

My world tilted. He could have said that his fairy godmother turned out to be a devil in disguise, and I couldn't have been more shocked. It was one thing to think out the possibilities with Officer Thorn; it was something entirely different to hear the reality from a victim.

This revelation crashed like a wave over Thorn's desk, but she remained immovable, a stone in the face of a storm. "I need you to be as specific as possible."

Zale wasn't looking at either of us any more, but at least his breathing came more regularly. "I—I remember exactly how it started," he told his hands. "It was after our last Ostara show. We were moored at Grendale then. He—he said something to me after the show—at the party. After that it was every time—after every payday. The day right after each payday."

The temptation to ask *why* was overwhelming. I had to bite my lip to keep it in.

"He was after money?" Thorn asked. "Just money?"

"Half," said Zale, miserably. "Half my earnings. It started out as less. 'Just a little off the top,' he said. Then he started asking for more. Last time—I mean, the time before last—he wanted half. The things he said . . ."

"Zale," I broke in, thinking, "the payday before last—that was before you came to Belville, right? But your most recent payday has been in the past few days?"

"Two days ago," the boy confirmed. "We were going to split everything out after the first show. That's how it goes: we split the first night, and everything else on the last night. Captain tries to do it so we can have some spending money in a new port. That's what everyone says, anyway. They say it makes good advertising for the show."

"So Coal was murdered on payday?" Officer Thorn clarified. "But before anyone was paid."

Zale nodded.

There's something else there, I thought, watching him revert to staring at his fingernails. I knew that particular brand of silence. Sometimes customers who wanted something they couldn't ask for used it, too.

"And what about the others?" Thorn continued. "Did he collect from them the day after payday, too?"

"Others?" Zale's head jerked up and he looked genuinely startled. "Not—?"

Officer Thorn's mouth pressed into an impatient line, so I cleared my throat. "Not *who*, Zale? Is there someone in particular you're worried about?"

"I—" Zale glanced between us, elbows drawn in, like a buoy trapped between the breakwater and the rising tide. When he spoke again, his voice was wispy. "I always wondered if he had something on Hemming."

"The animal trainer?" Officer Thorn was now taking notes.

"I don't know anything," Zale said hastily. "I just always wondered. Maybe that was why—why he let him hang around so much."

"Is there anyone else?" Thorn looked up from her notepad.

Zale shook his head, eyes wide.

"You're sure?"

"I—I don't know anything," Zale repeated. "I just thought—I just figured it was us. I thought he wanted to be head animal trainer or something. Coal. I thought he just wanted control of the animals. He said it was only a matter of time before he had *all* my pay—my job—"

His confession ended in a gurgle, and at that, a new wave of understanding hit me. "Zale," I asked, leaning forward, "when you sent that note to Officer Thorn, who did you think was going to be murdered?"

Zale's response was a fish-like stare.

But Officer Thorn pounced on this line of questioning. "Did you think it would be Coal?"

Zale hesitated. Then shook his head.

At this, Officer Thorn set aside her pencil and began tugging at her ear. "Then *who* were you writing about?"

"I—I thought it would be me," Zale whispered. Once the words were out, the dam broke. "I thought he was going to kill me. I thought he would take over. He said it all the time. How easy an accident might be. How much I was like his stepfamily. Intruding—that's what he said. Worthless. Greedy. I took it from him in the first place, the work. That's what he said. I thought he'd make it look like an accident and Hemming would just give him my job. Then he'd get my pay too, all of it. He always said I shouldn't have run away in the first place, that I should have stayed on dry land, that if I had any kind of backbone he wouldn't have to—to—to take my money, and do my work—"

The poor boy wasn't sitting still any longer. As he spoke his hands flailed, and he'd gone from staring at his fingers to glancing wildly all over the room. At last I rose and put my hand on his shoulder, steadying him. His monologue ended, but he was still panting and shaking in his chair.

And Thorn's gaze was still even-keeled. "So. You wrote to us because you believed that your blackmailer would become your murderer—that very night. *Before* getting any money from you?"

Zale's mouth opened and closed before he could get the words out. "He said it had to end. One way or another."

"He said that to you? In what context?" Thorn asked.

"He said it to the animals," Zale said. "He—he used to talk to them a lot. Sometimes he'd stay there all night. I just overheard. That's all."

"And you thought he must be referring to you?"

"I—he—he'd just been yelling at me," Zale admitted quietly. "The day before I sent the note—the day before the murder. I had the evening shift. He came back from dinner all upset and saw me and said something about how I never work hard enough, and then he went to go talk to the animals and stayed there until I left."

The references to Coal being upset and even sleeping in the stables were interesting, and I could see Thorn writing them down. Meanwhile, I tried to focus on our witness. "Zale, if you were afraid for your safety, did *you* consider coming here? To Belville, or the station?"

Zale blinked and then shook his head vigorously. "I don't go ashore. I never do."

"You're ashore now," Thorn pointed out, looking up from her notes.

"I never do," Zale repeated, looking uncertain. "But— today—you had my note—I thought, if I stayed with you—"

"Is there someone else ashore that you're afraid of, Zale?" I guessed, when his voice faltered. "Someone working with Coal, maybe?"

"No, he never met Coal," Zale said definitely. "But I can't go back. That's all. I just can't. That's why I never go ashore."

This didn't make a lot of sense to me, but the look in Officer Thorn's eyes was knowing. "Is that what Coal had on you, lad?"

Zale nodded, going quiet again. But the admission seemed to calm him a little.

I turned to Thorn, making a mental note to ask her what that was all about later. In the meantime, I asked, "In that case, remind me, how did Zale's note get to you?"

"It was damp," Thorn said, her own voice very dry. "I didn't think much of it at the time."

The two of us turned to Zale for an explanation, and he shifted, a small light of pride coming into his eyes. "It's Prissy—one of the ceffyl dwr. She's very intelligent. She took it for me. I told her how to recognize the police station, and she did."

Delivery via mist goat, I thought, amused in spite of the situation. *Maybe I ought to tell Mel about that.*

"And that's how you got the lock ashore too, right?" Thorn guessed.

Zale nodded. "I—I didn't want to go myself, and I knew they would ask, and . . . and Prissy gets anxious if she doesn't get exercise."

Officer Thorn nodded, like this was the most natural thing in the world. "Is there anything else you want to tell us, Zale?"

The boy fell back on his usual refrain. "I don't know anything." I believed him, and I felt deeply for the fear in his eyes. That haunted look flashed as he added, "You won't—my name—the case—"

Thorn nodded, again making sense of something I could barely follow. "I haven't told anyone, and I don't plan to, Zale. How about we walk you back to the ship?"

Zale accepted this with the first glimmer of eagerness he'd shown all day. But Thorn's glance at me over his head told me that we weren't yet done—not by a long shot.

* * *

After the trip to the carnival—and a brief stop on the way back at the tavern, where Thorn insisted she was "checking in" but where in fact she was picking up several flagons of lemonade and a basket stuffed full of fresh bread and butter—the officer and I sat down in the station once more. This time, I didn't bother biting my lip or watching my tongue.

"What in Beyond was all that about, Thorn?" I asked, as she was tucking into the bread. "Zale never going ashore, and not wanting anyone to hear that he'd been here?"

"Not uncommon. We get a training on it at the Guild," she said. As a sign of just how kindly she was feeling toward me, she even offered me the first piece of bread. "Thousand Furs-type stories."

"Yikes." The bread was warm in my hands, but I shivered as I perched atop Thorn's desk to eat and talk. People all over Beyond are used to the idea that fairy tales repeat themselves as a matter of course, but there are some tales that seem worse than others. In most versions of "Thousand-Furs," the main character runs away from a misguided, even lecherous parent, and opts to take work serving in a completely new place. The climax of the story is often the unpleasant, dramatic confrontation that occurs when the parent finally catches up with the child. "So you think Zale left home—and that's what Coal had on him? Coal was threatening to tell his family where he was?"

Thorn nodded. "Probably would have been easy to figure out, for Coal's part. Especially if Coal and Zale were friends, working together. Put together the fact that Zale never went ashore, probably turned down every chance to be in the show, never spoke of a family . . ."

"Easy, indeed," I mused.

"'Specially when you think of how similar Thousand-Furs and Cinderella stories can be," Thorn went on. "Domineering family relationships, work as a way to escape, so on."

I shivered again. "Don't you think, in a way, that makes it worse? That Coal would hold something like that over Zale, I mean. When they could have been friends, or at least understood each other."

"Understanding's not always a good thing," Thorn said darkly, polishing off her first slice of bread and reaching for another. I swatted at her hand and pointed out the jar of peanut butter nestled into the basket, a mute reminder to *eat protein.* Since I was usually a devoted cook and mindful of my food—when not in the depths of a murder investigation— Officer Thorn was familiar with this sort of thing from me. She opened up the peanut butter without complaint and continued musing aloud. "So now we have a whole new angle on Coal."

"Not just a victim, but a perpetrator, too," I agreed. "I wonder if he *was* blackmailing others on board? Zale might not have noticed if he was."

"If you ask me, all signs point to yes," Thorn said. She wiped peanut butter from her thumb and set aside her knife to count off the points on her fingers. "We've got longevity—this didn't just start yesterday. Ostara was nearly four months ago, by my count.

"Greed. 'Just a little off the top' was never enough.

"Time. The day *after* pay day? Hardly ideal. If Zale was a

bolder lad, he might've gone and spent the cash by that time."

"So, your thinking is that *on* payday, on the evening after the show, Coal was busy collecting from others who might've been less conservative," I mused. It made sense, even if it did make that pit in my stomach twist.

"Then there's the fact that everyone on board was hot on the collar during our initial interviews," Thorn concluded, tapping a fourth finger. "Seems high time we have another go."

"Tomorrow, I hope," I said, glancing around. Thorn's office had no window, but I knew from our walk that it was well past afternoon now.

"If you insist." Officer Thorn winked at me, a brief flash of humor. Then she was back to business—and another piece of fragrant bread. "I doubt Zale will go telling any tales. The question is, who do we want to focus on? Who else was being blackmailed?"

"But also, *why*?" I asked, distracted. "I mean, what was Coal doing with the money? Or planning to do? It's not as though he had any fancy things or clothes."

"Not that we found," Thorn reminded me. "But that's how it goes, sometimes. He might have been saving up. Biding his time until the ship docked somewhere he really wanted to make a go of it. Blackmailers are often planners, you know."

"I don't," I admitted, gladly. "But also, we didn't find any savings, either."

"So they were well-hidden. Or," the officer said thoughtfully, "he was robbed. *That* could be the motive for the murder."

"Robbery, relief from blackmail, anger over blackmail, or even self-defense," I said, ticking off my own list. "Looks like we went from a murder with *no* motives to a murder with too many."

Officer Thorn grinned a buttery grin. "That's precisely why a good police officer is always ready to ask for some help."

17

A Fateful Meeting

It was evening before I left Thorn's office. As soon as my feet hit the cobblestone street, I remembered my promise to Saki.

The café's sure to be closed by now, I thought, looking up at the cloudy, darkening sky. *We got too carried away talking everything over . . .*

. . . And really, it is such a shocking development . . . Did I notice anything that first morning? I did, didn't I?

"Musing over murder by moonlight?" A friendly voice asked, startling me from my reverie.

I turned, and blushed as I saw Sakura herself coming toward me. "I just got done with Officer Thorn and remembered that you wanted to talk. I was just about to look you up. You can see how far I got," I explained, with a wry smile.

"That I can." Sakura grinned. "Come on, walk home with me. Unless you think William will be worried?"

"No, he's probably still closing up. We've been experimenting with staying open later," I said as I fell into step with Saki. We paced back up the street before turning onto the neighborhood alley that led to Sakura's home.

"Every time I mention doing something like that, Glacial growls at me," Saki remarked flippantly.

Despite the strain of the day, I chuckled. "Probably because poor Glacial is in the café kitchen baking up treats before dawn most days. I always see her lights on when I go down to the lab."

"There's nothing 'poor Glacial' about it," Sakura protested. "She *likes* baking. And being up early. She doesn't do anything she doesn't want to!"

"Perks of being a retired mercenary?" I asked, referring to a well-established rumor. Glacial was something of a legend in Belville, in part because she rarely spoke to anyone except her friend and business partner, Saki. She made the most wonderful cupcakes, but if anyone ever tried to compliment her on one, she flushed like a cherry and disappeared into her kitchen. That, combined with her very short, slim stature, made it amusing to think she might once have been a fearsome warrior-for-hire.

Sakura knew exactly what I was fishing for, and she mimed sewing her lips shut. "I'll never tell," she then added, her face splitting in a grin. "But I repeat: Glacial never does anything she doesn't want to. We'll leave it at that."

By this time, we'd reached the trim two-story house where Sakura rented rooms. The apartment had originally been her brother Ryuko's, but seeing as he spent most of his time with Mel these days, Saki had it all to herself. I have to admit, I did sometimes wonder if that was why Saki had tried so hard to set her brother and the friendly postmaster up in the first place.

"Come in," she insisted, with another of her sly glances, just a brief little light in her blue eyes that seemed to say, *I know exactly what you're thinking, and I don't mind one bit.* "I have some leftovers from the café at home. When was the last time you ate?"

Rather than answer, I gestured for Sakura to lead the way. As she let us in the front door and slowly up the interior steps, my stomach *was* rumbling. I was a little embarrassed at how carried away Officer Thorn and I had become. *But it's really important to think this one through,* I reminded myself, thinking of Luca and the shine in his eyes as he'd told us all about his research yesterday.

At the head of the staircase, Saki turned and black sparks of magic flared in her hands as she went to open the door on one side of a long hall. I noticed all this, but didn't really process it, my thoughts still full of Luca. When I ran right into Saki before she'd finished opening her front door, she laughed. "At least I know it wasn't me and my fake legs that slowed you down."

"Taking the stairs, you mean? Don't be silly," I protested, blushing. "Anyway, given how thoughtful you are about everything, how could you call your feet 'fake'?"

"Oh, fair enough," Saki agreed airily, leading me into her apartment with a wave of her hand over her shoulder. Another burst of magic swirled around her legs—prosthetic, from the knees down—and instead of the low, sturdy heels she wore at the café, her feet now sported fluffy white slippers with rabbit ears. Ever since I'd known her, Sakura had been like that: effortless, fashion-forward, and self-possessed. Her fairy-made prosthetic legs seemed just as natural to her as my flesh-and-blood feet were to me—and far more graceful, at that. Something *pinged* in the back of my mind, and I thought again about Coal's bare toes. As I followed suit—much more clumsily, shedding my boots—Sakura added, "I've just been feeling a bit moody lately. Maybe it's you and Mel running around mooning over love that has me feeling like I'm missing something."

"Missing something right under your nose," I snorted, my orange-stockinged feet sliding over Saki's shiny wood floors as we made our way to the kitchen at one end of the narrow apartment. If it had been anyone else, I wouldn't have said anything . . . but *everyone* in town knew about Trent's feelings. Turns out, not all witches are effortless and mysterious.

Saki giggled. "Sometimes it's easier to choose *not* to notice something. And actually, that's exactly what I wanted to talk to you about."

"Great segue," I teased, dropping into a chair. It was nice, I thought, to be the "William" in a conversation sometimes. I leaned back, stretching out my shoulders, settling in.

Meanwhile Sakura bustled around her corner kitchen, keeping her face straight. "I didn't want to mention it out on the road," she said, as though we were discussing the early summer blooms. "Everything's much more difficult now, isn't it, with the investigation going on?"

I inhaled scents of cheese and thyme from the hand pies warming on the stove, and sighed. "I mean, it's not like Thorn could *not* investigate Coal's death, difficulty or no."

"Of course. But it brings up memories," Sakura observed very matter-of-factly for someone who had never known Owl—or Gloria's meddlesome assistants, either. But I knew she and Gloria were good friends now, and wasn't surprised at her familiarity with the subject. "And for my part, it makes it a little more awkward to admit what I wanted to talk about—in public, anyway."

"What do you mean?" I sat up, head tilted.

"Coal," Sakura said simply. With a wave of black sparkles, she levitated a teapot, cups, milk, and honey onto a tray, and then guided that and a basket of warmed pies over to the table. Following this display, she took her seat across from me and paused before explaining, "I had a bad feeling about him that first morning he came into the café."

My stomach plummeted, even as I reached eagerly for tea and food. "But you set me up with him!"

"To see what vibe *you* would get. I thought you'd back me up. I didn't account for how emotional you'd be about someone who even tangentially reminded you of your boyfriend," she replied, leveling a look at me through lavender earl gray-laced steam.

I flushed. "I guess your bad feeling was more the 'he's a bad actor' rather than the 'he's in danger' type of feeling, then?"

"Specifically, the 'he's scanning me for weaknesses and saying exactly what he thinks I need to hear' sort of feeling."

So she knew. Right away, just like that.

Sakura took one look at my slack jaw and neglected pastry before giggling again. "Oh, come on, Red. Shadow witch," she reminded me. "I know when someone's lying. And more to the point—I know when they're lying in order to get me to do something."

"So what was it you figured he wanted you to do?" I spooned honey into my tea, giving myself time to think before answering my own question. "For my part, he definitely wanted work at the shop. And you're right . . . I *did* think he was coming on too strong. But I also did feel for him. I guess that means his lies worked."

"It's not wrong to opt for sympathy rather than suspicion," Saki said, laying her hand briefly over mine. "That's why you have me to watch your back. And William. Did William ever meet Coal?"

I smiled gratefully at my friend before sipping my tea, gathering myself again. "No, we were met at the carnival with news of his death. Or *likely* news of a death, at the time. Why?"

"Because my feeling was only that—just my *feeling*," Sakura said, sitting back. "I thought at first maybe I was being unfair to Coal because of my experience last fall. Or that, as a potential employer, I was seeing a particular side of him, maybe."

Nursing my warm cup, I thought this over. Sakura was referring to a dangerous mystery we'd gone through together, its central character a metaphorical wolf in sheep's clothing. I could understand why she had strong feelings about that. "Sort of a scammy side," I mused in agreement, and went on to fill Sakura in on some of the blackmail details Thorn and I had learned. "So do you think that was how he went about it? He played this sympathetic character, and then used that to gain information?"

"Honestly, that's what I was worried about," Saki nodded, swallowing a bite of cheese and puff pastry. "But what I wasn't sure of was how much he was playing a character versus being genuine."

"You don't think everything that he said was a lie?"

"No. That's why it was hard to pin down my feeling," she explained. After a moment, more carefully, she said, "And that's how the best of them do it, you know."

The best of them. Somehow, the phrase made me immediately

think of Owl manipulating Luca. From Sakura's steady gaze on me, I could tell that this was exactly what she had intended. But I didn't fully get it, and that must have shown on my tired face.

"A lot of people who scam or trick or even abuse others start naturally—almost accidentally," Sakura continued, still staring evenly at me, still in that gentle voice. "In the beginning, what they share happens to be the truth—a truly sad situation, or a true burst of anger, maybe. Sharing that gets them what they want: sympathy, or obedience. Then next time, the circumstances are different, so they have to exaggerate a little. They find that exaggerating works just as well as the truth. From there, they go on and on, further and further . . ."

"Experimenting," I concluded automatically, fiddling with my pastry's flaky crust.

"Exactly. And over time, with each experiment, that little nugget of what was true gets covered up—or should I say, expanded. Now it isn't simply a story of an absent father that garners sympathy; it's a saga of a wicked stepfamily that garners investment, aid, even gifts or confidences. And it gains more nuance—throwaway lines, the appropriate clothes. It becomes a persona, a role—an emotional costume."

I glanced up at Saki, thinking of Coal's clothes that day at the Pomegranate—sizes too big. *Had that been a deliberate choice?* "So, you're saying Coal is exactly the opposite of what we thought. Or what he wanted us to think."

"Possibly." She sipped her tea delicately. "But I could also be saying that Coal was exaggerating his appearance without even thinking about it. I don't know where on his journey he was—that's why I wanted an outside opinion. I couldn't tell if he was trying to manipulate me on purpose, or if he simply didn't know how else to act. Because putting on a costume like that can be a defense mechanism, you know."

"Or a choice." My teeth ground on the words, surprising even me.

"Maybe it's a good thing we didn't get a chance to talk before you and Thorn made your discovery today," Saki said gravely. "It feels like a betrayal?"

"It does, but even more than that—" I set down my tea cup and pushed it away, so that I wouldn't break the china handle. "Luca's already invested in this case. In Coal. I didn't want him to be, but everyone told me I shouldn't protect him, even *he* told me that, so I backed off, and now—"

"Isn't it better if Coal isn't quite like Luca was?" Saki prodded.

"It isn't *better* if it makes Luca's old reality look just like some cursed *costume!*"

I was breathing too heavily. Somehow, my poor tea cup had ended up on its side.

"Ah." Sakura smiled as she lifted her fingers, magic lifting the hot water and herbs away from her table. "Feels better to know, in any case, doesn't it?"

I scrunched my face up at first, but as I understood what she meant, I let the tension go. "Thank you for helping me put my finger on what was bothering me."

"Any time." Sakura finished her cleaning spell, and then poured me some more tea. "We can't say anything for certain about Coal just yet, of course. You and Officer Thorn still have to find that nugget of truth. But as for Luca . . . Sometimes costumes *do* look like someone else's reality. The important thing to remember is intention."

"Luca's intentions have only ever been to be kind and

helpful," I said without really understanding where Saki was going with this. *Even to awful people like Owl,* I added in my head, reaching for tea to soothe the lump in my throat.

"You're probably right. In which case, there's absolutely nothing that can compare." When I frowned uncertainly at this, Saki leaned forward and smiled. "Think of it like gold, Red-the-alchemist. Fool's gold never passes for real gold, when put under careful scrutiny. You only have to pay attention and think it over. Sometimes costumes are impressive . . . but the real value is always in sharing honesty."

18

Shards of Glass

I left Sakura soon after that. Though I hadn't eaten much, cheese and pastry sat heavily in my stomach. The last thing I wanted was to go home. The neighborhood around Saki's house was full of the sounds and smells of dinner time—happy families, wood smoke drifting from chimneys in the twilight chill. It made me think of the cooking I'd planned to do that night: momos, a sort of dumpling recipe that I hadn't yet perfected. I'd thought it might give me a suitable distraction.

But I found I didn't want to be distracted.

Or, maybe, I just was already too distracted by the case.

In the hazy shadows, I paced the town. The schoolhouse was quiet, the tavern loud and bright. The shops were all shuttered, and even the grocer's was still. But the houses remained lively; there were even people out in Market Square, playing in the park. Children, running to and fro with a ball that sparkled with fairy magic.

I realized that I, too, wanted to run—my feet were itching to run. It was a familiar feeling, the one aspect of my family's heritage that I understood. I could run very fast—unnaturally so. My mothers, my entire clan back home—they were Seers, magical, and like all clans of Seers in Beyond, our clan's magic came with side effects, all linked back to a mythical patron. Much like Sakura, my family members had insight into things I did not. I had never had any aptitude for predicting the future or divination, and so I had left all that behind, training to be a scientist instead. But still I had the marks, the glittery hair, the speed, the itchy feet, things that ran in my blood. Things I masked, because I didn't want to answer uncomfortable questions. So many things I didn't want to face.

It wasn't until I shivered that I realized I'd been standing still, watching them. My shop and William were just a few steps behind me; I could go home, and think of my recipes and listen to the kids in the Square, and put all of Saki's talk about abusers out of my mind. Let a good night's sleep give me a more level-headed perspective. *Try again in the morning,* as my mother might have said. Or, in the more curt words of my old alchemical teacher, *get your thoughts right first.* Cooking always helped me do that; it was like alchemy, but the stakes were lower, and the results more tasty. Even William liked momos. I could go in and just focus on that.

Instead I kept walking.

"Red, I keep telling you, the back door is always open— well, that is, I *was* about to lock up, since it's after closing, but I always forget and end up locking it right before I head upstairs, so really you never have to knock, you could have just come in and—"

Luca's green eyes were luminescent as he spoke, an old familiar reproach. My hand found his on the door and I tugged him out into the alley behind the bookstore, and I kissed him.

Feeling the warmth of his lips on mine was exactly the distraction I'd needed. It didn't even feel like a distraction at all. In fact, it felt like an antidote.

"Hi." This time his voice was different, slower. The way he wrapped me up in his arms had me thinking of old castles and warm hearths, and it reminded me of what Gloria had pointed out an eon ago that morning—that tragic tales can have sweet endings.

"Hey," I said belatedly as I leaned my forehead against his, just breathing in the moment. "I want you to know that you're okay. You're real. And brave." When Luca shifted, hands drifting down to my waist, I chuckled self-consciously and added, "I know I'm not always very good with words. And you a scholar, of all things."

At that, he laughed, his voice deep and soft in the cloudy moonlight. "Is it not very good of me to admit that I thought you used the perfect words, then?"

"Oh. Well, if that's how you feel, that's fine," I decided, smiling as I kissed him gently once more.

But there was something more there than *fine,* and I couldn't string together the sentence. Luca didn't move away, either, and we stood there with our faces so close, my arms around his neck, until at last he murmured, "Sometimes the best things come from the worst parts of our lives."

I stirred, upset again. "Luca—"

"It's alright, Red. Sweet love, I keep trying to tell you, it's alright that I was wounded when you met me. I'm happy that you are part of my healing. Without you, I'm not sure how I would have found the strength. But I *have* found it, and our lives are different now. It's alright."

My jaw dropped open, brushing his cheek. Luca, with his

sometimes old-fashioned turns of phrase, had called me *my friend* before, but never *sweet love.* I heard all of his words, and I held on to them. But it was as though I couldn't see anything past that point.

Finally, groping in the dark, I managed, "I just—wanted to give you more. I wish you never had to be strong in the first place." I had to say it very carefully; the words were sharp. So much of what made Luca beautiful to me was his courage and heart, but that was also what pained me most—that he should ever have had to suffer at all.

"Not even alchemists can turn back time." Luca shifted, kissing my forehead. "What I have now is enough. What I went through then is done."

"But—" I leaned back, and caught sight of the small smile on Luca's lips. The expression reminded me to pause; I knew he was amused at me. Sometimes, he could feel truly ancient. I took a deep breath, letting my hands slide down to his chest. "Well, if that's how you feel . . ."

". . . Then that's fine?" Luca suggested, his small smile growing. "Come on, Red. I think we both could use a drink."

* * *

Walking back down the road hand in hand with Luca was a totally different experience. He'd always had that sort of cheer that just quietly makes everything better, even if you have no idea how or why. Lingering under the streetlights, I realized how much I'd been missing that during my long days of investigating.

Maybe, I thought, wryly, *everyone was trying to tell me that I shouldn't protect Luca . . . because if I let him investigate with us, then he can protect* me.

It was a humbling thought, but one I couldn't possibly be mad about. Luca *was* my best friend, after all, and much more—even if I couldn't exactly tell him so. I'd figure that part out in time.

Half listening to Luca chat about his day, my cheeks warm as I thought once more about that phrase, *sweet love,* I nearly ran right into William as he loomed out of the evening dark.

"Glad to see you're so worried about worrying *me,*" he grumped, plopping himself down in our way.

"Didn't she tell you where she was going?" Luca asked, a concerned look coming back into his face as he looked to me.

I rolled my eyes. "I was going to." *Before I kissed Luca and forgot about everything else, anyway.* "It's, um, been a busy day. Sorry, William. I figured I'd drop in, probably . . ."

William huffed. "I saved you the trouble. You're welcome. Are you lovebirds going to the tavern? Because I could use some gossip."

"Dusty didn't have enough news?" I teased, my guilt melting into a grin. The three of us fell into step naturally, making our way around the Square.

"Dusty got to see the carnival that first night. He said it's amazing. And that you did okay taking apart that lock," William reported. "And he also says he's heard about dangerous waterfolk too."

I groaned. "Oh, gods, not him *and* Sir Rowan. I already spent a morning trying to convince Sir Rowan not to immediately suspect everyone who's related to Melusine, just because he has some knightly issue with ladies of water," I explained to Luca, who chuckled.

"He did have a point," William corrected me.

"But seeing as we aren't legendary kings, I don't see how it's relevant," I argued light-heartedly.

"It *is* an interesting dichotomy in the literature, though," Luca said, eyes alight. "On the spectrum between considering water creatures untrustworthy tricksters or sympathetic healers, there's very little middle ground. In fact—"

"Please, not until I've had dinner," William interrupted. "Red didn't feed me *all day*. I can't focus like this."

"You don't actually need food," I reminded him, laughing. As a magical creation, a familiar, William isn't technically "alive," not in the way many of us are. His only real *need* is to recharge himself via starlight. "And anyway, I'm sure you and Dusty could have got lunch if you wanted some."

"He had to go fix a broken pipe in Johann's apartment," William said, as though Dusty doing his job—acting as town plumber and general tinkerer—was a personal slight against him. As we neared the tavern lights, my grumpy companion raced ahead, no doubt to regale the tavern hostess with a tale of his woe.

Luca caught my weary look, and laughed. "Maybe his complaining will get us a table faster?"

"Ugh," was all I had to say about that. But I smiled. I had, I decided, missed *both* of my best friends.

Whether thanks to William or not, I couldn't say—but we soon found ourselves seated in the cozy, smoky noise that was Lavender's Tavern. A chill had driven everyone inside, and the twinkling lights strung along the wooden eaves were swinging with the energy in the air. Lavender herself, a bastion of town life, oversaw the organized chaos from behind her bar. Waitstaff with hands full of food and drink wove their way through tables brimming with gossip and friendship.

"Well, it seems like everyone in town isn't quite as worried as I would have thought," I observed to Luca and William after we'd ordered our dinner. From our snug booth, we looked out into the wide room.

William snorted. "Because it wasn't one of *them* that got murdered. You know how it is, Red."

"Yes, but—I don't know. Officer Thorn was pulling a little of that earlier, I think—thinking of the crew and cast members as just 'carnival folk.' And they *are*, of course, but I really don't think that makes them any different from us . . ." As my musings trailed off, I caught sight of Luca smiling at me across the table—probably thinking of how far I'd come since the day *I*'d been a traveling outsider in town—and abruptly I blushed and changed the subject. "It's just as silly as the 'evil waterfolk' story, right?"

I looked to Luca, but he hesitated. In fact, he and William exchanged a glance.

"What is it?" I asked, my suspicion rising.

"Just that there *are* predatory types of waterfolk," Luca said at last. "Actually, that's why I've been a little worried about you being so distracted, if we're being honest."

I frowned. "You've been worried that much? Why didn't you say anything?"

"We did talk yesterday. And there's been plenty to say about naiads and Melusine," Luca said reasonably. "There didn't seem to be any point in adding more trouble to the mix, before it was necessary anyway. But since you're more and more involved with the crew now, and if we're talking about worry anyway . . . Well, that's what's been on my mind, at least."

He looked to William, and William cleared his throat. "*I* have been telling you this whole time. I literally said it last night. Didn't you pay attention when Thorn told you about the rumors, Red? Aicha kandida."

I didn't fail to notice how my best friends were now ganging up on me. I rubbed my hand through my pony tail, mind whirring at this development. "No. I mean—I do remember what you're talking about. She said the illusionist told you both something, right? No, the sharpshooter. Siren. She said something about someone on board. But I didn't get it. Is that a water creature?"

"The aicha kandida was mentioned? Officer Thorn wasn't that specific." Luca, too, looked surprised—*so*, I thought wryly, *at least the conspiracy hasn't gone as far as discussing me and the things I miss behind my back.* For my benefit, he added, "That's one example of the kind of waterfolk I was talking about. Traditionally, the aicha kandida is a very beautiful person or creature who lures victims into the water in order to drown them—sometimes even eat them. There are actually a lot of waterfolk like that in history and lore, but to *meet* one in person is very rare these days. They're, um, well, the conventional wisdom is that they can have a tendency to be . . . violent. Not quite human. In fact, prone to eating humans. Did I say that part yet?"

"But Coal wasn't eaten," I pointed out.

"Drowned, though," William countered, with a look I knew well in his doggy eyes. This was a point of contention he'd been holding on to for a while. "That would be within the scope of an aicha kandida's powers."

We paused as the food showed up—a veggie burger with no bun for William (who had probably most just wanted the fries) and an *enormous* spring salad for Luca and I to share. After all the bread I'd eaten with Thorn, I was craving veggies, and

Luca was always game to eat just about anything. This little bit of normalcy helped me gain perspective.

"I don't know how you two keep all that mythical information in your heads," I said ruefully once we were alone at our table again.

William stopped levitating french fries into chili sauce long enough to ask, "How do *you* remember all that nerdy stuff about rocks and plants and potions?"

"Not nerdy. But point taken," I conceded, smiling. "Okay. Aicha kandida. Do we remember who the sharpshooter was talking about when she made that reference?"

Luca and I both looked to William, who took his time swallowing an enormous bite of black bean patty before saying smugly, "*I* do. Three guesses who."

The tone of his voice was all I needed. As my nose scrunched up, my misgivings skyrocketed. "Anastasia."

"Which means Magica and Weep, too," William reminded me. "Assuming they really are all related."

"Three suspects to look at more closely, then. Why didn't you say anything earlier?" I asked him.

"Because someone left me in the shop during all the important investigating today," William retorted.

"But if you're going back tomorrow," Luca interrupted gently, with a look that assured me he knew I *would* be, even though I hadn't yet caught him and William up on the latest developments, "then maybe it would be best to talk to them specially . . . *separately*. See what they say about their life before the carnival, for example. Or how they relate to the rest of the cast and crew. Just make sure not to do it alone."

"Not alone," I promised faithfully. "No more being distracted. Now, with that decided, I have to tell you both what we found out today . . ."

19

Prey in the Night

The next morning Officer Thorn was, once again, eating bread when she rapped at my back door. I took one look at her breakfast-on-the-go, handed her a travel mug of tea and a deviled egg, then grabbed my own things and joined her.

"Not half bad," she decided, peering at the egg in the morning light.

"A trick from traveling," I told her. "Boil it, peel it, cut it open and mix in seasonings, then close it up again . . . Makes it cleaner. Not that you're ever messy."

"Never," Thorn agreed contentedly. "But I don't need your recipes, Red. I want to hear what that dog of yours had to say about the case."

I rolled my eyes, and grinned at the same time. *So she assumes that I blabbed about everything to William. Well, she's not wrong!* "And Luca, too. But you'll be glad I told him. Listen to this . . ."

As we made our way from my alley to Belville's quiet streets, I filled the officer in on my friends' thoughts about aicha kandida and drowning—and the importance of following up the sharpshooter's rumor. It didn't take long. Before I'd finished, Thorn had already veered toward the forest.

"Hey," I protested. We'd just hit the crest of the hill at the south edge of town, and the lake was in view.

"We're missing something," was her only response.

Fortunately, her direction told me more. She was headed straight for Trent's Hut.

Oh, I thought, realizing she meant that we were missing a Witch. *Well, that does make sense. He was the one to figure out about the saltwater, so he'll probably have good insight in the interviews.*

If, I worried as I hurried after Thorn, *he's even awake at this hour . . .*

He wasn't.

Officer Thorn fixed that.

Trent's "Hut"—a title given specifically to the residence of a town Witch—lived up to its name with a vengeance. Ever since he'd moved to town, Trent had been hitting up my shop for mending potions, garden fixes, and extra strong glue. Over the two past years, he and the Hut had settled into a sort of stalemate: the herb garden surrounding the little house was thriving, but the chimney was still somehow crooked and the shingle roof still looked like it might slide off at any minute. The fence was freshly painted but still a bit uneven, and Trent had given up on the gate entirely. That last part was for the best, because Thorn probably would have crashed straight through any gate that morning.

She marched herself straight up the garden path and began pounding on the Hut's wooden door. (Luckily, its hinges had always been one of the sturdier parts of the property.)

I caught up with the officer just as a light shone from the slats in one window, and muffled cursing emanated from within the Hut. "He might be busy, you know," I hissed to Thorn.

"No one's too busy for justice," she replied with unshakable confidence. "Of course he's not busy. Don't be silly, Red. It's before ten in the morning."

"Oh, my clock *isn't* broken," Trent grumbled as the front door creaked open. "It *is* before ten. So why are you here?"

"Official business," Thorn informed him without a trace of pity.

Trent stood in the sliver of the doorway thinking about this for a minute. Even his pajamas, a particularly beat-up old shirt and flannel pants, looked rumpled and unwilling to be up at this hour. But as the situation settled around us, the Witch straightened, eyes widening. "There hasn't been another murder?"

"There hasn't," I confirmed, before Officer Thorn could say something dramatic and misleading. "But we're headed down to the *Luna II* for more interviews, and William and Luca think there could be someone dangerous aboard—dangerous and magical, I mean. So Thorn thought—"

"I get it." As Trent's gaze slid from Thorn to me, he grinned crookedly and shrugged one shoulder, as if to say, *what's one to do?* "Fine. Be out in a minute."

The door closed. A flurry of purple sparks escaped the nearest window. A *thud* and some more muffled cursing traced Trent's progress through the dark Hut.

"He'll have to be more organized than that if he hopes to impress Sakura," Officer Thorn observed, a stoic mix of familial and impassive. She'd taken Trent under her wing when he'd moved to town; in fact, for both of us, Trent was something akin to a younger brother. But that didn't mean she wasn't going to call it as she saw it.

"*Thorn*," I reprimanded. "That's none of your business."

"It's *her* business he should be worried about," she continued, grinning at the opportunity for a near-pun. "Only a few months in and already a fixture in town. Anyone who can pull that off will need a partner who's—"

The door opened abruptly and Trent spilled out, clothed now but a little out of breath, one lock of dark hair still sticking up at the back. "Don't you dare finish that sentence."

"I'm just saying," the officer insisted, with a very smug-older-sister smile. "If you—"

"Okay," I interrupted loudly. "Let's go. The folks at the carnival aren't going to interview themselves, now, are they?"

* * *

It wasn't until we three found ourselves seated in the ship's lounge across from Anastasia that I started to regret my enthusiasm.

She was just so *showy*. And sure, there *was* a show that night—but that was hours away, and she wasn't remotely in costume. Or, perhaps I should say, she wasn't in her carnival costume. Instead, she was very elegantly draped in a maroon velour dressing gown, bejeweled slippers, and a hair net studded with pearls. Despite the early hour, her eye makeup was dark and smudged. She spent so much time turning aside to blot her eyes with a monogrammed handkerchief that I half suspected there was a mirror hidden within its folds.

"It's simply all been a shock," she announced as soon as we were settled. "We're all in mourning. But the show must go on!"

I bit my lip. Sakura's thoughts about manipulation and costume were at the forefront of my mind. But honestly, Anastasia's actions were so over-the-top that they hardly seemed like a costume—more like a fairy-made neon sign.

At this point, I couldn't help thinking, *it might almost be a relief to find she's the murderer.*

It wasn't a very kind thought, but it was also a serious one. I considered it more carefully. Anastasia *had* been one of the closest people to Coal, as far as we could tell; she might have one of several motives—he could have been blackmailing her, perhaps, or they might simply have fought. Or maybe she really *was* some kind of predatory water spirit, luring people in, and Coal had just been unlucky . . .

"The investigation is ongoing also," Officer Thorn reminded our interviewee sternly. "New evidence has come to light. I'd like you to tell me, in detail, about your relationship with Coal."

"Relationship?" Anastasia repeated, sounding—just for a moment—genuinely surprised. Then the polish and drama came back to her voice. "*New evidence,* you say? Did you find his money? Everyone knew he was stashing it, though he never told anyone where or how much—suspicious boy."

"All we need right now is straightforward answers," Officer Thorn insisted. She gestured to Trent and added, "Our special consultant will tell if you're lying."

Trent and I exchanged a sly glance, seated on the couch to either side of the officer. I had my notebook out and was taking notes; he was glowing faintly, just enough to remind everyone he was a Witch. But we'd agreed on the road that we were actually looking for something more insidious than new details or lies. I was looking specifically for any discrepancies from the stories we'd heard the first night. Trent was using his magic to scan for traces of magical blood as well as dishonesty. His information wouldn't be infallible—we'd seen the limitations of such scans over the winter, during a town-wide panic. But he might be able to corroborate the rumors about an aicha kandida on board.

"I'm so sure I've said everything already," Anastasia said, addressing her handkerchief again. "It's all such a blur. Oh, what a tragedy! To happen to someone so young!"

"At what age," Thorn said doggedly, "did you meet Coal?"

"You mean what age *he* was, of course? Why, he was only a little boy. It seems so long ago now."

Thorn tried again. "He lost his mother at six. Is that right?"

"Oh, yes, poor thing. A terrible loss, of course. So that must have made him . . . let's see . . . oh, how could I have forgotten? He was eight when our families joined. My own twins were just turning nine, you see." Anastasia ended with a proud smile before recalling that we were discussing a murder victim. Abruptly, she returned to dabbing at her dry eyes.

I made note of the age, just to hide the skepticism on my face.

Meanwhile Officer Thorn had found her tactic, and she stuck with it. "And he was ten when his father passed away."

"Yes. Another dreadful tragedy! Oh, my beloved! And now the whole family gone!"

"Excepting you and the twins, of course," Thorn muttered. Before Anastasia could respond, she said more professionally, "What did you notice about Coal when his father passed away?"

"About Coal? I'm sure I couldn't say. He was always a quiet boy, in any case."

"No acting out? No new behavior?" Thorn pressed.

"That was eight years ago," Anastasia said defensively. "Surely I can't be expected to remember. It's not as though he ever confided in me. Awfully self-contained, he always was. I always said it was due to losing a mother so young."

"So he didn't share his plans with you? Hopes, dreams, that kind of thing?"

As Thorn spoke, I realized what she was driving at. She wanted to know if Anastasia and Coal shared secrets—if, perhaps, Anastasia might have unwittingly become a victim of Coal's blackmail, or if somehow he'd dropped hints about his illegal behavior. I doodled around a timeline of Anastasia's story as I listened.

"Not once," she said. "As I said, he was a quiet boy. He wouldn't even play with the other children."

Magica and Weep, I thought. *If I had heard this story two days ago, I would have assumed it was because Coal wasn't allowed to play with them. But where is the truth?*

"He didn't express any concerns to you," Thorn continued, "even recently?"

"What had he to be concerned about? With me providing a roof over his head, and my children bringing the carnival more and more success?"

If I was a blackmailer saving up a bunch of money, I thought as I wrote, *I just might have a plan in mind for some kind of dramatic revenge against such an entitled and distant caregiver . . .*

And what if that's exactly why Coal wasn't spending his ill-gotten gains? What if he had plans for revenge, and Anastasia or her children found out about them?

20

Step Siblings

The interview might have continued that way forever: Anastasia and her handkerchief, Thorn and her detailed questions. But when it became clear that Anastasia either truly had no idea what Coal was up to, or she was a very good liar, Thorn nudged at Trent.

The Witch stood and, making some excuse about needing to do a magical survey of Coal's room, got Anastasia to escort him from the room.

As they left, I leaned in and whispered to Thorn. "Is it hardhearted of me to think that the idea that she might find out about our 'new evidence' if she helps Trent is more exciting to her than anything else we've discussed?"

The officer snorted. "You can't let suspects like that get to you, Red. You meet all types in interviews."

"Well, all the more reason I'm not a police officer," I retorted.

"Go on," was all she said. "You're up next."

This was the second part of our plan. Officer Thorn agreed with Luca about the need to interview Coal's stepfamily *separately*. But because it had been so difficult to get the twins to talk—or to get them away from their mother—we'd devised this distraction. Trent would continue gently questioning Anastasia, hopefully finding out more about the aicha kandida accusation, while I'd find Magica and Weep so that Thorn could have a chance to interview them alone.

Finding them was quite easy, actually; they were practicing their act. Their mother's devotion to her children's career was so evident that I'd been pretty certain I'd find them there. The harder part was convincing them to take a break. They absolutely refused to split up, which was a little frustrating— for me, but also for Weep, I think. Magica was the one who seemed truly concerned. Finally, Weep agreed to come along just to get me to stop bothering him. Magica trotted along behind.

Thorn gave me a look as I entered the lounge behind the pair of them. We'd *hoped* to get them alone . . . *I tried,* I mouthed, taking my place beside her with my notebook.

She shrugged, and I knew exactly what she was thinking. *It's better than nothing.* And then she got to work.

But this interview didn't go as smoothly as the first.

"What are you?" Thorn blurted.

I looked up in alarm. *Trying a very different tactic, isn't she?*

"Your heritage, she means," I said, when the silence and confusion became too thick in the room. *Someone* had to clear things up. "We, ah, neglected to write that in our notes after the first interview. For a full profile."

I was just stringing together words, but they must have sounded police-y enough. Weep shrugged.

"Basically human," he said, looking a little bored.

Thorn said nothing. I raised an eyebrow. *Mostly human, with near-literal gold hair and leaves sprouting from your head and silver eyes? I don't think so.* I looked at Magica.

Magica was staring at Thorn. Without even glancing my way, she finally broke and said, "He says that because we're—we're in between. Dad was a dryad. We don't remember him. Not really. M-mother's a water spirit. Of course. It's why she's so good. Ah—with the carnival. And all the water. And very beautiful, too."

"Has she ever told you about herself? Her powers?" Thorn asked.

The twins seemed puzzled. I could imagine why. Anastasia *did* do an awful lot of talking, even talking *for* her children when given the chance. But what did she really say about herself?

"What powers do *you* have?" Thorn added.

Again, Weep shrugged. "None."

"Hard work," said Magica earnestly. "That's what Mother says. Hard work is a virtue. We can do anything. If we work hard enough."

"What acts has Anastasia done in the carnival?" I asked, going for a more roundabout approach.

"None," said Weep, as if I'd asked him how many wings a manatee has. "She runs it."

"Sh-she *used* to do acts. Before us. Before Father. She did all kinds of things," said Magica reverently.

This struck me a little strangely. Anastasia wasn't young, of course, but she also didn't seem quite old enough to have done 'all kinds of things' *before* having adult children. *Agelessness—is that a helpful characteristic in narrowing down water spirits?*

With my luck, it probably wasn't. But I noted it anyway.

"*No* power?" Thorn resurfaced into the conversation. "Unlikely. No soft powers? No affinities? No glamours?"

"Nothing," Weep insisted. "Just, like Magica said. Work."

"We—we should really get back to it," Magica added. "If that's everything?"

The tense, confused silence returned. While it perplexed me, I was also very aware that we had a short time frame, and there was no space for silence. I cleared my throat. "I have an idea. Weep, why don't you talk Officer Thorn through your act? That'll probably help clear things up. Magica, you and I can start walking back to the practice ring. I just have a few extra things to ask you along the way."

Magica looked to her brother, who looked as impassive as ever.

"Just very small things," I promised, standing up. "This way, you'll get back to work sooner. And it'll keep Officer Thorn happy, right?"

Officer Thorn startled, like I'd pulled her perfect hair. "Fine. That's fine. Do that."

The response was so strange I had to repress an eyeroll, or better yet, the urge to *actually* pull her hair. *Hopefully she and Weep can make some sense out of each other*, I thought.

With one last reluctant glance at her twin, Magica stood. "Well—if that's what we should do—"

"Come on," I told her kindly. "I'll be out of your hair before you know it."

* * *

Magica, of course, had lovely hair. She'd described her mother as *beautiful,* but truly, the twins were every bit as striking. As we walked back down the long corridors, Magica paced at my side, her gold tresses as high as my shoulder, her small feet taking two steps to my one. The dryad, or tree spirit, heritage she'd mentioned made sense; after all, the leaves entwined with her braids were real. So was the nervous energy that had her bouncing with each step.

In fact, there was so much energy spilling off her that even I couldn't think straight. After a minute's quiet walking, I couldn't take it any more. I paused at a corner, reaching out to brush her elbow to catch her attention. She jumped like a scared cat.

"I'm sorry," I said, as gently as I could manage. "I didn't mean to scare you. I just wanted to tell you that you're not in trouble. In fact, you did very well answering Officer Thorn's questions."

"Really?" Magica's face lit up. The sight took my breath away. *Does she actually have some kind of magic? Maybe a glamour, like Thorn said?*

"Definitely," I replied, trying to keep an even keel. Still, I couldn't help but smile as I added, "She's not always the easiest person to talk to. I don't know what that was back there—she might just be a little stressed over the case. We really want to solve this, you know. That's all."

"*Is* that all?" Magica asked. Then immediately she blushed and began walking again, as though to remove herself from the scene of speaking up.

"Well," I said, walking with her, "I can only speak for myself, of course. I'm just here to help in any way I can. Officer Thorn would probably tell you she wants justice—that's usually what she says, any chance she gets."

"Any chance?" Magica echoed the phrase, skipping a step. She seemed . . . delighted. But the emotion was short-lived. She was serious again when she added, "I want to help too.

That's why I said those things."

"And they *were* helpful." I pulled to a stop again, and this time, Magica wheeled to face me—but she kept her distance. As I watched her, I thought of what Sakura had said to me about intentions and fool's gold. "Magica, can I ask you something? Just as one friend to another."

Magica's gray eyes went wide.

She's either a little bit innocent, or a large bit like her mother, I thought. *Too bad I don't have Trent or Saki's abilities. Who knows if we'll catch her alone again.* Taking a deep breath, I asked, "If you could do anything, what would you do?"

"Help Mother," she said promptly. But then her large eyes wavered, and she said, "I—I want to help Officer Thorn, too. Like you. But I can only do one thing. I've—already worked very hard at it . . ."

"Magica," I said very softly. "You don't have to work so hard."

The tone in her voice, that hesitation. Neither, I knew intuitively, could be faked. I knew . . .

"I wondered," Magica whispered, eyes downcast. "But then— I *couldn't* wonder. Because practicing is all I know."

. . . I knew why seeing her face light up earlier affected me. *Because you're so invested in anyone who even tangentially reminds you of your boyfriend,* Saki's amused voice echoed in my brain.

Thorn may have been right about this being a Cinderella story, I thought, as a new well of sympathy opened up within me, *but in this case, Coal wasn't our Cinderella.*

21

An Invitation

"**M**agica," I said more urgently, because I could feel her shock at her own candid thoughts. She was slipping away from me, pulled back to the practice room by an inexorable tide. "What did you think of Coal? Did Coal wonder things like this too?"

Her feet, which had been inching over the rough wood floor, went still. She bit her lip. "Coal didn't wonder."

"Is that because—"

"Coal didn't have to wonder," she continued, as though a dam had broken. "That's what he said. He was the only one of us going to get away. He told me all the time. He said he'd go to big cities. And be very famous. And how he'd *know* what it's like to be successful. To have a dream. He always told me—he said we were sad. Pathetic. That Mother gave up on her dreams. That she blocked others' dreams. He told me I have no dreams. I can't dream because I'm always working. I can't wonder because I can't dream."

"Hold up there," I interrupted, finding that line of reasoning abhorrent. And perhaps a little too *true*. "That's not the case any more, is it? You just told me that you *have* thought of things outside of your act."

Magica gave me a look like she'd seen a ghost, and mentally I kicked myself. I didn't want to upset her; that'd just make her run away all the faster.

"Wait," I said, responding more to her body language than anything spoken. "Why did Coal say that? About your mother? Please, Magica, it's important. It'll help me, and Officer Thorn."

A little bit of that brief light came back into Magica's eyes, and she ventured hesitantly, "Coal would always say those things. I don't know why. But—"

"Yes?" I coaxed.

"Mother didn't want Coal to leave," Magica said all in one breath. "She wanted us all to stay. Here. In the act. As a family."

"A family?" I repeated, doing my best to hide a bit of skepticism. "But Coal wasn't in your act, was he?"

"Not any more. Coal wanted to go," Magica added, breathless now. "It wasn't very—nice. He really wasn't kind. But I shouldn't—I should—I have to go and practice."

Before I could protest, she'd whirled and disappeared down the hall. For a split second I considered following her, but I had a feeling that'd only make her more upset. And as I stood there pondering, I heard footsteps behind me in the hall.

I turned and saw Weep. "Oh, are you done talking to Officer Thorn, then?"

He nodded, then shrugged at me. For a moment I thought he'd walk past me without speaking. Then, almost as if it was an afterthought, he turned back to me and said, "She's talking to the Director now. She said to tell you if I saw you."

"Thanks," I replied, though truthfully my gratitude was mixed with a bit of *well why didn't you say that sooner, then?*

Weep nodded once more and then continued silently walking, like a ship steaming away in the night. I watched him for just a moment, perplexed. There was nothing in his manner that suggested he was angry, or vengeful, or upset in any way. He simply wasn't concerned with me or my affairs.

Anastasia's a bully, I thought, working through the situation the way I would think through an alchemical experiment. *Who knows what else she might be, but at its simplest, she's egocentric, and probably has been for a very long time. Coal reacted by keeping his distance, and coming up with his own plans. But her children reacted differently. They were more exposed to her, for longer, of course. Weep seems to have simply retreated into himself; he acts untouchable. Meanwhile, Magica . . .*

. . . has borne the brunt of the unbalanced family dynamics. This wasn't a fact—a hypothesis only. But it seemed a very reasonable one, based on the new insights of our interviews. I continued thinking it over as I returned to the lounge.

Magica's focus on pleasing her mother and her reluctance to say anything negative is consistent. If we could get her to meet Saki, of course that'd be ideal, but my bet is that she's totally genuine. And it seems like, all on her own, she has been dreaming of a different life—even if she can't quite admit it yet. So how does that fit in with Coal's activities? He was clearly rude to Magica, but would he have gone as far as blackmailing her? The drama about the act could have been enough cause. Surely Anastasia would have reacted very poorly if she thought Magica might leave the act.

This was all conjecture. My trained mind went immediately to gathering more evidence. *Who might have insight into this? Who could say if it has any bearing in Coal's death?*

Before I could come up with any ideas, voices interrupted my thoughts. From the sound of it, Trent and Anastasia had rejoined Officer Thorn in the lounge, and the carnival's director—Fontus—was still there too, gathering information.

"I can't tell you any more about the investigation while it's *ongoing*," Officer Thorn was saying as I entered the room. For a moment, I was simply glad she was talking in long sentences again. *So was that thing with Magica and Weep just because she was thinking of something else? Or was it because of one of them?*

"Ah, Miss Alchemist," Fontus enthused, distracted from the conversation. He strode my way and I sidestepped him subtly, managing to make it to the couch next to Thorn.

"Where have *you* been?" Anastasia asked, her voice far less friendly.

"Just collecting a few more details for my notes," I said in my best completely-harmless voice. I cast a quick sidelong glance at Thorn, so she'd know I had information to discuss later.

"You've all been working so hard." As Fontus reclaimed ownership of the conversation, I was a little startled by his use of the word *work*. It seemed to be coming up so often. I snuck a glance at Anastasia, but her eyes were fixed on the handsome director. Trent, too, was observing. "You simply must let us show you our appreciation for all you've done for us during this investigation. Please—"

"It's not done," Thorn interrupted. "The investigation isn't over."

"Oh—of course," said Fontus, with the ease of a dancer tripping and recovering in a second. "But if you can stand to take a break for even a moment, please, you *must* attend our ball tomorrow evening."

From the back of the room, Trent coughed. "A ball?"

"I believe I've brought it up before. It is our custom to end our tour in every town with a ball," Fontus said proudly. "Isn't that so, Anastasia?"

"It's sure to be the event of the season," enthused the grieving stepmother.

Meanwhile, Officer Thorn's shoulders were set like an ox's. "You can't leave town with the investigation still going."

"Of course, we'll stay an extra day or two if you need us," Fontus said. "We'll think of it as a holiday. But our business in Belville was slated to be done tomorrow, and done it shall be! We must look to the next port, you know."

"*Murder* is hardly a holiday," I heard myself protest.

Fontus looked at me for a moment—really looked at me. Then he threw back his head and laughed. "What excellent defenders of justice you all are! Please, do tell me you'll come to the ball. We haven't had guests like you in *ages*."

Hopefully because you haven't had a murder *in ages*, I thought. But I kept that one to myself.

"It may even help your investigation," Anastasia added silkily from her divan.

She did have a point there—but I was a little suspicious that she'd made it. I'd also realized who she'd reminded me of, that very first night: the haughty look in her eyes had mirrored *Coal's*.

"We'll come," Officer Thorn said woodenly.

"Perfect," Fontus exclaimed, diving into the details. At a look from Thorn, I began writing everything down. Honestly, though, it went in one ear and out one pencil . . . I kept wondering about Anastasia as I wrote. She was coming across as pretty duplicitous. But was that enough to point to her as prime suspect?

22

Some Day . . .

"You have to hand it to him," I murmured to Officer Thorn, when at last Fontus and Anastasia were leaving. "He doesn't seem to be afraid of anything." Not scorn, not murder cases, not large and unamused police officers . . .

"Neither are a lot of criminals," Officer Thorn said with a *hmph.* "They think all this glitz and glam will keep them from getting caught."

"It does sound like this ball tomorrow's going to be glitz- and glam-iest," Trent said as he came over from his corner to join us. "You two have fun with that."

My jaw dropped. "I'm not going! If *I* have to go, then *he* has to!"

"Wouldn't you rather a certain bookseller came?" Trent suggested, grinning.

"No one's going unless I say so," Officer Thorn declared. "We have work to do before then. Come on. I'm tired of sitting in this lounge."

"But you've only interviewed three people," I pointed out as she rose, stretching.

Thorn's spine creaked as she rolled out her shoulders. "Interviews require breaks. And break-fasts, ha ha. I'm hungry. You two coming with me to the kitchen?"

Trent and I exchanged glances. "It's called a galley," he said as we fell into step behind the police officer.

"As long as it's not called 'closed' or 'empty,'" she hummed to herself in satisfaction. "So, what do we have? And Red, what was all that strangeness about Magica?"

"*Me*, strange? What do you mean? You're the one who suddenly started talking like a schoolkid in detention," I protested.

Trent chuckled. "What, so you didn't get anything?"

"*I* got plenty." I nudged Trent, sending him into the wall in the narrow hallway. He just kept chuckling as I went on to prove my point. "Officer Thorn, remember our initial thoughts about Coal? About his situation? I think they'd be better applied to my interviewee. Now, that's not to say he had anything on—"

For the second time in two days, I ran into Officer Thorn's back. It was an interruption, to say the least.

"Magica?" she clarified, her voice sharp.

"Well, I was *trying* to be discreet about it," I said, rubbing my forehead where my goggles had been jostled out of place. "But yes. Maybe you got a similar vibe from Weep?"

"I didn't get any vibes," Thorn retorted, a little more abruptly than usual. She also started walking toward the galley with more force than before.

What is it with her and this investigation? Or, more specifically, her and those twins? I glanced at Trent, but he just shrugged. Between our confusion and her sudden speed, we had to trot down the stairs to catch up with Thorn.

"I got something, anyway," Trent told us, breaking the ice.

Officer Thorn said nothing, only kept walking. So I turned to the Witch and asked, "Could you figure out about—you know—what William and Luca said?"

"Not exactly. I can't get that specific. But we're definitely in that arena," Trent said. "If not looking at something worse."

"*Worse*? What could be worse than eating—"

"Breakfast," Officer Thorn interrupted loudly, veering into the galley. She addressed the cook, Circe. "Anything break-fasty still available?"

"More like second-breakfasty," Trent whispered to me.

"Or third," I agreed, hiding my grin.

It was clear that Thorn was focused, and that we'd have to shelve our discussion; the ship had too many ears, anyway. I squinted and resisted the urge to pull my goggles down over my eyes as I tried to adjust to the darkness of the galley. The portholes along one wall faced the wrong direction for sunlight, and the overhead light was dim. In fact, all the chairs and tables were empty; there was only Circe at the counters that made up the actual kitchen, and Hemming sitting there at the bar, watching her work.

Watching her work? I looked more carefully between the two, wondering. It made me glad to think that Hemming might have a friend on board aside from Coal and Scylla and the mist goats.

"Coffee," Circe said promptly. "There's always coffee. Bit of leftover fruity porridge from this morning, if you like."

"I would," said Officer Thorn, pulling up a stool at the bar. Trent and I followed suit; he gladly nodded in response to Circe's questioning look, but I shook my head. Sakura's café had spoiled me; coffee that had spent all morning brewing no longer sounded appealing.

While Circe got to work ladling out steaming porridge and thick brown sludge, Officer Thorn looked Hemming up and down. "Any news from the stables?"

"Zale's got the wind up," Hemming answered slowly, as though thinking it over. "Take it you talked to him yesterday?"

"We did. He's in no trouble," Officer Thorn said, some of her earlier gruffness easing off. "We're just collecting some more perspectives on Coal."

Hemming's eyes widened, the wrinkles at the edges of his face giving him a particularly surprised look. "Never knew the two lads to talk."

"It sounds like they probably didn't," I told him. Behind the cover of the bar, I kicked Thorn's shin. Gently, of course. From my own time with Hemming, I knew he probably had no knowledge of Coal's penchant for blackmail; no doubt Coal had been able to get everything he wanted from Hemming *without* having to resort to such things. I made a mental note to explain this to my comrades later.

For the moment, though, the officer seemed to catch on. "Our showing up with questions startled Zale," she said deftly. "I'm sorry about that. Surely he hasn't slacked off as a result, though."

"Not nearly," Hemming agreed, with all the ponderousness of an iceberg. His tone at least was considerably warmer than ice, especially as Circe passed him a coffee mug, too.

"I don't believe you two have met Belville's local Witch, Trent," Officer Thorn continued. "He helps out as my assistant when needed."

"Seems you're well set for assistants," Circe said, nodding at

Trent and smiling at me.

"It's just too bad she couldn't get ones from the Guild," Trent quipped, grinning crookedly at his new acquaintances. "Thanks for the food. Sometimes that's the best part of helping the police."

"Second to *solving cases,* of course," Thorn said. After she'd taken a bite of her porridge, though, she added, "I must say, Circe, your cooking *is* good."

"Hmmm?" The elven cook, who had been looking at Hemming, turned and smiled at us. When we'd first met her, her hair had been purple and spiky. Today her hair was a bright teal, tied back in a bun. "Oh, please, Officer. I'm sure I told you you can call me Caty. I don't go for this stage name business, not the way the others do."

There was an opening there; I could sense it, but wasn't sure what to do about it. Fortunately, Officer Thorn had had training on these sorts of things.

"You did say that. And didn't you also mention feeling a bit . . . 'out of place,' was it?"

Hemming shifted, and Circe glanced down, flushed. "I suppose I did," she admitted. "Though I never meant to speak ill of anyone here, of course."

"Not anyone?" Officer Thorn pressed.

"Not—oh," Circe said softly, as the implications of the officer's question echoed around the room.

This time Hemming shifted and grumbled, too. "No one's giving you a hard time, Caty?"

"No—nothing like that." She glanced at him quickly, now pink from her scalp to her collar. "I see what you're getting at, Officer. But I really couldn't say anything about—the murder, or Coal's affairs. I kept my distance. I always have."

Another strike out, then, I thought. Trent was happily chowing down as he watched the conversation, and I doubted he'd detected any trace of a lie. To be honest, though, I was a little pleased by the way this conversation was going. Maybe if Circe/Caty could inspire Hemming to look beyond the stables . . . Well, it seemed like not such a bad thing.

"Who would you say *hasn't* kept their distance?" Officer Thorn asked.

Caty and Hemming exchanged a very, very brief look.

"Some have no distance to keep," Caty observed finally, noncommittally. "Some make it their business to be everywhere on the ship."

"Anastasia and Fontus," I guessed immediately.

Thorn kicked me this time—perhaps I wasn't supposed to put words in suspects' mouths—but Caty gave me that knowing look again, and nodded. "And then, of course, children of an age find it hard to stay apart."

This confused me—*does she mean Weep and Magica, maybe?*—but what was even more confusing was Hemming's reaction. Behind Caty, his ruddy cheeks darkened.

"I can't imagine how anyone on board can stay apart from anyone else," Trent said casually, scraping the last porridge from his bowl.

"We old timers manage, I suppose," Caty said, with a rather fond look at Hemming. "I do wonder how Captain Pleasant puts up with it, sometimes. All our squabbles and dramas, getting in the way of him running his ship."

Officer Thorn's ears pricked up. "Would you say they *have* done so, then? Got in the way?"

"Just look at our situation now," Circe answered levelly. "I doubt we'll be able to leave port until this is solved, will we? And having the ship searched was certainly disruptive. I hear they've had to delay maintenance on the engine that he'd hoped to have done."

That was news to me, and mildly interesting. *But even so, I can't see Captain Pleasant getting so worked up that he would murder anyone, least of all Coal. Besides, if he was to murder someone, wouldn't he do it out on the open water rather than at port?*

Still, Hemming's words about *affairs of the heart* being dangerous rang in my mind . . .

Right at that very moment, just as I was thinking of passions and plots, a new step sounded in the hall and the captain himself arrived in the galley.

"Ah," he said, looking around at all of us. "I haven't interrupted anything, have I?"

23

Diamonds and Dust

"**W**as just leaving," Hemming said, rising the moment the captain spoke.

Surely that's a little odd, I thought, watching the animal trainer leave. *It's not like he's incredibly social, but still, he didn't seem to mind our company. Or Caty's.* Hemming saluted the captain as he passed, a familiar sailor's gesture, so perhaps nothing was wrong between the two of them. *Maybe Hemming just doesn't like crowds.*

But as Officer Thorn invited Captain Pleasant over to the bar for a seat and a chat, Caty, too, made herself scarce. In her absence, our meeting with the captain started to feel more official—almost businesslike.

"We're doing a round of follow-up interviews," Officer Thorn began briskly as Pleasant took his seat. "Can you spare a few moments?"

"Of course, if it will help your investigation," the captain said, mild. His uniform looked as crisp and clear as ever, but his eyes were red-rimmed and shadowed.

"We hope to wrap up everything as soon as possible," I said,

175

thinking of his manner just two days before, when he'd told me his feelings. My heart ached for him all the more because of what we'd found out. *They treated Coal like a criminal, he said,* I recalled. *Little did he know, perhaps, that Coal in fact was a criminal!*

"Right. And I don't mind telling you, new evidence has come to light," Officer Thorn added with a particularly appraising glint in her eye.

Captain Pleasant rose to the bait like a mythical fish to a plot point. "New evidence? Then you know who did it?"

"Not yet," Thorn responded patiently. "But we're looking for some new perspectives. Is there anything you can think of, anything out of the ordinary, that you didn't tell us the first time around?"

"Well—I—couldn't say exactly." Captain Pleasant glanced at me, then at the floor. While he wasn't looking, I nudged Thorn. Her nod assured me that she remembered our conversation about the captain's feelings.

"Just wait," she whispered to me.

Several seats down, Captain Pleasant cleared his throat. "There is one thing I didn't think to tell you at the time. I wonder if it would help."

"Just one?" Trent leaned around Officer Thorn's other side, curious. I'd almost forgotten he was present.

"Just . . . the one." Captain Pleasant hesitated. "Coal had big dreams. He wanted to travel—to see worlds beyond this carnival."

"He told you that?" Officer Thorn pressed gently.

"He didn't have to," said Captain Pleasant. "It was obvious."

Obvious to someone watching him, I thought, simultaneously making a note and praising Officer Thorn's instinct to give the captain time to reflect.

"And how was he going to make that happen?" Thorn asked.

Captain Pleasant smoothed back his perfect hair, then let out a nervous breath. "I'm not sure," he admitted. "Sometimes—when you're on one path—it's hard to leave. So hard. I would have helped him if I could."

"He didn't share plans with you, or ask for help?" Trent asked.

The captain shook his head, eyes shimmering.

I glanced up at Officer Thorn. I sure wasn't about to tell this grieving man about our suspicions—there didn't seem to be any point. The officer must have agreed with me, because with a few kind words of closure, she motioned to Trent and me to leave.

As soon as the galley door swung shut behind us, we huddled—almost as though we really were the trainees Thorn sometimes pretended we were.

"What'd you get from him?" Officer Thorn asked Trent in a hushed voice.

"Honestly, I'm not a human lie detector," Trent protested, similarly hushed. "Witches can be deceived, you know. Especially when lying isn't their strong suit. I thought I was here to suss out people's elemental affinity!"

"Maybe we should have brought Saki," I teased quietly.

"She talks too much," Officer Thorn said, without a trace of irony.

"What she said. Plus, there are murderers here," Trent protested.

"Oh, but you're not worried about me?" I grinned, despite the situation. "Wow, thanks, Trent—"

The Witch sputtered. "I'm just saying, you *know* how she

attracts danger—"

"Um. Excuse us?"

Thorn, Trent, and I immediately broke our huddle. We turned to face another group of three—the clown troupe, dressed today in sensible blues and grays. While I searched the recesses of my brain for their names, Officer Thorn took over.

"Where are you headed?" she asked, managing to sound only *marginally* interrogational.

The trio exchanged uncertain looks. "Our break room?"

"You have your own break room?" Trent blurted.

Officer Thorn cast him a look, then crossed her arms, her purpose returning. "Perfect. We'll just come along with you, if you don't mind."

* * *

As it turned out, the trio's names were Triton, Oceanus, and Apsu. Stage names, of course, but they seemed much more attached to their monikers than Caty had. They led us down the hall and a set of stairs to what turned out to be a converted personal room. They had, they explained, moved their three bunks into one room, used another room as a dressing area, and preferred to hang out in this third room. As a living room it left something to be desired; the light from the porthole was filmy, and the air smelled faintly of lake weed. But there was plenty of seating. Apparently, the trio's decorating taste ran to large pillows, bean bags, and blankets that could double as rugs.

They were hardly more than boys. As they settled onto one low couch, I could see how young they looked—and how similar. *They did say they were brothers, I think,* I reminded myself, trying to remember their initial interviews from the confusion of our first night aboard. Three pale, chiseled faces turned to Officer Thorn as she plopped herself down into a beanbag chair.

"So," she said, not without a little difficulty. Over her head, Trent caught my eye and smirked. He'd chosen to curl up on a rug, while I remained standing by the door. I pulled out my notebook and tried to look serious as the officer continued with her now-familiar line: "We're looking for some new perspectives on Coal."

This time, however, the reaction she got was anything but familiar.

"*Perspective.* Is that what they call it these days?" Triton, the largest of the three, wearing a shark tooth necklace. His voice was tight and his blue eyes flashed as he spoke.

"That'll make for interesting investigating." Oceanus, whose oversized tunic bore a painting of a blue dragon. The sarcasm in his words was sharp.

"Can you prove any of it, though?" Apsu, the smallest, sporting a hooded scarf made to resemble a famous lake monster. He glanced from Thorn to his brothers, his hands tucked under his legs.

"We can prove it," Trent said confidently. The wisp of purple magic that flared and disappeared over his palm seemed to impress the trio as much as his words.

"Magic," Apsu concluded, eyes aglow. "Why didn't we think of that?"

"Because we haven't had a moment of peace," Oceanus answered dryly.

"We've already got a lot of evidence," I added, only fudging a little. Combined with Trent's show, it seemed to have an impact on the boys. They visibly wavered, tempted.

Officer Thorn broke in. "Why don't you start over and tell us everything, from the beginning."

Nessie and dragon looked to Triton, owner of the shark tooth. He straightened as he spoke for all three. "Since you already know, I guess there's no point lying. I don't know how long he was after anyone else for, but for us it started a year ago. Last summer. He *promised* in the beginning he'd only need a little. Then he started making excuses. 'You have three shares to live on, and I only have one,' he'd say. Or, 'it's getting harder and harder not to tell the captain—you know how fond he is of me.' So we gave him more. We had to."

"And this was every pay day?" Officer Thorn prompted, as I scribbled furiously.

"Not at first," Triton answered. "First it was our savings."

"All our savings," Apsu echoed mournfully.

"A whole year," Oceanus added, the frustration in his voice agreeing with his brothers' tones.

"It wasn't all the time, like I said," Triton continued. "Just here and there. Then lately it was every pay day. It had to be. Nothing was ever enough. Just like we weren't ever *good* enough, on account of our blood."

"We've heard similar things before," I told them sympathetically.

"Was that what it was all about?" Clearly, Trent hadn't had lessons in tact at Witch school. He leaned forward, asking the question that Officer Thorn, for all her brashness, tended to dance around. When the rest of us stared at him, he explained, "I just figured, because your water magic seems to be more faint than the others.'"

"The other naiads, you mean," Oceanus said with a sigh.

"So it's true. What of it?" Triton, the leader, was defiant. *So much for having taken to Trent,* I thought, as he went on, "So what if we only have a quarter naiad blood? We're as dedicated as anyone else to this show."

Now that the lead was out of the bag, so to speak, Officer Thorn clearly felt no compunction following up on it. "So that *wasn't* the reason for the blackmail, then?"

"Uh—no. That was something else." Triton's eyes darted between his two brothers. The three shifted toward each other, closing ranks.

"That was just another thing Coal used as ammunition," I reasoned, in the suddenly uncomfortable silence. "That also tracks with other things we've heard. But if he wasn't blackmailing you about your identities . . ."

Apsu, the youngest, broke first. "It wasn't anything illegal!"

Oceanus snorted. "Not yet."

Officer Thorn shifted beside me, her manner becoming more pointed. Triton gulped visibly, and his thoughts were just as clear: *better to just come clean, then.* "It was early days," he said, by way of explanation. "We'd just started, really. We hadn't gotten to know everyone. We thought we had all these ideas about how to make things better. Sure, we drew up some plans, but really, it was just between us. We wouldn't have gone so far as—"

"Mutiny," Officer Thorn concluded. "Is that it?"

The three boys looked uncomfortable.

"We wouldn't have," Apsu insisted.

"But we did write things out," Oceanus said.

"Just between us. Just daydreaming," Triton was quick to tell the officer. "But—when you look at it on paper, as an outsider—yeah, that's what it looked like. Mutiny. That's what *he* said."

"And so he was threatening to take it to the captain, who would exile you from the ship?" I thought aloud as I wrote more notes.

"And Fontus. It'd ruin us. We'd never get another gig at a carnival," Triton explained. "We'd be blacklisted forever. No one wants someone like that on board."

"Why'd you write it down?" Trent asked.

Triton deflated. "We weren't thinking."

"More to the point," Officer Thorn said, watching the boys carefully, "how did Coal get his hands on those papers?"

"Right here, in this room," Oceanus admitted, when Triton wouldn't speak. "We . . ."

"It was me," Apsu interrupted. "It was me. I should have put them away. I forgot."

"He saw them. He *stole* them," Triton said, straightening once more to put an arm around his little brother. "We used to have him over all the time then. That was before we knew better."

Children of an age, I thought, recalling Caty's words earlier. *So maybe this is who she meant. The brothers were being friendly, and Coal . . .*

. . . Took advantage. Well, I realized, steeling myself, *this fits exactly what Saki was telling me, about how behavior like this can develop. And while Hemming might have thought the trio was being cruel to Coal, it was the other way round!*

"It wasn't just us," Apsu said plaintively in the silence.

"But you already knew that," Oceanus added, looking closely at Officer Thorn.

She shifted again, her beanbag chair protesting loudly. "Yes.

But if you have names of other victims, it's best you tell me, so I can check with them all."

"We probably shouldn't," Triton said, with a warning look at his siblings.

Officer Thorn rumbled. "I understand the thought. And remind me, where were you three on the day of the murder? And where was Sleepy?"

The brothers looked askance at each other as their situation sunk in. Without other known blackmail victims, they had to top the officer's suspects list. Of course, they didn't know we knew about Zale; could that be who they were referring to?

"We were in the practice room, getting ready, all day," Triton explained hurriedly. "We had to prepare for opening night. All three of us were there, and Sleepy, too."

"Anyone else?" Thorn asked.

"Weep. And Magica. Until she had to go help her mother," Apsu supplied.

"Everyone was in and out," Oceanus said quietly. "But we never even saw Coal that day. Like we told you before."

"Noted. Is that all you have to say?" Officer Thorn stared hard at all three boys.

Apsu looked up at Triton, a question in his dark blue eyes. The older brother shook his head. I could have sworn I heard him say, *"We really shouldn't share her name."*

24

A Stitch in Time

After an afternoon of chasing down the rest of the carnival staff and ship's crew, I still couldn't be sure who Triton had been talking about—or if I'd even heard him correctly. In fact, the only thing I could be sure of was that Sakura qualified for sainthood.

We'd made it to the Pomegranate just barely before closing, when Saki was gently herding all her other customers to the door. And in about two seconds, we'd overtaken a circle of couches by the front window and lounged in the silence, having claimed the café as a kind of pseudo-headquarters.

"I had no idea interviews could be so taxing," Sakura observed as she brought a tea tray over. I struggled to sit upright on my plush blue couch, and she winked. "You three must have been on your feet all day."

"It certainly feels like it," Trent grumped from his sofa under the window.

"New recruits always have to toughen up a little," Officer Thorn observed airily, leaning over the table between us to help herself to a cup of steaming tea. The porcelain teapot sported green flowers, so I knew that the tea inside was green tea. Sakura was rather particular about details like that. Today's offering smelled faintly of lavender, and several pots of honey accompanied it on the tray.

As I leaned over to pour a cup for Trent and then for myself, Saki sank into the seat next to me. "I hope you aren't having to 'toughen up' because the case is proving difficult?"

"We must have talked to everyone, and yet nothing is any clearer," I confessed, giving her a brief overview of what we'd done.

"We did accomplish *some* things," Trent said when I'd finished. He spoke to me directly rather than to Saki. "One: we know that Anastasia *is* some kind of elemental water creature, possibly dangerous, and that Coal was definitely blackmailing multiple people, so any of them might have wanted him dead. And two, we got you invited to a ball."

"I'm pretty sure Thorn was the one invited," I protested.

"You're going to a *ball*?" Sakura asked, blue eyes lightening.

"No! Officer Thorn said it was silly!" I looked across the table for support.

"Actually," said the officer, "I think it's the perfect plan. Exactly what we need. Incredi-ball, one might say."

"One would *not* say," I retorted, groaning. "Explain to me why this is the perfect plan?"

"It's a chance to see them all in a natural setting, for one thing," Thorn said, popping a macaroon from the tea tray into her mouth. "You can catch them unawares. See who slips up. Test out all those theories of yours."

I frowned. "I'm not the only one with theories—"

"Plus, if you're acting as the main guest from Belville, it lets Thorn move in the shadows," Trent put in, unhelpfully.

The officer pointed at him in approval. "Exactly. It's cover."

"It's more like coercion," I said, though I felt certain at this point that no one was listening.

"*Plus,* it'll be the perfect excuse to give you a makeover!" Sakura squealed at my side.

I turned to her in despair. "Not you, too! What is it with everyone lately and how I look? What does it matter? We could be talking about a *murder* right now, not a party!"

"Oh, Red, don't be so silly," Saki told me, taking my elbow affectionately. "We *are* still talking about murder. This is how you can help investigate."

"You're the best person for it," Officer Thorn agreed.

"See?" Sakura continued, beaming. "Thorn can't get all dressed up, it'd hamper her in case of emergency. And I can't go, because I hate boats—you know that. Trent, of course, nothing can be done about *him,* and—"

"I never agreed to getting dressed up," I protested, while Trent just grinned, no doubt pleased as punch to have been ruled out of the festivities. "Send in Glacial. Wasn't she a mercenary or something?"

"Glacial has cooking to do," Sakura said solemnly. "Also, she can't control her temper like you can."

I sputtered. Never had I thought that being even-tempered would turn out to be a hindrance. And a little voice in the back of my head wondered what *would* happen if Glacial ever lost her temper . . .

"Fact is, someone's got to go tomorrow, and it's going to be you," Officer Thorn said, interrupting my mental images of cupcakes and hot tea flying through the air in all-out café warfare. "If it makes you feel better, I'm sure half the town has paid for tickets already. And I'll see to it that the bookseller gets invited, too."

"Luca?" This caught my attention for real. I tugged at the belt around my tunic. "I'm not sure he'd want to . . ."

"He'll want to," Trent said. "Trust me."

"Trust *him*," Sakura said gently. I knew from her meaningful gaze on me that she meant Luca, not wise-cracking Trent. She added, "Sometimes to get to the truth, you have to put on a costume. Just remember your intention. Think of it like wearing a lab coat."

I hated to admit it, but the metaphor was very apt. *Sakura has always been too good at words for my own good.* I knew I'd lost the battle, but there *was* one last hill of concern. "I don't actually own anything to dress up in . . ."

"Really?" Officer Thorn flipped her perfect hair.

I raised an eyebrow at her. There was a lot of attitude in that one word for someone who never appeared in public without their uniform.

"Leave that to us," Saki assured me.

But I was far from assured. "'Us?'"

"I have a feeling Gloria will know exactly what to do," Sakura answered, the smile on her lips almost evil.

"If you're going shopping, I want to go too," Trent said. When the three of us looked at him in surprise, he added, "What? Just because I don't wear fancy outfits doesn't mean I don't have opinions on them."

I laughed, but Officer Thorn clearly still had business on her mind. "That's *if* you're not needed on police business."

"Is dressing Red and Luca up not police business now?" Trent protested.

"Oh my goodness, *please*, let's focus on police business," I broke in, relieved. "What else do we need to do? What else is left?"

"There are still victims of blackmail aboard that we haven't found. Mark my word on that," Officer Thorn said. "That means motives."

"But what about opportunity?" Trent piped up. "All this running around talking to people is forgetting that no one had access to his room anyway."

"Not true," I protested. "There's the matter of the missing key. And *someone* must have taken his boots."

Saki put her head to one side. "He was missing his boots?"

"Yeah, and we never figured out why," Trent said. "His feet were dry."

"But his boots might not have been," Saki said to him. "After all, why do we take off our shoes when we get home?"

"Because they're dirty," I realized slowly. "His boots *should* have been dry—he and I were talking, right here, until the rain stopped that morning. So there must have been something on them—some clue!"

"Took you all long enough," Officer Thorn said smugly. "But it's no use. The search of the ship turned up nothing, and we can't possibly do a tracing spell for the boots, as we don't have anything left of them to compare traces to. If we get desperate, we could send a team to search the lake, but that'll take time."

"They could find the key, too," I said, thinking.

"And the murder weapon," Trent reminded us. "Assuming Sleepy isn't it."

Saki looked interested. "Can't naiads manipulate water?"

"It was saltwater that killed him though, and you're *not* getting involved," Trent said.

"Excuse you! If you're going to sit here in *my* café and talk about murder—"

I tuned out the argument, which looked like it could go on for a while. As Trent and Saki turned to each other, heated, I thought about what Saki had said. *Naiads can manipulate water; in fact, a lot of waterfolk can. Even a very old shark. But the water in Coal's lungs wasn't what we'd expect anyone but Sleepy to use, because of the salt . . .*

How much *salt*? I wondered suddenly. After all, Trent had made that identification: I myself had never tested that water. *What if it was only trace amounts?*

"Trent," I said, nearly shouting to be heard over the lovers' quarrel. "Trent! How much salt was in the water you found on Coal?"

"How much?" The scowl on Trent's face faded into confusion as he turned to me and thought this over. "What do you mean, how much?"

"I mean what I said. You found water and salt in his lungs, right? But how much of each?"

"We aren't talking about alchemy, we're talking about magic, Red," said Saki. Despite her issues with him, she leaned forward, taking Trent's side. "It's very difficult to be exact about things like that."

"Yeah, and honestly, I've spent so much time sensing water and salt all over the carnival ever since that I'm not sure I could say any more," Trent said slowly, as though the gravity of this was just now hitting him.

Officer Thorn tugged hard at one ear.

I kept thinking my new line of inquiry through. "It just occurred to me. We assumed saltwater meant ocean water. But the simple presence of salt in water doesn't *mean* it's from the ocean. It might be contaminated fresh water, for example."

"Contaminated by what?" Thorn asked.

I bit my lip. "Other than 'something salty,' I couldn't say for sure."

"Need I remind you about the giant saltwater-breathing *shark* on board?" Trent added.

"Maybe it was a drop of saltwater *and* a bunch of freshwater," Saki agreed. "A spell wouldn't know the difference between the two."

"This is not helping me narrow down suspects," Thorn rumbled.

"Well that's what you get for relying too heavily on magic," Saki returned tartly. "Spells can't solve problems with just a snap of the fingers, you know."

"It was only a thought," I told them, interrupting the squabble. "I'm just saying. Whenever we make it back to the carnival—whether it's for a party or not—let's keep an open mind about where that water could have come from."

25

Pumpkins and Mice

The next morning, I'd fully given in to the impossibility of my situation. I'd even curtailed the shop's hours, since Sir Rowan was off and William refused to even contemplate for a millisecond the idea of staying home while I went to a masquerade ball.

"Gloria and Saki are probably going to be all excited about it," I warned him, as we ate our late breakfast at the shop's sales counter. "Basically the minute we close for the afternoon, I expect they'll be here."

"The sooner the better," William said, casting a beady look at my ponytail.

"What is *with* everyone these days?" I shuffled my hair to my other shoulder so he'd stop staring at it. "I look exactly the same as I always do. Why is it suddenly such a problem?"

"Because times have changed," my familiar declared.

"Big words from someone eating a pumpkin spice muffin in early summer," I teased.

"You're the one who made it for me," he retorted. "And if you don't start eating yours, then I'm eating it next."

"I know, I know. I'm eating," I told him with good humor. Still, I slouched on my stool, leaning over the muffin and a mug of chai. I had a feeling that the day ahead was going to require a lot of caffeine and sugar. Even in the quiet store, the colorful potion bottles lining the walls reminded me of strangers in fancy dress. For as much as I enjoyed teasing with William, and for as determined as I was to help my friends, I couldn't deny the deep misgivings I had about the evening's ball.

"Hey, Red and William!" Luca's voice mingled with the bells above the front door as he stepped into the shop. Sunlight from the street behind him streamed onto the floor behind him. Suddenly, my nerves didn't seem *quite* so insurmountable.

Luca grinned especially at William as he came over to lean on the counter across from us. "Looks like you aren't in charge today, huh?"

"For once," William grumped. "I ought to get manager's pay."

"You ought to remember you have prime window seat rights and, usually, the freedom to set your own schedule," I told him. "I think those two things alone are probably worth manager's pay."

"*Usually,*" William echoed huffily.

"Police business takes precedence, as Thorn always says," I reminded him cheerfully. "So, Luca, what brings you out this morning?"

"Trent came over last night and filled me in on everything. Seems like the town's still pretty quiet, so I left Frank in charge," Luca said, smiling at me. In a friendly aside to William, he added, "Frank doesn't get manager pay, either."

"Because the world is unjust," William observed.

"Also the reason we have to go to a ball tonight," I said, amused but remembering the more somber events at the carnival.

"I'm sure we can make tonight a better one than last time," Luca said, his gaze steady on mine, like he'd just read my mind.

I blushed. "Well, I hope so. With any luck, this'll be the night Thorn solves the case. If we're *really* lucky, maybe she'll solve it before we have to go to the party."

"Come on, Red, aren't you a *little* bit curious about it?" Luca chuckled. "I bet they put on quite a show."

"That might be a little what I'm worried about, on top of everything else," I admitted. "I don't think my nerves could stand too much fireworks and acrobatics and turning mice into water-horses, or whatever it is they have planned."

"What if the mice are actually made of fireworks, and they perform acrobatics?" Luca suggested brightly.

I couldn't help it; I laughed. "That just sounds *too* over the top."

"Isn't that what carnivals are all about?" He beamed.

"You both are ridiculous," William sighed, polishing off his muffin.

"Maybe Thorn should just send *you* in, then," I teased, nudging him.

"William Investigates," Luca agreed, speaking as though he was reading off a book title. "Criminals and Muffins Beware!"

William acted like he couldn't hear us, but I saw his tail wagging.

"Anyway," I added, more soberly, "I guess you are okay with going, then, Luca?"

My boyfriend turned his green eyes to mine, the mirth fading into something softer, and warmer. "Yes. Where you go, I go, Red."

"Well . . . thank you," I managed, feeling my cheeks heat up. "I have to admit, that does make me feel better about it."

* * *

Of course, no ancient three-legged mink is known for their patience, so Luca had to say goodbye soon after our jokes about the ball. Once I'd finished my muffin—which was smeared with peanut butter and extra pumpkin seeds for protein, so despite William's protests, it really was too healthy for him to bother stealing—and helped a young family pick out some glow-in-the-dark baubles, I retreated to my lab.

The one problem with Officer Thorn's investigations was that, inevitably, my custom orders suffered for my absence. (Well, perhaps I should say that falling behind on orders was my one problem *aside from all the danger and death*. Funny how running a business changes your perspective of things!) Neither William nor Sir Rowan showed any interest in filling the orders, aside from helping package them or hand them out. And truthfully, I'd studied for years to get to this level in my career, so I couldn't expect either of my assistants to fill my shoes.

Studied for years so that I could make Lavender's special purple glow lights and Lumi's specifically tailored magnetic healing bangles. Some alchemical masters would have found such mundane orders to be beneath them. But for me, the thought came with a smile. Honestly, I *love* handling Belville's orders, big and small. It makes me feel useful, and it reminds me what I loved about alchemy in the first place.

As I donned my gloves and goggles and prepared my

ingredients, I remembered Weep and Magica's devotion, and the clown trio's dedication. *Clearly, carnival work can inspire passion like mine, too.*

But Coal never felt it. He was born to the life, I continued musing, letting my hands move and mix solutions on instinct. *He said himself his family was involved in it, and yet he wanted to leave it; that seems obvious. And in Belville, perhaps, he was about to. Why else would he have been sounding Saki and me out about work?*

So, then, the real question, I decided, *is why now? Why was he thinking about leaving now, here? And who felt that they simply couldn't* let him go?

The timing of the murder and Coal's foray into town seemed too sequential to be ignored. But his blackmail victims—Zale and the brothers were the only ones we'd found so far for sure—surely they would have been happy to see him go. Unless they didn't know he intended to leave? Perhaps they heard he'd been in town, and were worried he was planning to share their secrets?

I heard the bells ring out in the store, but didn't look up. I'd achieved a perfect purple glow in my first light for Lavender, but my thoughts were nowhere near as satisfactory. There was something there—something I was missing; I was sure of it . . .

"Where's Red?" The unfamiliar voice speaking my name caught my attention. "I'm here to talk with her, and I don't have much time."

26

Twelve Strikes

Hastily, but carefully, I finished up the reaction in my little glow light. Once it was stable, I set aside my gloves and stood to poke my head through the window into the store. "Someone's looking for me?"

"Here," William called, drawing my attention to the middle of the shop floor. There, he sat staring intently at one of the carnival performers.

Siren, I realized, with a little shock. When we'd spoken to the sharpshooter the day before, she'd been reticent—even more so that on the night of the murder. Of all the people aboard the *Luna II* that might want to talk to me, I'd have figured that she and Anastasia would be vying for last place.

But thinking of her in that context served as a reminder. *Siren was the one who heightened Officer Thorn's suspicion of Anastasia in the first place. She didn't want to talk yesterday, but maybe now she has another tip to share? Or—hopefully not—bad news?*

"Like I said, I don't have time to be stared down," Siren growled directly at William.

William shimmered, a deep blue. He was blocking her path to the lab.

"It's alright," I told him. "Unless you're worried about something in particular?"

"Not in particular," he admitted, cocking his head. "But I'm going to be paying attention," he added, obviously for Siren's benefit.

"Pay as much attention as you want," she scoffed, although her voice didn't sound quite as confident as her words might suggest. When William stood and moved to one side, she shot past him like she'd been launched from a cannon.

"Hold up," I said, half afraid she'd try to run right through my lab door. "I have to unlock it first. We'll go out on to the back patio to talk. That okay, William?"

"Fine," he rumbled back. He had so many wards up on the shop and its grounds that I wasn't surprised that he could monitor our meeting from inside. He might not be able to hear what was said, but he'd probably have no trouble tuning into our energy, feeling if anything dangerous came up.

Siren was already waiting at my door, so I proceeded with the plan. I waved her through my lab quickly—it was the one space I was most protective of—and joined her outside in the sunshine. Amid the potted plants that crowded the patio, Siren managed to find the lone bench, a gift from Ryuko in his early days of carpentry. She sat all the way at one end, her hands tight on the wood next to her knees. Her outfit wasn't carnival attire—plain, deep black boots and vest over a fitted fuchsia dress that set off her deep tan—but it still felt intentional, like she was making a statement. I thought of what Saki had said about costumes. *What is Siren hoping to convey? Is the perfect appearance meant to distract from her nerves?*

I sat at the other end of the bench and waited.

"The boys spoke to you yesterday," Siren began without preamble.

"Triton and all? Yes, I was there when Officer Thorn interviewed them," I answered, still confused.

"You've been interviewing everyone," she continued. "You know something new?"

"We're learning, yes," I said cautiously, and decided this was going down an unhelpful road. "Have you noticed something you wanted to talk about?"

Siren pressed her dark red lips together. Aside from her edgy makeup and sharp attitude, she actually would have looked a lot like me from a distance—medium build, light brown skin, long black hair. Her eyes were teal, arresting, lined in black. She was curvier than me, and when you looked only at her clothes, she oozed confidence. Something definitely seemed to have her worried, though.

"The director told me to keep my mouth shut," she finally growled.

"Fontus?" I asked, surprised.

Her eyes flicked to me and away again, not appreciating the interruption. "Yes. Fontus. He didn't tell you, did he, that he's going to be replacing the crew at the next port? Oh, yes," she said, smirking at my gasp. "He admitted to me this morning he'll be posting notice, which is basically carnival code for clearing house. That goes for acts, too, not just crew mates."

"Does everyone know this?" I asked.

Siren shrugged, like what other people knew didn't concern her. "Word gets around. Everyone knows what's on the horizon."

"Sounds tense," I ventured.

"You can bet there are a lot of hopes riding on this ball," Siren answered obliquely, her lips twisted back in a grim smile. "Last night's show was electric. Everyone's trying to prove their worth."

I frowned. "But there's something in all this that's worrying you?"

"It's like this," Siren said at last, leaning toward me. "The carnival's fine. It's always been. This little town, Coal being gone, that doesn't change anything. So the reason Fontus wants to ditch the crew and cast . . ."

I could see that the end of her sentence was *is that someone is dangerous*, but I didn't quite get it. "We've always known the murderer was probably on board," I said, not seeing why this was news.

"And that wasn't a big deal when we all figured it was someone who snapped on Coal," Siren agreed, rather coldly. "But if Fontus is in a big hurry to get rid of someone, then that means he thinks they're going to strike again."

"Or they know something," I couldn't help but point out. Siren was still staring at me. I swallowed. "Do you? Know something?"

"Not in particular," she drawled. "That's why I came here rather than the station. This is all rumors and hearsay. But I *will* say that I agree with Fontus."

"You think the murderer will strike again?"

Siren nodded. "And when better than tonight?"

I stood. "Look, if that's how you feel—even if it's hearsay—then we need to involve Officer Thorn."

"If you think it's worth it, alchemist," Siren said, rising to her feet. She was shorter than me by a few inches, but I had a sudden feeling that she'd been looking down on me, leading me along. *Aha, I thought. She wanted backup before facing Thorn. She wanted to know we'd take her seriously. That's why she came to me . . .*

"Go on," Siren added. "We may have all day, but we don't have all night."

27

Herald of Changing Tides

"I'm in the office," Thorn called out as soon as I opened the front door at the police station. "Waiting for a wire from the Guild. Make it quick, please!"

"Officer Thorn," I called back, leading Siren through the waiting room, "you're going to want to take the time to hear this."

She was literally sitting at her desk hunched over a little gilded magitech device, waiting, the way I'd hunched over my lab work earlier. When she caught sight of my guest in the doorway, she straightened.

"Come in, both of you, and shut the door if you like," she said, waving us to the two chairs haphazardly set before the desk. "What is it? New developments?"

"More like background developments. And maybe some more danger than we thought," I said, as Siren shut the door. She moved almost too carefully, like a spider who'd caught a fly in a trap. But as soon as the thought came, I shook it out of my head.

Siren sat beside me and stared straight ahead. Not at Thorn, not at the magitech wire communicator, not at me, not at the maps on the wall. It was as though she was visualizing the shape of her story before she shared it.

"You're here to represent everyone at the carnival, Siren?" Officer Thorn prompted.

This got the sharpshooter's attention. "No. What I have to share can't go beyond this room."

"I hear you," Officer Thorn said carefully, looking at me. I shrugged; I had only vague suspicions of what Siren might say next. "However, if I need to use something as evidence, I can't guarantee it remains a secret."

"If we get that far, it'll be too late then," Siren said. She shifted, addressing me. "I told you the reason I came to you is because I overheard the boys."

She did *say that,* I recalled, nodding. I'd been so distracted by the rest of her news that I hadn't thought too much about it. But now that I heard her say it again, something in her tone—*the boys*—it reminded me of the way Triton had spoken. *We shouldn't share her name . . .*

"About blackmail," I said slowly, putting the pieces together at last.

"Exactly." As though satisfied by my deduction, Siren shifted to face Thorn. "They thought Coal was blackmailing me. He wasn't—not for lack of trying. He did come to me a few months ago. He said he knew what I was, and he wanted hush money, otherwise he'd go to Fontus about it. I told him he'd see the barrel of my gun before he saw so much as a penny from me. But that didn't stop him hounding me about it with every pay day since, hanging around and making hints."

Officer Thorn stroked her long chin as she listened to Siren go from possible victim, to possible suspect, back to victim again. She didn't seem surprised by this development. My jaw might as well have been on the floor.

"You *threatened* him, Siren?" I asked, before I could think better of it.

"Why not?" Siren's glance at me was not a little haughty. But behind that proud flash, I caught a glimpse of something familiar: the self-possession that's necessary when you're a traveling merchant or performer on your own. I might once have looked the same way, myself.

"None of our other victims have admitted to doing the same," Officer Thorn observed.

"They probably didn't think to. They're young. That's not one of my faults. You get it," Siren said to me. She must have watched the understanding dawn on my face. "When you're alone for long enough, you learn to be proactive about these things."

"How long," I asked quietly, thinking of Luca's research about water folk, "is 'enough'?"

Siren smirked. "You don't get as good as I am with as many weapons as I can use without centuries of practice."

Across from us, Officer Thorn glanced down at her magitech device, then settled her elbows on the desk and leaned in. "The tip that Anastasia might be a predatory water spirit came from you, if I remember right."

"I thought you'd put it together sooner," Siren said carelessly. "Your dog probably did, just now. *I* am one, of course. Aicha kandida, full-blooded. That was so long ago now that it may as well be another life. I gave up those ways ages ago, but that doesn't mean I can't sense it on someone else."

William. No wonder he was so alert. "You figured she is one because you are one, and therefore you have special insight," I summarized hesitantly. "But why conclude that she's dangerous, when you're telling us that you're not?"

"I'm not telling you I'm not dangerous." For a brief moment, Siren's grin was wide and sharklike. "But I've moved beyond those ways. I find it more interesting to amaze people for my money. Anastasia, on the other hand, is about as hungry as they come."

"Hungry for attention—that much is obvious," I agreed. "But hungry for . . . people?"

"It was only a tip. A feeling. I can't give you any evidence," she replied.

"Let's circle back to *you*," Officer Thorn said, focusing on Siren. "You assumed we would deduce what you are."

"Were," Siren corrected easily.

"Nonetheless. Am I to understand you take no pains to hide it?"

Siren rolled her head on her shoulders, that fluid dismissive motion again. "I don't advertise it. Naiads tend to be superstitious. I don't need that kind of attention. But if a narcissist like Coal could figure it out, surely *you* could."

"Coal seems to have been very perceptive of others' weaknesses," I interjected gently.

"You might be right about that." Siren considered me, then turned to Thorn again. "I'd rather deal with consequences than hide."

"Did anyone else aboard know?" Thorn pressed.

"Not anyone who spoke of it to me," Siren said indifferently.

"But you weren't worried about Coal saying he'd go to Fontus," I pointed out.

"No." Siren laughed, a quick and heartless sound. "It'd probably tickle Fontus to think someone like me was in his carnival. The man has no self-preservation at all. Nothing matters to him but the success of his show."

"And yet, he must have some self-preservation to have kept Anastasia under control until now, if you're right in your suspicions," said Officer Thorn.

"If anyone was doing it, it'd be him," Siren agreed more soberly. "But I can't say anything about their relationship. I make it not my business."

She was so determined about that fact that, for just a brief moment, I wondered if jealousy came into play there.

"And he's the one who's been stirring things up now," I recalled, leading Siren to summarize the rumors and announcements for Officer Thorn. While she spoke, Thorn and I both watched her closely. I couldn't detect any falter in her manner, or any discrepancy in her story. She seemed to be telling the truth about everything.

But she admitted herself that she has no evidence for anything. And seeing as she's the sort of person who spreads rumors and responds to blackmail with her gun, I doubt she's holding anything back now that she's decided to share . . .

So I thought, anyway, but from the way Thorn steepled her fingers as she considered Siren's story, it was clear the officer felt differently. "This all has you worried enough that you came into town and sought out Red?"

"Obviously," Siren said.

"And yet, you don't seem like someone to be frightened of vague threats."

Siren looked from the officer to me and back again, then slid to the edge of her chair. "Listen. I'll stand by everything I said so far. But something else has occurred to me."

"Something else?" Officer Thorn prompted.

"Fontus or Anastasia would obviously have wanted to shut the kid up." Siren was clearly referring to Coal; her tone was emotionless. "If that's all this was, it'd be one and done, over with. Or even if it was Anastasia's nature getting the better of her, that doesn't bother me. But if it was someone else, that worries me."

"Why?" I asked, interested in spite of my better instincts.

"Because Fontus and Anastasia want adoration," Siren said simply. "That has nothing to do with me. But if it was someone else who killed Coal, someone less single-minded—"

She let the phrase dangle, watching Thorn to gauge a reaction. I puzzled in silence. From what Luca and William had said about dangerous waterfolk, many of them played on their victim's deepest desires. *Siren's insight about what those around her want makes sense—and she certainly seems confident of it. But how clearly can she read such an emotional group of people when it's clear she's not very emotional at all?*

"You came here because you have an idea who it is," Officer Thorn said flatly.

"Yes." Siren glanced at me from the corner of her eye. "Alchemist. I know you're thinking over the facts. There's something that won't have come up in your research. Lore," she explained, addressing Thorn again. "Just old tales. That's what I've always thought. But there's no way to be sure. I've never met any others."

"Any other what?" I asked. From the hard look in Thorn's eyes, I figured my friend was getting tired of the tales.

"Half-bloods," Siren answered, matter-of-fact. "Children of demons. Most of us are made, not born. I've never encountered any like Anastasia's brood."

"Weep and Magica," I said, my stomach turning. "But that's

assuming Anastasia is what you say, and that her children are indeed hers."

"It's my assumptions," Siren reminded me. "My skin I'm worried about. I'll stick to my story—you can stick to yours."

"You haven't shared your full story," Officer Thorn reminded her dryly.

"I forgot." Siren smiled slowly, not looking at all contrite. "It's like this. There's an old tale that half-blood demons are wilder than the rest of us. We who are full-blooded can learn to control ourselves. But if we go so far as to have children, particularly with someone who *isn't* like us . . . that heritage tends to sneak up on the kids in nasty ways. Not often in the male children. They usually don't survive. I'm not saying there aren't male demons in the world. But the tales I always heard were specifically about the girl children. They might grow up just fine . . . until an accident happens. They kill one—just one. And then they lose control."

28

Voices in the Dark

Whatever kinship I felt with Siren was not enough to keep me in the station to discuss her theories with Officer Thorn. Not remotely. In fact, everything about what Siren had shared—from the cold smile down to the words she chose—unnerved me. I left the station as soon as the interview was over, checked on William in the shop, and then kept moving. It did occur to me to stop by the café, but I knew Saki would want to talk about the ball—and I couldn't face that yet.

So, just as Luca had turned up in my store earlier, I turned up in his.

As I stepped over the threshold, the first thing that greeted me was Frank's whispery voice. "What are you looking for?"

"That's a little intimidating," I replied, seeking and finally locating the mink atop a nearby bookcase. "Is that how you greet everyone?"

"Some people appreciate not wasting time," was the mink's cool reply. "Luca is in the back room shelving books."

"Point taken," I said, although I still wasn't so sure that

Frank's manner was customer-friendly. *What is it with talking animals and being grumpy?* I shook the thought away, thanked Frank, and headed for the back.

"He's suspicious of everyone right now because of the carnival," Luca explained by way of greeting. I'd barely stepped into the room. He turned, smiling lopsidedly, as I came and sat on the carpet beside him. The cozy little room was empty aside from us, and Luca had left his hood down, exposing the twisted horn and mossy tattoos that remained from an old curse. He pointed at one of his pointed ears, adding, "It's amazing how much better I can hear without the hood."

"Why don't you leave it off all the time?" I asked, still thinking of Siren and her brazenness.

Luca shrugged. "It's comfortable, for now. It keeps my head warm. Is that really what you want to talk about? It seems like something's wrong."

"Ugh." I sighed in agreement with his deduction, shifting so that I could lean against the stone fireplace. Luca and his stack of books sat just to my right, an anchor. "There's been a development in the case. Remember the sharpshooter, Siren? She came over to my shop not too long after you left."

"She came to find you specifically?" Luca asked, his voice slow and considered as he continued his work.

"Yep. At first I was kind of honored, in a way. I mean, it's not unusual for people to be intimidated by Thorn. But I had this feeling like Siren was . . . cool, and if she liked me, I must be too." Involuntarily, I shivered, and Luca looked up. Without his glamoured hood obscuring his face, his expressions seemed different, clearer—sharper. "She didn't *do* anything," I hastened to explain. "She just wanted to talk. Actually, I think she wants to make sure *we* do something.

Basically she had three things to say: that Fontus seems to be on high alert for another murder and is planning to replace the crew the next chance he gets; that Siren *is* in fact an aicha kandida, though supposedly she no longer preys on people, and that's why she thought Anastasia might be one—"

"Whoa." Luca sat back on his heels. "How sure are we?"

"About Siren no longer hunting people?"

"No—that's actually well-documented these days. There's been a big ongoing study of that kind of thing in Brass, decades long. It does seem like elemental beings can change their nature, usually if they undergo some life-changing event that creates an innate desire for change." Luca tilted his head. "I meant, how sure are we about Anastasia?"

"Oh. Well, Siren is quite sure. But that leads us to the third thing—"

"That wasn't the three things?" Luca looked worried.

"Well, it may have been three, but it wasn't everything." I bit my lip. "Siren had this story—she said it's basically folklore among other waterfolk—that if one of them has a child, that child might be . . . essentially, corrupted by their heritage. So she thinks Anastasia's twins are like that. She thinks they're dangerous. Specifically, she thinks *Magica* is dangerous, because the folklore she was told has this slant where only the females end up corrupted. Is any of this making sense?"

Luca pushed his remaining books aside and sat next to me, his back against the shelves. "A slippery slope argument," he summarized. "One murder leading to more. That's what Siren wanted to talk about?"

"Yeah. It all got very—transactional, I guess. Like after Siren told us the story, finally, she went into this whole reasoning about how she doesn't want to leave a lucrative job at the carnival, and she doesn't want to 'run away,' but she also doesn't want to deal with Magica—because she really is convinced Magica is behind all this. And she, Siren, she thinks that Anastasia and probably Fontus know all about it, but they can't control Magica. So they're trying to hide it, and Siren wants Officer Thorn to swoop in and . . . fix it. The way she talked about it in the end was more like she was deploying the police like some kind of weapon. Or like an insurance policy, almost."

"Siren's logic is sound," Luca said. Though his voice was mild, his eyes were inscrutable when I lifted my gaze to meet his. "It's her starting point, her premise, that you have trouble with."

"She was just so—heartless," I agreed. "And I know that must sound funny, coming from me, because I'm always going on about science and experiments and—and, well, I know I'm not good at recognizing emotions—not my own, anyway."

"Red—"

"And it just makes it worse because it's Magica," I went on, unable to stop now that I'd started. "I was starting to really like her, I think. Or feel for her. She's perceptive, but she's in exactly the position we thought Coal was in. And wouldn't this all be exactly what Coal would have wanted us all to think, that Magica is some kind of evil stepsister? She fits right into that role, doesn't she, just like she fits into Siren's story—it makes a kind of sense—but it's *not* sensible—or am I not being sensible? Am I being too emotional over all of this, just like Saki and Gloria and—"

"Cinnabar," Luca interrupted firmly. My mouth snapped shut at once, of its own accord. I'd never heard him use my real name before. "Stop. Breathe."

My breath shuddered in my chest, and I realized with some surprise that I had to wipe my eyes dry.

"You're alright," he added softly, watching me. "You're just being human, that's all."

Another shuddering breath turned into a shaky chuckle as I searched my pockets for a handkerchief. "You sound like you've been talking to my mothers."

"I'd like that," Luca replied, the sincerity in his voice a flash of warmth against all the confusion I'd been carrying around.

I had to blow my nose and catch my breath again before I worked up the courage to ask, "Luca . . . do *you* think it's possible that Magica could be behind all this?"

"Are you asking me because our parallel situations make me a suitable 'control' subject to measure her against?" he returned, a small smile quirking up one side of his mouth.

The humor and honesty of it caught me off guard, and I laughed, if briefly. "That's not what I meant, promise. I just think . . . you have better insight into these things than I do."

"I think that's a lot less true than you believe," Luca said gently. "Magica and I might have similar experiences, and I do feel empathy for everything you've told me about her, but she is very different than I am. She has her brother to think of, and her mother might be a more difficult shadow to escape than Owl ever was. Besides, I am very self-centered."

I sat up, aghast. "Luca, how could you say that? You never—"

"Hold on," he said, smiling ruefully as he held up a hand. "I don't mean it in a bad way. It's helped me rediscover who I am. But that's just it . . . the farthest from this forest that I've ever been is when I went to help you in Seaside. I was stuck on my own for a very long time, and all I could do was read about other people. After I was cursed, aside from Owl the first real person I truly *met* was you, Red. And there was so much going on at that time, and I had so many emotions I'd never let myself notice before, that I had to parcel some of them away. So even to this day, I'm still working through some of them.

"And I know you know that," Luca said, heading off my interruption with a soft look. "And I know that's why you've been worried about this case from the start. But that's my point. I'm here, in my little bookshop, working through my own past. Red, *you* are the one who has been so many places, and met all of these people, and listened to them speak. You are the one who is brave enough and caring enough that you try to feel my pain for me, when I don't even want to see it. Your intuition is what's really valuable in this case."

"Luca . . ." I couldn't manage to say any more; I was crying again.

"Not that I'm telling you that you trying to feel my pain for me is a *good* thing, mind you," he added, quietly, wryly. "I'm just admitting that sometimes there is some good that comes from it."

"I'm pretty sure I heard you say that I have permission to take on as many feelings as I like," I teased. I knew it wasn't at all what he'd said, but it was worth it to see his face light up.

Even as we collapsed into giggles, Luca's words echoed in my mind. *You are brave enough and caring enough.* If only I was also eloquent enough, like he was, to be able to tell him what all of this meant to me . . .

"Come on," he said, taking my shoulder and interrupting my thoughts once more with that look like he could tell what was going on in my head. "We can talk more about this later.

Right now, we have to get ready for a ball."

29

A Magical Transformation

Next thing I knew, I was trussed up and in a chair at Gloria's salon, with about a dozen things I didn't understand happening all around me.

"You know," said Johann, Gloria's assistant—and currently wielder of an emery board and nail clippers in one hand, and several tubes of scented lotion in the other, "if you came in more, this wouldn't be so mysterious to you now."

"Or so difficult," added Gloria, through a mouthful of bobby pins. She seemed to have sprouted extra hands, and they were all tugging my hair in different directions.

"You really could use a break more often," Sakura agreed, hardly looking up from a makeup chest holding everything but the salon sink.

"This doesn't feel like a break," I muttered rebelliously. But since they'd wrapped me up in a poncho and a towel and a face mask which Saki had promised would have "magical" results, I don't think they could hear me.

An hour later, though, my tune had changed.

"Okay," I admitted to Saki, while Gloria and Johann were in

the salon storeroom arguing over scents and finishing touches, "I will confess that I feel strangely accomplished, for having just *sat* here."

"I told you it's magical." She winked at me from her stool, where she sat happily pasting colored glass gems to my toenails. I'd *tried* to tell her that it was unnecessary—after all, I'd been the one to make those faux gems for Gloria, and if I wanted them all over my feet, I could have just stepped in glue and then walked around the floor of my lab. But to be fair, Sakura's method was a lot less messy . . . and probably much safer.

"Couldn't you have just used magic to do, you know, all this?" I asked, waving a manicured hand around my newly moisturized face and the haircut I was still a little afraid to look at.

"That's called glamour magic, and not only is it borderline amoral, it's also temporary," Saki informed me in her best disapproving-teacher voice. "Besides, it's more meaningful this way. Like I was trying to tell Officer Thorn, sometimes magic is more of a danger than a tool. Having shortcuts isn't always good."

"Try telling that to some alchemists I know," I joked. "Still, I hope you are planning on doing some kind of instant-setting spell on that glue."

"Oh, that I *will* do, don't worry," Sakura said, smiling fondly at her nail art. "This was just a little spur-of-the-moment whim of mine, since we had the spare time. And your feet really are pretty. Don't laugh! You, Red, have to remember to appreciate what you have more often."

The reminder was poignant, not only because I knew Saki was referring to her own prosthetic feet, but because of Luca's comment earlier about my intuition being valuable. "You're right, Saki," I said softly.

"Of course I am," she returned, pert. "There! All done. Doesn't it look nice? You don't even need fancy glass slippers at this rate."

"Or maybe I *should* have glass slippers, to show off your work," I laughed. As I twisted my feet to look at the swirling patterns Saki had created with blues, teals, and silver, the little gems flashed and twinkled back at me.

"You could do this all the time," Sakura reminded me. "You don't need a ball as an excuse."

"Yes she does," Gloria called as she emerged from the storeroom, Johann in tow. "I'm not going through all this work again without a very good reason."

"I thought you told me I should come more often so that it's *less* work," I retorted, grinning.

"I don't think either one of us has the patience for all that work, though," Johann said, peering over my shoulder at my new blingy nails. "So don't come to Gloria and me expecting *that* every month."

"Maybe I'll start a pop-up business in the café," Sakura said airily as she rose and went to the sink to wash her hands.

"I don't think Glacial would approve," I called after her. Behind me, Gloria and Johann were using some kind of spray that reminded me of jasmine under starlight, and they were passing a tray of something sparkly between them; I caught glimpses of it in my peripheral vision every now and then. It was strange not to have my goggles or my ponytail, but Gloria had been very insistent. *You'll live without them,* she'd informed me curtly. And she was right. For a moment, sitting there, I felt entirely present and alive.

Even though I had nothing to hide behind.

"Thank you," I said eventually, to all three of my miracle-working friends. "Thank you for taking the time to do this, and help me out—and just putting up with me. You even closed the salon, didn't you?"

"Just proving that fairy godmothering can go both ways," Gloria said gruffly.

"You're going to be great advertising for us, anyway," Johann added with more enthusiasm.

"You're welcome," Sakura said pointedly, through giggles. "My, such gratitude before you've even seen what you look like!"

"You haven't looked yet?" Gloria asked, the way someone else might have said, *I gave you a present and you haven't even unwrapped it yet?*

"I'm a little scared," I admitted. This prompted more sounds of rage, so I added in a rush, "Not because of you! I'm sure you do good work! But you have to admit, the last time I looked in a mirror in your salon—"

Johann interrupted by stepping deftly around my chair with a large handheld mirror, bringing me face to face with my own reflection. While I looked, he said, amused, "They're not *all* enchanted, you know."

"But . . . I look like me," I observed, no doubt showing off all that intellectual prowess which kept me in business as an alchemist.

Sakura giggled harder. "What did you think I was going to do, use makeup to turn your face green?"

"Or create something impossible out of this mane you call hair?" Gloria added.

"I think what your dear friends are trying to say," Johann

explained with a smile, "is that of *course* you look like you. That's what we do here. We simply bring out all that potential that's hidden under the surface."

I suppose I had thought, when Saki and Gloria had gotten so excited about a makeover, that they wanted exactly what the word implied—a total overhaul of my normal appearance. A do-over, almost. Without even meaning to, I'd assumed from the beginning that my natural appearance wasn't good enough for a fancy masked ball.

Clearly Gloria, far wiser than me and experienced in her art, had had a different vision. Of course, the usual lab attire was gone, and Saki had somehow managed to undo the dark circles under my eyes, too. But aside from that, nothing was erased or replaced; instead, my own eyes stared back at me, more sharply and deftly outlined than usual, and my hair hadn't all been cut off or dyed, but instead styled in the sort of lovely braid that looked impossibly simple. Jeweled flowers nestled among the iridescent streaks in my hair, highlighting them rather than hiding them.

"Hidden under a purposeful layer of neglect, more like," Gloria said, breaking the spell of my reverie. "I still don't know how I got the indent from your goggles out of your hair."

"Amazing expertise and years of experience?" I suggested, smiling hopefully at her in the mirror.

Her eyes met mine, and she smirked. "You better be glad I have both in spades."

"This is all very well, and we *do* have a lot to be grateful for, but Luca won't be thanking anyone if we take so long that Red misses the ball entirely," Saki reminded us. "Her hair and makeup might look wonderful, but we can't send her out in a salon poncho."

"Oh no." Suddenly, I recalled that I'd given Saki and Gloria permission to go shopping for me—and that they'd probably taken Trent with them. "Do I really want to know what else you have in mind?"

"You ought to have more faith in us," Johann said, shaking the mirror playfully to remind me of my earlier awe.

"You'd be surprised what they've got in that consignment shop across the Square," Gloria admitted grudgingly.

"Everything's set up at your place," Saki told me. "Let's head over there now, and let Gloria and Johann clean up here."

"Oh—are you sure we can't help clean?" I asked, as Saki tugged me from the chair.

"Are you kidding?" Gloria gave me a look. "Go and dress before your hair reverts to its natural wild state. Just—make sure you stop in here on your way to the ship."

* * *

William was waiting for us at the back door, his tail wagging.

"Come *on*," he insisted, bounding halfway up the stairs before we'd even made it inside. "Thorn's already been by twice to remind us about the ball, and it's going to start soon. I don't want to miss any of the drama!"

"What about my dramatic transformation?" I asked, framing my face as I climbed up the stairs after him.

"Eh. You look like you. Nice hair jewelry, though," he said, before bounding into the kitchen.

"Some people just don't appreciate details," Sakura observed, grinning as she followed us into the apartment.

"Some people are busy thinking about practical things like

time," William retorted easily, tail in the air as he leaped onto the couch. Though he was a sorcerer's familiar and generally prejudiced against witches as inferior magic-users—the list of inferior creatures in William's world is a very long one—he and Sakura seemed to enjoy annoying each other. There was an undertone of respect.

"Saki was actually just giving us that lecture," I admitted. "I think it's my fault we're running behind. But you said everything was set up—?"

"Over here," she answered, leading me to my bed. In the little studio, the only truly private space was the bathroom; I wasn't surprised my friends had made use of the one large flat space. They'd laid out a lovely turquoise gown, velvet cape, and silver shoes.

"Gloria and I were all set to get you this very practical, sedate button-up dress with a blouse underneath," Saki admitted. "Something that still had an official look to it, since you're technically at the ball to help Officer Thorn. But in the end, Trent talked us out of it. He argued that if you made a big impression, you'd actually fit in more easily with the carnival crowd."

"Typical Witch reasoning," William snorted from his post.

"And the mask we have for you is actually his handiwork," Sakura continued as though she'd heard nothing. "He just put it together with some odds and ends from the thrift shop."

She held out a golden carnival mask made to cover the upper half of the face. It was trimmed in white ribbon, and from the center of the forehead, a twisting, pearlescent horn rose.

I stared at her, my throat dry, my feet itching to run.

"You probably never paid attention to the details, but everyone's supposed to wear an animal-themed mask at the carnival ball," Saki said.

Something in her eyes told me that she *knew* that wasn't what I was speechless about.

"He got the unicorn idea because of Luca," she added finally.

Of course, this only gave me *more* questions. Did Trent give me a unicorn mask simply to match what he knew about my boyfriend's true appearance—or did he somehow know, perhaps *from* Luca, about the unicorn magic that ran in my family's blood?

I thought I'd hidden it all so much better than this . . .

That's not my world, after all.

But—the mask was right here, and it was beautiful. It *was* part of my world, right in front of me. There was no arguing with it.

Sometimes costumes do *look like someone else's reality, and that's okay.*

"It was <u>very</u> nice of him, don't you think?" Saki prompted at last.

"Whatever it was, I have to admit I'm glad," I said. And I was. After years of trying to make myself appear as normal as possible, something about this mask was incredibly freeing. "I probably would have been right there with you and Gloria, choosing the practical outfit. And I never would have thought of a mask . . . But that would hardly do all your hard work justice."

"Neither will you standing there and staring at it all," Saki chuckled. "Go on, try everything on. If anything doesn't fit, I'll magic it into place, don't worry. But you have to actually be wearing it for that to work!"

Laughing, I gathered up the clothes and made my way into the bathroom to finish getting ready. On the other side of the frosted glass door, I could hear Sakura threatening—jovially—to turn William into a coachman or, worse, a noble steed. The thought that soon we'd meet up with Luca put a flutter in my chest.

A costume, I thought, looking at the dress again. *Getting dressed up like this almost made me forget how serious the ball might be. And yet—even if this dress isn't very practical—it does give me more courage.*

30

One Party to Rule Them All

Luca was waiting for us on the corner outside the shop by the time we were ready.

"I saw the lights go off upstairs as I walked up," he said, coming to meet us as we emerged from the alley. "Officer Thorn stopped by the bookstore on her way to the ship, and she gave me our tickets. She said she'd been talking to Fontus and everything was all set. I was thinking—"

The moment I stepped onto the sidewalk and into the streetlight, Luca stopped talking. His reaction was so priceless that I had to chuckle at him. But, honestly, he was just as breathtaking in his fancy getup. Instead of the robe that I had *always* seen him wear, he now sported tailored trousers and a fitted black coat over a high-collared white shirt. He looked a little bit like Jade had once looked, but because his head was unglamoured, the tattoos and horn that made him unmistakably *Luca* were visible.

"You were thinking?" Saki prompted, amused.

Luca gestured helplessly. "I wasn't."

"Let's go," William said to Sakura. "Otherwise they're just

going to stand on the corner staring at each other all night."

"I think they might do that no matter what," she replied, laughing. "Let's go get Gloria and Johann while we wait, then. They wanted to see the final look."

As the two meddlesome jokers walked off, I stepped a little closer to Luca. In a way, he looked exactly like himself, and yet nothing at all like himself. It was the same feeling I'd had looking in the mirror in the salon earlier.

"I guess I should have known," he managed to say after a moment. Pointing at a silk cravat at his throat, he explained, "Trent came over with this for me to wear, so I could match you. Actually he had a *lot* of instructions about what to wear. I only barely escaped. I think he was vicariously going on a date himself, through us. I should have expected what your dress would look like. But, um . . ."

"I know," I confessed, laughing self-consciously. "I had no idea what to expect either. Saki told me their first idea was to dress me up like a schoolteacher. I kind of would have found that more believable."

"Oh, no," said Luca, taking my arm. "I don't mean to say you look unbelievable. I think you look perfect—as always. It's just a different kind of perfect. Which is good . . . it reminds me how amazing you really are."

"You haven't seen the mask yet. Trent made me a unicorn mask," I said, still half surprised myself. Luca had known about my family's legacy and reputation before I met him, and so I knew he understood. "I haven't put it on yet, but I think it'll all be pretty . . . dazzling. Though I could say the same thing about you," I murmured, blushing.

"Well." Luca waved his free hand at the horn that rose above his forehead. The look in his eyes was deeply understanding.

"I figured, why not? And anyway, it's time. That's something else you've reminded me of lately."

"That's me," I said, trying my best to be light. "Just your friendly neighborhood alchemical reminder. Reminding-device? Reminder clock?"

Luca interrupted my puzzling over word choice with a laugh, steering me gently to where our friends were waiting. "Don't worry. You're far more than that."

* * *

"You made it!" Gus's eyes lit up as our little party walked up the gangplank. A gateway had been erected on deck, carnival curtains strewn with vines and fairy lights, but he didn't need the lit archway to see us. Behind him, the carnival ring was shining gold against the night sky.

Fool's gold, I couldn't help but think.

But Officer Thorn was in high spirits; she'd met us on the dock, dressed in her usual uniform and an iridescent dragonfly mask. William had opted to go maskless, and in his enthusiasm had already bounded right up to Gus. I took a deep breath and put my mask on, then glanced at Luca. He smiled as he took my hand.

It felt almost—natural.

"They aren't letting you dance too?" Thorn asked Gus. Her usual slightly-too-loud voice was necessary now, as strains of upbeat classical music streamed from the carnival ring.

"I'll be in shortly," he assured her. "Just seeing to the last guests, you know. One of the crew will take over for me in a little while. We're taking shifts."

This seemed to appease the officer, who nodded. Not even

her winged mask could hide the fact that she held more authority than the rest of us put together—even on someone else's ship.

Gus gave us directions, but he didn't need to. We followed the fairy lights and music up the curving staircase on the main deck. Once we'd ascended to the top, we were in a completely new world.

I hadn't had a chance to see the carnival itself, and for a moment I regretted that. As I took in the ball, the steampunk aspect of the *Luna II* finally made sense. Until that moment, I'd figured that the magitech wheel and gadgets were really just window-dressing. Now, however, they'd been put to use.

The music was loud not only because of the crowd, but because it had to fight with the whir of well-oiled machinery. The center of the ring was lifted several feet and spinning slowly, like a massive merry-go-round, as the orchestra played atop it. Golden magitech lamps mingled with the fairy lights. Hidden pumps powered fountains of what I sincerely hoped was lake water—minus any fish—placed all around the floor, bubbling and spraying near tables laden with sumptuous food. Pistons as large and solid as trees lifted the carnival bleachers up so that the carnival ring was now twice as wide, ringed by a forest of pillars and deep shadow underneath the seats perfect for the kind of mischief that reportedly happens at balls. Across the ring I could see that the bleachers were at ground level as usual, but from there they spiraled up and up, towering several stories over our heads. Billows of steam from the machinery created deep blue clouds beyond, giving the carnival an ethereal feel, like we were up in the sky. People milled around this elevated playground and filled up the stage before us.

I turned and looked at Luca, my forest-bred small-town bookseller. Behind the leafy mask that accentuated his dark horn, his eyes were wide as saucers. "It's like a floating castle garden. I've never seen anything like it," he told me shamelessly.

"Most people here probably haven't," William observed as he eyed the crowd.

"Yeah, I think that's the point," I said, a little more cynically. But as the clown trio twirled by, each with a different brightly-dressed partner in their arms, I couldn't help but smile. "They do a good job, I will admit."

"We're not here to criticize the decorations, Red." Officer Thorn squared her shoulders. "First things first. Food."

I protested as she grabbed hold of my arm. "That doesn't sound very investigativ—"

"Detecting needs fuel," she declared, towing me—and, effectively, Luca—through the crowd. William disappeared on his own, but I knew he'd be somewhere nearby. Though he'd played off his determination to come along as excitement, I could tell he was in a highly protective mode. *After all, there is a murderer here somewhere . . .*

The nearest banquet table was covered in white silk and strewn with golden decorations—little gears and carnival favors, naturally. But most of its surface was covered with platter upon platter of canapes, charcuterie, and cakes in all colors. In the back of my mind I had a bad feeling about who might have made all that food—I doubted Caty had time, and given all this magitech, I suspected animated (read: probably unethical or even illegal) help. *Not here to judge decorations, not here to bust them on the morality of robot abuse,* I reminded myself. I sighed. The list of *nots* was getting longer. Why couldn't I just enjoy myself like a normal person?

Oh, right, because a murder happened here only a few days ago.

Luca, of course, was supremely unbothered, bless him. I was more grateful he'd come along with every minute. He piled a golden plate high with tiny phyllo dough pies and bruschetta so potent I could smell the basil and garlic in the air, talking the whole time. "Well, this certainly seems like an example of the amazing things magitech can do, right, Red? There's never been anything this mechanical in Belville before. We have to make sure to record this. Maybe someone can draw up some prints. I'm a little surprised, Red, that you don't have more of this kind of thing in your shop—especially after the way you figured out that lock—you have a knack for tinkering!"

I opened my mouth to tell him that in my opinion magitech meant trouble, but someone beat me to it with a very timely example.

"Our little friends from Belville! How wonderful you could make it." Anastasia swooped in, quite appropriately, given the graceful swan's mask and wings rising above her pure white, bejeweled dress. It was so bright I could barely make out the twins, hiding in the shadows of their mother's silken wingspan.

I gritted my teeth and chose *not* to point out that most of the carnival's audience was probably from Belville and neighboring towns. In fact, judging by the crowd, nearly everyone *except* Gloria, Johann, Trent, and Sakura had come. If not for all those 'little friends,' Anastasia and her carnival friends would be dancing with themselves.

"Anastasia," Thorn answered from my side. "Even in a mask, you're unmistakable."

My friend paused slightly over the word *unmistakable,* and I knew she was holding back a pun. Luca sidled up to my other side, holding his plate over to me in a *here, this scene deserves popcorn* gesture. Between the two of them, the tension in my jaw eased.

"I consider it a duty to shine brightly at these little events," Anastasia said, taking barely any notice of us. "It gives the good people something to look up to. It is our duty to help the less fortunate, don't you think, children?"

"Sure," mumbled a blue-bejeweled otter mask in a suit. Weep.

Magica said nothing. Now that I'd acclimated a little to Anastasia's garish dress, I could see her, standing off to the right a little. Like her brother, she wore an outfit of cerulean blue and black—hers a ruffled tutu and tights rather than a suit. She, too, had a blingy otter mask on, but it didn't quite suit her; somehow, the ears felt more mousy than anything.

She was also staring directly across me at Officer Thorn.

I pursed my lips, thinking about this. *She does that a lot, doesn't she? Does she have something to confess—did she see something, maybe? Or was Siren's story somehow true?*

"Getting murdered's pretty unfortunate," Officer Thorn declared with a marked lack of decorum, even for her.

Anastasia gasped and stepped back like Thorn had whipped out a venomous snake. "You *can't* still be going on about that, can you? And at an event like this?"

"Mother," Magica said, very quietly.

"We're not under suspicion," said Weep.

"Exactly right, my boy," Anastasia agreed, pulling myself. "Myself, I don't see how *anyone* at the carnival could be. We're a family. And we've worked hard for all we have! Just look at what we created," she said, gesturing to the ball around us.

"Just because it's beautiful doesn't mean it isn't dangerous," Luca said mildly. "I think it's a good thing to have—"

Anastasia peered at him for only a moment before interrupting. "If anyone here was under suspicion, I'm sure they'd already have been arrested. We may as well put the whole thing behind us, because it's clear the true culprit will never be caught now. Everyone knows that if a murder isn't solved right away, it will never be solved. I once had a fan who was a very great detective, and he told me that you can know at once if a police investigation is going to be any good. 'Ana,' he told me, 'if it *isn't* any good, then you better leave quick.' That's what he said to me. Well, now I am leaving!"

She swept off as suddenly as she'd come, shaking her skirts with an imperious, "Children, come! We have duties to perform!"

But she didn't make it very far.

Weep went easily enough, fading into Anastasia's wake. She *did* cut an impressive figure; as she and her massive white wings moved across the dance floor, everyone turned. I myself didn't want to give her the satisfaction of watching her leave— and besides, I was more worried for my friend. I turned to Thorn, full of indignation and ready to sympathize.

But Officer Thorn wasn't looking at me.

As it turned out, Anastasia made it nearly to center stage before realizing she'd lost something. There was a *whoosh* of quickly-turned wings, and a demand rang out: "Magica!"

Magica was staring at Thorn.

Anastasia's voice could have cut glass. *"Magica!"*

Thorn was staring at Magica.

"Magica Willow!" The entire ball ground to a halt.

Magica spoke so quietly her voice blended in to the whir of

magitech. "No."

31

A Dangerous Waltz

"*What did you just say to me?*"

Magica trembled. She was alone now, and in the shadows no longer. The crowd's entire attention was focused on this unforeseen drama between her and her mother. You could have heard a pin drop . . .

In fact, what I heard was a plate settle onto a tablecloth. Luca set aside his dinner. Without looking at him, I knew exactly what he was doing, and I moved to join him. Together, we closed the distance and flanked her, turning to face Anastasia.

I knew in my bones that Siren had been wrong.

"*Magica,*" the starlet shrieked again. "Just what do you think you are doing? Are you going to give in to them so easily?"

The silence was almost unbearable. I stood to Magica's right, not touching her; I wasn't sure if she would want me to. But perhaps I should have risked it. In the end, it was Luca who did so. I'm not sure I've ever felt anything stronger than the rush of admiration and gratitude I felt for him as he shifted, putting his hand on Magica's left shoulder.

The girl between us looked up then, and in one quick tug,

233

she pulled her mask from her face. She was crying. "No," she said, and the only reason we could hear her at first was that everyone else was waiting with bated breath to find out what was going on. "I won't leave. I don't think it's—I don't think it's right. I don't think there's anything wrong with—with their investigation."

She's been trying to help from the start, I thought. *What I thought was almost ominous was her trying to get me to understand—to see how her mother's opinion was hampering her!*

"Magica, silly child." Anastasia's manner had changed: she cooed now, more like a dove than a swan. "You're just confused. What do *you* know about police matters, poor thing?"

Magica's voice shook. "I—I know they're *trying,* at least . . ."

"Of course they're doing their best, child, but you know what happens when amateurs try to measure up. That's why we must work so hard. These little townsfolk, they're in over their head, the p—"

"*Don't!*" For just a moment, just a very brief second, Magica sounded exactly like her mother. Her one word rang out shrilly, sharply. But in the startled stillness afterward, it became clear how different they were as Magica went on, her voice low and ragged. "Don't say such things. You're always saying those awful things. Don't you think it will come back to haunt you? Don't you think everyone *knows?*"

Anastasia was on her back foot now, and Magica was gaining steam. She threw her mask down. "I have tried and I have worked to be so *good,*" she continued, nearly choking on the last syllable. "I have done everything, but it is never enough. Nothing is ever enough for you. Nothing will *ever* be enough for you. And everyone here knows it! Everyone knows how you are. They know you are bitter and how you hate anyone who gets anything you don't have. You act like your life is perfect and mine is the one that needs work. But all I have done is *try*. You're the one who never tries at all. You just *lie*! You let us believe in lies. You let me keep working, thinking that one day it would be enough. You let Coal think you'd take him under your wing. You bring people close and then you make them smaller and smaller until all they can do is look up to you. But you *can't* do it to these people, because *they know who you are!*"

Even without being able to see Anastasia's eyes behind her mask at this distance, I could hear the danger in her voice. "Magica . . ."

"*No*," Magica said, more firmly this time. "No! I will tell them." She turned to Officer Thorn, who still stood by the food table, watching the scene unfold with an unusually blank look, her mask removed. In a rush, like she thought that at any minute her mother might tackle her into silence, Magica said, "Mother is an aloja and Weep and I are half. Our father was a dryad and she loved him very much but he gave away her secret, so we had to leave. Then she married Coal's father and he died by accident, but he left her all this money and a place in the carnival. She always told us we have to work hard to be beautiful and wealthy because no one else will help us—"

"Awful, traitorous, lying child!" Anastasia erupted.

"—and she liked Coal best and I always thought it must be because Coal was more like a naiad but Weep and I are more like our father but Coal and her were maybe too similar so they would fight all the time and that's why she would try to lock him in his room," Magica finished in one breath. She looked around, almost surprised no one had physically stopped her.

Luca and I were ready to intercept, but as the crowd settled, it turned out there was no need for us. Weep had caught his mother, preventing her from running forward. She'd sunk to the floor and was sobbing in his arms.

I glanced around the ball, looking for any other protesters. Siren stood behind a nearby fountain, and I thought I caught a look of disdain on her face. I could intuit why: while Siren had confessed to being an aicha kandida, and thought Anastasia was too, it turned out Anastasia was actually a generally mild-mannered or traditionally "good" water spirit.

But it sounds like she was guided by betrayal and unexamined grief, I guessed, *which she then passed on to her children. Meanwhile, for as dangerous as Siren could be, she was guided by an interest, however self-centered, in working with others . . .*

It wasn't a time for contemplating cosmic ironies, though. I kept scanning, noting Captain Pleasant and Gus near the stage. Fontus was seemingly absent. Other than that, no one looked like they might jump in.

"Thank you," Officer Thorn was saying, with some difficulty, "for letting me know, Magica. Is there anything else you'd like to say, or—anything we can do for you?"

I glanced sideways and saw that Magica looked like someone had asked her if she would like the moon as a reading lamp. "You—believe me?"

"Yes. I took a look at that lock myself," I said kindly, nudging her just to make sure she was still breathing. "What you've said makes a lot of sense."

"They had a fight the day before he was murdered?" Luca prompted gently from her other side. He gave me a look over her head, like, *better to draw out all the poison now.*

Magica nodded slowly. "Because of the blackmail. But I

don't—I don't know very much more than that. She always sent us away when Coal brought it up. Then Coal would say why couldn't we see that he could make dreams come true, if we would just listen, but I never understood it really, because I'm—"

"Magica." Officer Thorn interrupted, and for once, I was glad she did. I had a bad feeling that Magica's next words would have been something like *I'm not smart enough,* which was clearly untrue. The officer went on, "Did you ever hear anything about those dreams? The ones Coal thought he could realize?"

"He wanted to leave." Magica stared at Officer Thorn once more, silver eyes wide and leaves trembling in her hair, like she'd never heard anything as nice as her name before. "I just want everything to be made right."

Officer Thorn's face took on its own mask, one of determination. I smiled. I knew for certain that that was one dream my friend could *definitely* realize.

"Fools!" Anastasia cried as we paused. I had to give her credit—she knew how to seize a moment and reclaim attention. And . . . for a water spirit naturally inclined to being admired, maybe that made sense. "How *could* you believe that senseless girl. To treat her own mother in such a fashion! After all the things I've been through, and everything I have done for you, for *everyone!* Where would you all be without me? *Nowhere! I* am the key to this carnival's success!"

The word "key" dropped into my belly with a heavy *thud.*

That's been one of the worst, most confusing parts of this case all along. There were two keys to Coal's room, but Coal had his, and we never found the spare. Did I ever see Anastasia wearing a key ring? No, she seems more like someone who would have someone carry everything for her . . . she would send for it if she wanted it . . . she never did tell us anything about it. Did we ever ask her? She played it off the first night, but did we bring it up again?

. . . maybe we did, and she played it off like we were foolish, just like now . . .

. . . it's funny, she seems more like the pitiable, foolish one now, never seeing what the true cause of her suffering was . . . her daughter sees it better than she does; what a burden to bear . . .

Wait . . . if Anastasia was too wrapped up in her own world to actually think about any of our questions . . .

Maybe she never understood what we were talking about, with that extra key.

"Oh, my gods and goddesses," I whispered softly, moving away from Magica. I glanced toward the stage again, then to Officer Thorn. "Oh my goodness. I think I understand something. I think I know what we missed."

32

Ring Around the Rosie

"Anastasia," I said, walking very, very slowly toward her, like she was a deer about to turn tail. "You would fight with Coal about blackmail. Let me guess. He wanted to blackmail others. You didn't."

"Why ruin a relationship," she said sullenly from the floor.

Perhaps she meant it to sound sympathetic, but I smiled grimly, sliding the pieces into place. Coal's method of blackmail made instant money, but it turned people into enemies. Anastasia clearly preferred a *relationship*, where the people thought they were her friends, and would give much more than money over time. "But did you know Coal was already blackmailing your cast and crew mates?"

There were gasps from the crowd—I'd almost forgotten we'd had an audience. But no one protested. Not even Weep's gray eyes, fixed on mine, wavered.

"So, at the very least, you suspected it," I surmised from her silence. I continued moving forward, one step at a time. "And, if Coal was already blackmailing others just fine, why would he want to involve you? Perhaps because you had access to someone he didn't. Someone *big*."

Anastasia said nothing, but Weep did. He looked down at his mother, and he didn't ask the question. "Fontus."

"I would never," she said very quietly.

"But it's funny," I continued musing, turning over my shoulder to look at Officer Thorn. "Fontus isn't here tonight. At his own ball. What was it we thought about him once, officer?"

"Fearless," she said, clearing her throat. "That's what you called him. And it isn't as funny as you might think, Red. I looked into our director. Turns out anyone who acts that fearless has got *plenty* of fears deep down."

Anastasia looked up, startled. In my head, the final piece clicked into place.

"You didn't know that," I guessed, watching her. I stood still and let Officer Thorn catch up as I talked. "You thought he was perfect . . . like you. Both of you have perfect masks, perfect costumes. Maybe that's part of why you tried to keep Coal out of it. The last thing you wanted was for Coal to actually dig something up on Fontus—and besides, having him hanging around the director all the time surely got in your way. Because blackmailing seems to involve a lot of loitering around darkened corners . . ."

I glanced at the crowd around us once more.

"No need to reveal the director's secret," Thorn grunted as she caught up to me. "But suffice it to say, someone *was* blackmailing him. He and I had a little talk about it this afternoon."

"Not . . . Coal?" Anastasia whispered, still on the floor.

"Fontus wouldn't say," Officer Thorn said casually. Now she, too, was looking around. "Myself, I would have figured it was you."

"Because that's the thing about this ship," I agreed. "It's got *more than one* blackmailer on it already, doesn't it? But it doesn't have more than one spare key per room, no matter how fancy the locks."

Officer Thorn caught my drift and stood straighter beside me. "Anastasia," she asked formally, "when you fought with Coal and decided to lock him in his room. What was your routine?"

A drift of black amid the vividly-dressed audience assured me that William, too, was on the case. He was making his way around the back of the stage.

"My . . . routine?" Anastasia's face contracted into a pout. "I didn't have a routine. I'd just tell him to go to his room and then call for the spare key, the one that fits both locks."

Officer Thorn was seething quietly as she caught on. "How many spare keys are there?"

"One," Anastasia answered, looking confused. Beside her, Weep nodded.

"But when we asked you who has it—"

"You think I have time to worry about things like keys when I'm trying to carry this entire *carnival?*"

There it is, I thought with grim satisfaction. *She wanted to wash her hands and be done with it. Each time. Leaving just one person with undisputed access to Coal's room on the day in question . . .*

"Then we were lied to from the very start," Officer Thorn said, gnashing her teeth. She lifted her head to shout. "Where is—"

Cries of alarm and a muffled *whump* to one side of the stage interrupted her. The crowd shifted, and parted, and filled in again, gasps and screams covering the noise of footsteps beating a hasty retreat. I leapt forward into the confusion—

—only to meet with William, one battered boot in his mouth, shaking his head blearily as Gus beat a hasty retreat.

* * *

This time when my feet itched to run, I listened.

The crowd parted in Gus's wake, and no one had time to sort themselves out before I zoomed past. I raced at top speed, following the path of the disturbance. Luca, William, and Officer Thorn faded behind me. This was something I could do alone—something *only* I could do.

Just like only I could be so taken aback by a unicorn mask.

I was still wearing it—I hadn't paused to take it off, hadn't paused to think. Maybe that was also why the dancers were so glad to get out of my way. No one wanted to be rammed by a golden clay horn.

Gus was headed for the main stairs; that much was clear. He didn't know about me and my ability to run—otherwise why would he have bothered? But it turned out he must not have been thinking clearly to begin with. I was at the top of the staircase, and he'd just barely made it to the bottom, when the jet of water began.

Hemming and Sleepy were on the deck below.

I just barely made sense of the giant, pale shark in the moonlight before I had to dodge to the left, out of the path of the water. One glance down the stairs told me Gus hadn't been so lucky. He was sprawled on the steps, surrounded by mist goats. But he *wasn't* soaking wet.

Because he's a full naiad, and he can manipulate water.

"Going up for our performance," Hemming said as I ran up. He didn't question my unnatural speed, but he did seem confused as he stared at Gus. "Would've gone the back way but it's blocked when the seats are up. Sleepy just went off. Didn't mean to cause trouble, I've never seen him do that—"

"It's fine," I panted, pushing my mask up to see more clearly. "Can you get the ceffyl dwr to hold him?"

"Gus?" Now Hemming's confusion was potent, and sharp-edged.

"Nice try," said Gus behind me. He'd struggled to his feet, free of the mist goats. But all was not lost. Hemming, Sleepy, and I were between him and freedom.

And the animal trainer, though solid, didn't cut a very impressive figure in his wet and stained shirt . . .

Wait. I glanced again at the white stains on Hemming's shirt, so reminiscent of my own lab equipment, and the final piece clicked into place. *That coarse white scrub Zale was using. Salt.*

"What's going on?" Hemming asked. Beside him, Sleepy wavered in midair.

"Hemming," I said quickly, my gaze on Gus. "You said the stables were all in order, but maybe there was something very small amiss. Did a container of water go missing the day Coal didn't show up for work? Maybe something you used for cleaning?"

"Yes," he answered slowly. "One of the old salt jugs. Why?"

"Because Coal did show up that day. In fact, he'd stayed overnight. But he didn't do any actual work, did he?" I asked Gus. Behind him, I saw Officer Thorn at the top of the stairs, and knew I just had to distract him for a little while. "Instead, he was lurking somewhere, in the dark, maybe in one of the stalls, when he heard *you* talking to Fontus."

Gus's face was hard. "I don't know what you're talking about."

"And *I* don't know what you had on him, but that's okay. I know enough for it to make sense. You were blackmailing the director, and Coal overheard. Maybe he approached you—maybe he wanted in on it—or maybe you simply saw him hiding there. You picked up the nearest weapon: an empty jug. You can make water move, so it wasn't hard to fill it. Not very much for the average person, but for someone with naiad blood . . . it was exactly what you needed, right?"

"Coal wasn't killed in the stable," Hemming protested.

"And your timeline is wrong," Gus added, sneering.

"I didn't say you killed him then. You wanted to, but you didn't get the chance, right?" I took my time, watching Thorn descend over the slippery steps, listening. "He got away and came into town to think it all over. Probably he should have stayed there, but that wasn't his style. He thought he could deal with you himself, at least for a little while. He was planning to leave the carnival soon, anyway, and he most likely thought he could string you along for a few days before things got too dangerous. After all, he'd been blackmailing others in the carnival for months. Once the shock of overhearing you wore off, he probably felt untouchable, and that's why he risked coming back. He wanted that last payday, and he thought you wouldn't be a threat.

"But you couldn't risk him telling anyone, in the carnival or outside of it, right?"

Gus's hand was at his hip. There was, indeed, a beat up old flask there. I longed for my goggles and their night vision, to be able to see if it was the same one from the stables, but I doubted it was. He would have replaced that one, no doubt.

Either way, I had to proceed with just my wits.

"You told us yourself you were busy in the stable the day the ship got here, and even Fontus admitted to checking in on the animals. So you were all there, but Coal got away from you, and then he managed to sneak back into his room later. But you were ready, all day, with that water. And you knew where you'd find him eventually.

"And there never was a missing spare, was there?" I added, raising my voice to capture Gus's attention as he began to look around, seeking an escape. "That was just something you told us to shift suspicion. Just like the leftover salt from the jug that contaminated the water, distracting us—that was just luck for you, though. And the boots . . . you had to hide the fact that Coal *had* been in the stables earlier that day. Then we might realize that was where he met his murderer. Coal might have been a clean person—Anastasia herself told us that—but he hadn't had time to clean up his boots from staying in the stables overnight. If he had walked in the rain, they might have come clean, but I saw him myself, and he waited for it to stop before going outside. His boots were muddy. I didn't think anything of it—but it was stable mud.

"So, you took the boots and the key and the water jug, and you thought you were free . . . free to keep manipulating others and stealing money. In fact, you had plenty of time to straighten up Coal's room and most likely steal what he'd collected, too."

"*Stealing?*" After all the talk of murder, this is what Gus latched on to. "The wages *here* are theft! And that's just adding insult to injury, with the way the crew here treats anyone new. You're talking like I should feel bad about any of this. All I've done is make the best of my circumstances. Is it *my* fault

Coal went listening where he wasn't wanted? Is it *my* fault the director has a lucrative secret?"

"The murder is your fault," I bluffed, as Officer Thorn and a glowing William came up behind him.

"In another day I'd have been gone and it all would have been forgotten!" Gus returned.

"We'll see about that," Officer Thorn said, announcing her presence as she captured his wrists in a set of handcuffs. "I'll help you go right now. To the station, of course."

Over Gus's vociferous protests, there was a roiling, rumbling noise, like waves in a storm. As one, we all turned to find Sleepy taking an interest in the conversation.

"His real name is Marcus Augustus," the shark said, blunt snout lifted towards William. "He came to us because he was on the run. And I've been waiting for someone to realize it for a very long time."

33

True Love's Kiss

I guess it's a credit to the After Midnight Carnival that the talking shark wasn't the most incredible part of the evening.

Sleepy said a total of two more sentences before he was done with us; first, that he'd been listening to everyone's secrets ever since he'd been brought aboard—everyone assumed he couldn't talk, so they managed to say all kinds of things around his stall. The second sentence was an almost grudging respect for myself and William, who had used his magic to help bind an irate Gus. In fact, I got the impression that the shark saw William as an inspiration; perhaps he hadn't thought anyone would believe him before, until he saw that William had much more responsibility than simply performing tricks.

As soon as the matter was settled, and Officer Thorn and William had marched Gus off to the station to check the criminal record of a "Marcus Augustus," Sleepy resumed his usual can't-be-bothered attitude, and the show went on. Hemming shepherded the ceffyl dwr up the steps, and they did their little dance routine. Luca and I dutifully reported to Captain Pleasant and the remaining carnival folk. They all expressed surprise and innocence of any of Gus's doings, naturally, but they also effusively asked us to stay for the remainder of the ball—so we did.

* * *

"So," said Luca, grinning. "You sure know how to party."

I grinned back, nudging him. "You're the one who set the whole thing off. It was your support that helped Magica speak up, and it was her talking to her mother that made me think of the key."

"But *you* were the one to catch Gus and get him to talk. Besides, I think this place has been waiting to go off for a long time," Luca said modestly.

Together, we looked down, over the ball. We'd climbed the spiral seating until we reached the highest set of bleachers, a few stories off the deck of the ship. The lights weren't as bright there, and the music was reduced to a pleasant background soundtrack. The dancers themselves looked like twirling dolls, almost as untouchable as the stars in the sky above us.

Luca munched absently on a plate of chocolate-covered fruits. In one hand I held a champagne flute; in the other, my unicorn mask dangled. The breeze, when it came, was a welcome burst of coolness, bringing with it a faint *chink* noise as it clicked my mask against my glass.

"Listen," I said, thinking of all the little details, swirling around each other like the dancers below. "You can say I know how to party, but I *know* I don't know how to express how I feel. It's like I can't string the words together."

"Well," said Luca, reasonably, "you did pretty well with Gus earlier. Just treat it like that."

"What, you mean, talk to you like you're a suspect in a mystery that I'm just now putting together?" I glanced at him doubtfully, then laughed. "I was thinking of it more in terms of this mask."

I set aside my glass and pulled up the golden unicorn mask in both hands. Luca leaned against my shoulder as he studied it, too. "It's actually really nice," he said. "Good thing you didn't break it during your high-speed chase."

"Luca, you're not helping," I said, laughing again. "I was going to say, I don't feel like I'm qualified to wear it. Just like I don't think I'm—well, I'm not eloquent enough to be romantic. But I wish I was."

"Or you could think of it a different way," Luca suggested gently. "Cinnabar, you're *always* walking around with a mask on, thinking your loved ones can't see who you are behind it. But who you are is obvious to us, no matter what you're wearing. It doesn't have as much to do with *seeing* as it has to do with feeling.

"That came out more suggestive than I meant it to," he added after a moment. "Sorry about that."

A chuckle broke its way through my speechlessness. "It's fine. You know, that's the second time you've used my real name."

"And that's my point. Just because I don't use it all the time doesn't mean I don't know it," he told me softly.

"Sure, but—but—" I hesitated, overwhelmed by all my thoughts of masks and names and expressing emotions and carnivals and secrets.

"And just because you're a worrier and I like to joke," Luca went on, "doesn't mean that you aren't the light to my dark. I told you before, you're the good that came of a very bad time, and I won't ever forget that. And I'm not the only one who sees it," he added, pressing his hand over mine, over the edge of the golden mask.

I wanted to protest. I didn't see myself as 'light' to Luca's 'dark' at all. That wasn't even remotely how he felt to me. But again there were too many words in my mind to pick the right ones, and before I could string together a sentence, we were interrupted.

"Oh, there you are!"

It was such a quiet, relieved sound that I couldn't begrudge it. Luca and I turned to see Magica edging along the row of seats towards us.

"Hey, Magica," Luca said kindly. "Come sit with us. I don't think you and I met properly, my name's Luca, it's nice to see you again."

"Hi Luca," she said, perching on the edge of a nearby chair.

When her eyes slid to me, I finally managed to choose my words. "Hi, Magica. How are you? How are things down below? It must feel like kind of a . . . big night."

"It *was*," she said earnestly. "It's just past midnight now. Didn't you notice?"

"Uh, no," I admitted. "Are we supposed to leave?"

"Oh, no. It'll go on a long time," said Magica, as she glanced down at the dancers. "But, Red, you asked about me. And I—I want to leave."

I straightened, glancing back at Luca, and she went on hastily, "I don't mean right now. It's okay. I'm okay right now, I mean. It's just—everyone's been talking about dreams, and I—I think it's time for me to stay."

"To stay?" Luca echoed curiously.

"I know I'm not making sense," Magica said, flushed. "It's just, the carnival, it's always moving. Always a new town, new faces. Always practicing a new routine. Always a new drama . . ." she glanced down at the ball again, then met my gaze with more determination. "I want to stay. I don't want to jump into the next port or the next big thing, not yet. I want to take time for myself. I want to think about what my dream will be."

"That sounds completely sensical to me, Magica," I said at last. "We'd be happy to help you stay in town. Right, Luca?"

"Absolutely. You could do a lot worse than staying in Belville," he agreed over my shoulder.

"Oh, thank you!" Magica beamed.

But I couldn't help but ask the hard question. "About your family, and the rest of the carnival . . ."

"Weep wants to go with the carnival." Magica bit her lip, but soldiered on. "Mother will go too, of course. I tried to get Weep to stay here, but—we agreed—maybe it's time."

"You each have your own path," Luca said sympathetically.

"Right." Magica's head bobbed up and down as she nodded. "And I—I do think it's time. Captain Pleasant said I could. He said he might find new work soon, too. But everyone else—I think they'll keep going on, just as before."

"There'll probably be a trial, and they'll have to come back for that, at least," I said. "So you don't have to feel like you're saying goodbye to them forever."

Magica's nod was more absent this time, slower. Then her gaze fixed on the mask in my hand. "You were so pretty tonight, Red," she said, changing the subject.

"That's what I was trying to tell her," Luca laughed.

I blushed. "Thanks. I'm not used to dressing up like this."

"Oh, but it's so nice! Your hair, too," Magica said, warming to the topic.

"You like my hair?" I twisted a stray strand between my fingers, thinking. "Magica, I might have someone to introduce you to . . . someone who can help you make a new start."

34

New Work to Do

Needless to say, the party went on until early—or rather, not so early—hours of the morning. Good thing for us that the following day was a rest day! My shop and the bookstore would be closed anyway, so Luca and I met up for lunch after catching a little sleep. Lavender, who had heard all the news and more from her tenants, made us a special picnic box to take up to the hill below town. There, we spread out an old blanket and watched the huge ship on the lake prepare to set sail.

"It's almost too bad they couldn't stay longer," Luca observed, watching the activity on the upper decks of the *Luna II.* "Even just a day or so, to recover from last night."

I chuckled—laughing aloud was too offensive for my overly-sensitive head, brought on by too many glasses of champagne. "I think they're used to that sort of thing. Late nights and early mornings, I mean, not necessarily murders and blackmail . . ."

"Never those," Luca agreed, passing me a glass bottle of iced tea.

As I took it, I silently blessed Lavender for her foresight. The cool liquid and hint of caffeine had me feeling better from the first sip.

"Oh!" Magica's voice as she crested the hill behind us was faint and startled. "I'm so sorry, I didn't mean to interrupt you again . . ."

"It's fine," I assured her, shielding my eyes to look up at her thin frame, silhouetted against a bright blue sky. "Would you like to join us?"

"If you're planning to watch, it might be better to do so with company," Luca added gently.

"Oh, no. Thank you, I mean. I appreciate it, really. But I wasn't going to," Magica explained as she walked down to our blanket. "I just wanted to—well—I'm not sure exactly."

"Say goodbye?" I offered.

"Remind yourself that you're starting fresh?" Luca suggested.

Magica hesitated. It was so new to see her in an oversized tunic—one of my own, in fact—instead of a leotard. She'd left nearly all her belongings aboard; even though she'd had the support of Captain Pleasant and the rest of the crew, Anastasia's ire had been terrific. "Maybe both," she admitted. "It's big, isn't it?"

"Very," I assured her. "You're starting a new story."

"But there's no reason to worry," Luca added. "You're in the perfect place to do so."

"Yeah. I—I think you might be right. I think it's right I ended up here. That this was the port I finally . . ." Magica glanced down at the *Luna II*, then at us. "Did Gloria tell you she's given me an interview this afternoon? If I make her hair and she likes it, I can work at the salon."

"Good luck," Luca said earnestly.

"I'm sure you'll be much better at it than I am," I added, silently quite pleased with myself for having made the introduction between the two of them. After the late night last night, Luca and I had escorted Magica to a room at Lavender's tavern and given her notes to take to Gloria and Thorn, too.

Speaking of the officer, Magica had one more bit of news to share. "Officer Thorn said to tell you—the shark was right. Gus, I mean Marcus, well it turns out he was wanted in three different ports. Under the name Marcus Augustus though, that's why he was 'Gus' on board the *Luna*. I never would have guessed," she concluded, her eyes wide.

"Wanted for what?" Luca asked, intrigued.

"More blackmail, I'm guessing?" I said. "Seems like the sort of thing that becomes almost addictive, always looking for power over others. Adding new blackmail cases to your repertoire like jewels to a fancy mask."

"Not to mention adding actual money for jewels," Luca added.

"Blackmail, threatening behavior, and misrepresentation," Magica said meanwhile, as though reciting it from memory. "But she still wouldn't say what he did to Fontus, just that Fontus is safe and decided to go somewhere else. I guess someone new will be carnival director."

There wasn't much to say to that; I wasn't sure how much to feel sorry for Fontus, versus how much to wonder what mask he'd put on at his next stage. Given all the drama we'd seen among the After Midnight crew, I was inclined to think everything had worked out for the best.

Magica watched us apprehensively for just one more moment. Then she smiled. "You two are funny. Has anyone told you that?"

"Only everyone," Luca confessed, grinning widely.

"Basically every chance they get," I agreed, downing the rest of my tea.

"I'd like to be funny too," she said, this time glancing north, toward town. "I'd like—I'd like to have a different kind of story. A different kind of life."

"A life is all kinds of things," Luca told her. "That's what I've learned. The outward appearance is never the full story."

"Never," she said slowly. "Yes—maybe you're right. So far—so far I've always thought of life like a show. Like only the outside counted. But maybe . . ."

"No 'maybe' about it," I promised her. "If you're working for Gloria, she'll see to it that you think about what's on the inside, too. It may be salon work, but she's big on highlighting people's true selves and intentions."

"And you two," Magica said hopefully. "That is—I won't work for you—but—"

"We're friends," I assured her, at the same time Luca said,

"We'll always be here for you, don't worry."

Magica gave us both that look once more, that *you're so funny* look, and this time it evolved into a true smile. She waved and walked on; no doubt we'd given her plenty to think about.

"She's right, you know," Luca told me as he went back to pulling cheeses and veggies from the basket. "We *are* funny. At this rate, the town will be setting us up with our own carnival show."

I'm not sure what it was—the mention of the carnival, or Magica and her honesty, or the peer pressure of the town behind us, or maybe the utter simplicity of it all, sitting there with Luca under the warm summer sun among the heather and butterflies. Somewhere inside me, that last dam broke.

"Luca," I said. "That isn't quite right. We aren't just funny. We are love. I mean—what I mean is, what I've been trying to tell you, why I was so worried about you and I'm always messing around trying to step on *your* emotions instead of admitting *mine*—"

"I love you," Luca interrupted, grinning. "There, how's that for stepping on emotions? I beat you to it."

"I—well, fine then," I said, blushing and half laughing at the same time. "If it's all so obvious, then—"

"You do still have to say it," Luca insisted. "It'll be good for you."

"Ha! That's what you say. Probably the earth will swallow me up or lightning will come out of the sky—"

"*Cinnabar.*" Luca leaned over and kissed me, pressing me back. When we came up for air, he was grinning again. "It's not like you to deny the truth."

"Fair. But it's also not like I go around all day saying 'this hillside is green' or 'the sun is hot,'" I teased. "It's so true it's hard to say. I love you, Luca."

"I love you, too," he replied gently, kissing me again.

This time when we broke apart, stomachs rumbling, we realized that our view was a little more empty than before.

"I've heard of love giving you rose-colored vision, but this is a bit much," I said, gesturing to the lonely lake below us.

"We missed it," Luca realized, laughing. "How in Beyond did we miss a massive magitech pirate ship taking flight?"

"Oh, well, I wouldn't worry," I told him airily as I reached straight for a cupcake. "I'm sure the next big excitement in town will come sooner rather than later. Who knows what it'll be this time?"

Epilogue

A Note from Weep

To Red:

We just finished the trial, so I'm sending this to you before I forget. I'm not sure when the *Luna II* will be in Belville or Pine again.

Listen, I know how my family must look to you. Just because I'm quiet doesn't mean I'm ignoring everyone. And just because I stayed doesn't mean I'm okay with everything.

The truth is, Magica was always the one who needed to get away. Maybe she didn't realize it, but I did. Coal was mostly talk. Magica—well, she could learn to speak up more. Maybe you think that's ironic coming from me. But speaking up isn't just about words. I don't do anything I don't want to do. I'm fine with doing acrobatics in the carnival, and there's nowhere I want to settle yet. Magica, on the other hand—I'm not sure she's ever really *wanted* to be part of the carnival. I think she's always wished she could have a quiet life instead.

That's just me thinking, though. I won't say it's easier for me to write than it is for me to talk. I still think about every single word before I write it down. But I have to get this all out now, while it's time.

I'm glad it was Belville where everything fell apart. I know you and your friends will take care of Magica. She promised to write me–she's already sent me a few letters. I'm still figuring out what to write back. I will, though, don't worry about that. But in the meantime, I wanted to make sure you're looking after her.

And I wanted to thank you. We can't change anything about how the investigation went. I think it went the way it needed to. I even think it was good for Mother. She misses Magica, you know. You don't have to tell her that, though.

There's one other thing. Fontus showed up on the last day of the trial, after you'd left. He admitted to being blackmailed. Said it was all because he'd tried to help Gus start out on a ship a decade ago, and instead they both got involved in piracy and raiding. Their ship was caught, but a lot of the crew escaped. He thought he'd got away clean until he saw Gus at the carnival just a few years ago.

Maybe everyone goes through a phase pretending to be something they're not. Pirates, performers, partics. I've never bothered pretending. I'd like it if Magica could stop, too. Seems to me that you're the right one to help her do that.

Thanks.

Weeping Willow

P.S. Hemming said to tell you thank you, too, if I got the chance. I guess I made the chance.

Recipes

The recipes included here have been submitted by the residents of Belville, collected (and at times translated) by the author. Mistakes might have been made at any part of the process, but with any luck, these will bring a bit of fun and inspiration to you, our readers! Always feel free to experiment with the recipes included. And if you do, reach out to info@elle hartford.com to let us know how it went!

That said, without further ado . . .

Red's Snack-Worthy Falafel

Perfect for on-the-go meals in a busy, crime-solving life, but even better when served with dipping sauces and perhaps some hummus, sliced veggies, and a side of rice or pasta.

Serves 4

Ingredients:

- 15 oz. chickpeas, drained and rinsed
- 1 Tbsp minced garlic
- 1 med. onion, chopped fine

- 2 Tbsp fresh parsley, chopped fine
- 1 tsp ground coriander
- ¾ tsp ground cumin
- ½ tsp salt
- More salt and pepper to taste
- 2-3 Tbsp flour
- 1 ½ C vegetable oil, more as needed (if frying)

1. Add chickpeas, garlic, onion, parsley, coriander, cumin, salt, and pepper (to taste) in a medium bowl. Add 2 Tbsp of flour and combine well.
2. Mash the ingredients until they bind together into a paste (if you prefer using a mixer, you can do so). Add an extra tablespoon of flour if the mixture is too sticky. The result should be thick and hold its shape.
3. Form mixture into balls, about the size of a golf ball, and flatten slightly so they have distinct "sides."
4. To fry: add oil to a large skillet and heat over medium-high until oil shimmers. Shallow-fry falafel in batches to avoid crowding pan, 2 to 5 minutes per batch, flipping when browned on one side and adding more oil, if needed. Drain on paper towels.
5. Alternatively, you can bake them in the oven at 375 degrees Fahrenheit on a greased cookie sheet. Bake on one side for 10 min, flip, and bake an additional 10 min until golden brown and crispy.
6. Serve falafel by itself, with sauces, or with sides suggested above; or, store in an airtight container in the fridge and snack when desired!

* * *

Lavender's Large Summer Salad

Can a salad count as a meal? Absolutely, says Lavender, especially in summer when produce is plentiful. Feel free to adapt this recipe to suit your season, location, and taste!

Serves 2 (or one, if very hungry)

Ingredients:

- 4-6 C salad base: mixed greens, spinach, kale, etc.
- 2-3 C salad mix-ins: berries, sliced cucumbers, sliced tomatoes, carrots, radishes, shelled peas, summer squash, sliced peppers
- 1-2 C salad protein: nuts, sliced hard-boiled eggs, diced grilled tofu or meat of choice
- ½ C salad dressing (below)

1. Make sure all your ingredients are ready: wash the greens and tear them into bite-sized pieces, wash and chop your vegetables, prepare your protein.
2. In a large bowl, toss base, mix-ins, and dressing together.
3. Portion the salad into serving bowls and place protein (and more dressing to taste) on top.

Lavender's Go-To Salad Dressing:

- 3 Tbsp vinegar (white wine vinaigrette preferred)
- ½ C olive oil (extra-virgin or as good quality as possible)
- 1 Tbsp dijon mustard
- 1 Tbsp honey
- salt and pepper to taste
- 1-2 tsp optional mix-ins: minced garlic, chopped rose-mary, citrus juice, etc

1. Combine all ingredients in a jar, seal the lid, and shake thoroughly (or whisk in an open bowl).
2. Taste and adjust according to preference.
3. Use immediately or store in an airtight container for up to one week.

* * *

Gloria's Favorite Easy Floral Soaps

Gloria may be a little light on the technical composition of soap—she insists that's Red's domain—but her strategic ignorance makes this recipe beginner-friendly! It's also great fun for spring and summer decorating or gift-giving.

Makes 6 soap bars (depending on mold)

Ingredients:

- Soap mold, preferably silicone
- 2 lb melt-and-pour soap base (Red likes to use goats' milk soap)
- 10-20 drops of essential oil (lavender, calendula, or rose make good choices)
- 1 C dried flowers (lavender, rose petals, or a mix that accentuates your oil)

1. Melt the prepared soap base in a heat-safe, easy-pour container (for example, an extra-large glass measuring cup). You can either use a double-boiler method (boiling a few inches of water in a medium-sized pot, and nestling the cup/bowl with the soap in it within the pot so that it's above the water, heated by the steam) or one of those fancy technological microwaves! Whichever method you use, go slowly and gently, stirring the soap and keeping an eye on it every 30 seconds or so.
2. Remove your soap bowl from heat and add in essential oils. This is entirely subjective. Use the scents that smell best to you, or remind you of early summer flowers! As with melting, go slowly here. Add just a few drops at a time and smell the mixture as you go, making sure the aroma doesn't get overwhelming.
3. Stir in half of your flowers now, gently.
4. Pour the soap into your molds.

5. Sprinkle the soaps with the remaining flowers. Or, if you want to be really fancy, arrange the petals in colorful designs!
6. Let the soaps sit, undisturbed, until fully cool—about two hours.
7. Remove soaps and enjoy! Store them in a cool, dry place. Because of the addition of organic materials (the flowers), these soaps may have a shorter shelf life than others—try to use them or gift them within a few months.

* * *

William's Recipe for Peace of Mind: Camelopardalis

As usual, everyone's favorite magical familiar has his own unique twist on a "recipe." Enjoy!

"This one can be a challenge," says William. "You'll only be able to find it if you're in the Northern Hemisphere, and it can be pretty faint. However, it's close to the Dippers, which—if you recall a previous lesson—you should be a pro at finding.

"If Camelopardalis is too much of a mouthful, you can just call it what it is: a giraffe. Seeing as we've already talked about Cetus the sea-monster, I had to come up with another cool animal constellation to represent all the very significant and helpful animals in the carnival and in Belville, too. There aren't any myths associated with Camelopardalis—yet. Maybe while you're out stargazing, you can think some up.

"To find it, first find the Dippers. Then, look for Cassiopeia (the very first constellation I taught you about). Between the Big Dipper and Cassiopeia lies Camelopardalis. Look for that brightest stars, one of the legs, first. From there, you can trace out the rest of the body. Or at the very least, you can pretend to see the rest. Stargazing isn't an exact science–thank goodness!"

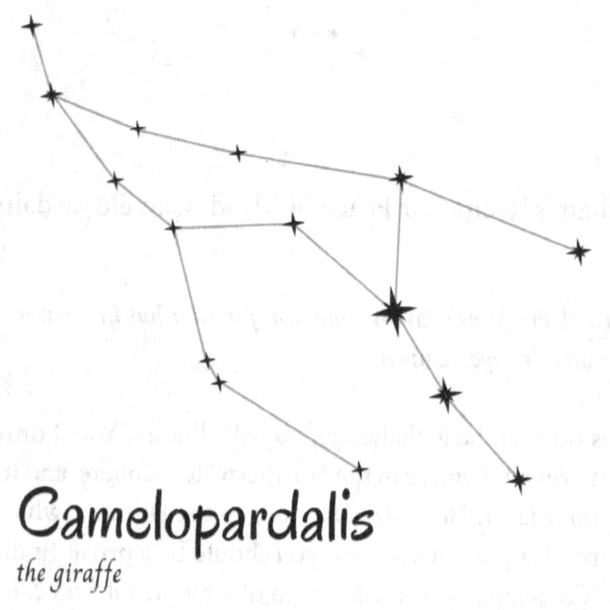

Camelopardalis
the giraffe

Acknowledgments

It takes a crew to run a ship, or to catch a criminal–I say something like this with every book, and this one is no exception!

Writing a retelling of Cinderella was difficult for me at first. I'm forever indebted to my newsletter community, many of whom shared their personal love for Cinderella with me when I most needed inspiration. At a surface level, it can be easy to dismiss Cinderella as a story about waiting for someone else to save you; but at its heart, I've come to believe it's a very necessary story about *being worthy of help*, even when you are at your lowest point. Once I understood that, this novel was even *harder* to write, believe it or not. But it has been very healing, too, and I'm so grateful to everyone who shared in this journey.

As always, that includes a heartfelt thank you to my family and friends, to the other authors who encouraged me, the sweet book community on Instagram, the Cozy Mystery Book Club, the Cozy Mystery Tribe, and my incredible ARC readers!

And on top of that, I'm very thankful to *you*. I hope your time in Belville has been magical! And if you have extra time on your hands, reviews give authors a reason to dance around the office like it's a fancy masquerade ball!

About the Author

Elle adores cozy mysteries, fairy tales, and above all, learning new things. As a historian and educator, she believes in the value of stories as a mirror for complicated realities. She currently lives in New Jersey with a grumpy tortoise and a three-legged cat.

Find more stories of Red and her friends at ellehartford.com. And while you're there, sign up for Elle's newsletter to get bonus material, behind-the-scenes sneak peeks, and terrible jokes!

Also by Elle Hartford

The Alchemical Tales
  Beauty and the Alchemist (book 1)
  Cold as Snow (book 2)
  Mermaid for Danger (book 3)
  Cry Big Bad Wolf (book 4)

Pomegranate Cafe Romance
  Worthy in Love (book 1)